T0326712

Praise for *Castro's Curveball*

"Tim Wendel's love and impressive knowledge of baseball suffuses every page of this passionate novel of love, loss, and the real freedom that wisdom and time sometimes bring."

—KEN BURNS, filmmaker

"A Cuba libre mixed with baseball, revolution, and moonlight, wonderfully evocative of a time that was and a pitcher that might have been."

—FRANK DEFORD, author of *Everybody's All-American*

"Well-known sportswriter and radio commentator Wendel explores the legend that Fidel Castro could've been a contender in America's major leagues. . . . Beautifully written, and with a ring of truth to it."

—*Library Journal*

"A superbly crafted meditation on heroism, duty, and the irony derived from recognizing everyone's imperfections but your own."

—*Kirkus Reviews* (starred)

"A skillfully rendered story that resonates with the ring of truth. . . . This book has the power to get under your skin and the wisdom to make you reflect on the meaning of your own life. Above all, it stands as an allegory for the story of Cuba itself, in all its tragic magnificence. Highly recommended."

—*Historical Novels Review*

Escape from Castro's Cuba

Escape from Castro's Cuba

A Novel

TIM WENDEL

University of Nebraska Press • *Lincoln*

Library of Congress Cataloging-in-Publication Data
Names: Wendel, Tim, author.
Title: Escape from Castro's Cuba: a novel / Tim Wendel.
Description: Lincoln: University of Nebraska Press, [2021]
Identifiers: LCCN 2020019522
ISBN 9781496222923 (paperback; alk. paper)
ISBN 9781496225429 (epub)
ISBN 9781496225436 (mobi)
ISBN 9781496225443 (pdf)
Subjects: LCSH: Americans—Cuba—Fiction. | Base-
ball players—Fiction. | Castro, Fidel, 1926–2016—Fiction. |
Cuba—Fiction.
Classification: LCC PS3573.E512 E83 2021 | DDC 813/.54—dc23
LC record available at https://lccn.loc.gov/2020019522

Set in Garamond Premier Pro by Laura Buis.

Escape from Castro's Cuba

Havana, Cuba—2016

1.

THE ASSISTANT CAMERAMAN held up the slate detailing the next scene, and once again the clapperboard snapped down. "And action," the director said.

With the cameras now rolling, I told myself to stay calm, hold my gaze. Thankfully, I only had a few lines today. All I had to do was sit in the ancient stadium in Havana, as the Panavisions moved in from either side, and pretend to be my old friend Papa Joe Hanrahan, who was once the chief scout for the Washington Senators. In doing so, I tried to ignore the fact that I had somehow found myself back in Cuba, a star-crossed land that always seemed to get the best of me.

"It is a beautiful game when it's played well, isn't it?" said the guy sitting next to me in the box seats behind home plate. I waited, softly inhaling for a long beat, as I had been coached to do, before nodding in agreement.

"It's more than a game here," I replied, trying to speak my lines slowly and with a measure of conviction. "You know, it could be called a way of life."

Of course, the real Papa Joe Hanrahan died decades ago. I had been recast as him for the movies. Davey Bucolo, who played my boss in the picture, visiting from Washington, seemingly hung on my every word as the cameras continued to zoom in on us, eavesdropping on our conversation in the crowd at the ballpark.

"That it is, my friend," Bucolo agreed. "Back in America, baseball represents the Fourth of July and mom's apple pie. But here they have been playing the grand sport almost as long as we have. For it has always been the game of an independent Cuba."

I nodded as he waxed on about the game here in Cuba. Its rich pageantry. The flair with which they play. All the crap they were laying on thick for this big-budget Hollywood feature. So much so that I couldn't help thinking that the Cuban government had a hand in it all.

Out on the diamond, players from the Habana Lions, dressed in the flannel uniforms of the late 1950s, took infield practice. I had to admit that it was a fitting backdrop for our snapshot history lesson of baseball in Cuba. We had rehearsed this scene several times, and the process had fallen into that comfortable place of being familiar yet not quite predictable.

Over Bucolo's shoulder, I noticed that a new kid had moved onto the field, taking over at shortstop. He fielded the ball effortlessly, flipping down his weathered glove at the last possible moment and then firing the ball on to first base in a single fluid movement. While he appeared to put hardly any effort into it, the ball flew on a line toward the first baseman. Arriving at waist level, the delivery tattooed the recipient's glove with a pop that any baseball lifer would recognize as someone with the goods.

Even though I was supposed to be hanging on Bucolo's every word, I stole another glance toward first base as another delivery arrived, courtesy of the kid at short. My old teammate Chuck Cochrane, who had been cast to type as an ornery coach, had his eyes on this new kid, too.

Then everything around me grew quiet, and I realized that Bucolo, who had put so much effort into his lines, had stopped talking and was looking at me. Everyone—him, the director, the people on either side of us, seemingly the very camera itself—was waiting for my reply. The only problem was that I had forgotten what to say.

"That kid," I began, knowing that what was coming out of my mouth was all wrong. "The one at short. He can really play."

"And cut," the director shouted.

In a heartbeat, Nicky Reid was alongside me, with his dog-eared script in hand.

"Billy, your line really is 'It's the thing that makes Cuba, Cuba, my friend. The mastery, the majesty of it all.'"

I nodded. "Sorry."

The director took a deep breath and gazed up at the gorgeous blue Cuban sky.

"Re-block the whole thing," Reid said. "We need to get this scene in today. C'mon, I mean it."

The makeup people descended upon us like flies, retouching our faces with a touch of rouge and powder.

"Find your happy place, Billy," said Darr Prescott. He had begun the picture doing photos and random video for an HBO feature about the making of the feature. But in recent days, as the pressure mounted on Reid to finish filming before his production visa expired, Prescott had become one of the director's trusted confidants.

"Remember your reflexology points," Prescott said, and he took my hand, squeezing his thumb into the fleshy part of the palm. "You're so tense," he said, pressing hard several more times before I pulled my hand away. "It's like you just saw a ghost."

I told Prescott, Bucolo, and anybody else who would listen that I'd be better this time. No worries. Just a momentary lapse. We needed to get this scene over with, I thought to myself, so I could find out who that kid playing shortstop was.

"HIS NAME IS Gabriel Santos y Valdez," Evangelina said that evening, as the sun set over the Hotel Nacional, still the best place to stay in Havana.

"So you found out?"

"How couldn't I, Papa?" she smiled. "After poor Nicky Reid about lost it, all in a tizzy, I had to figure out what was really going on with you."

"Everybody messes up their lines," I replied, "especially on this picture."

"Papa, you didn't just flub a line," Eván said. "It was like time stood still for you. So, I followed your eyes and saw that player. He is good. Real good."

"Chuck saw him, too."

"You two old-timers would know."

I let my daughter's comment drop. Instead, I asked, "Any idea where's he from?"

"Nobody's sure. Some of the ballplayers said he was from Bayamo or Holguín—somewhere on the east end of the island."

"He's just arrived in Havana then?"

"That's the story."

"Like I said, Chuck saw him, too."

Eván shrugged. "I can find him first."

The two of us sat at a small table in a corner of the suite. I had cracked the full-length window, enjoying the trade winds as dusk settled over the city. Six stories below us, the famous Malecón seawall swept away toward Old Havana and El Morro Castle, which stood high on the bluffs above the deepwater harbor.

"The kid can play," I said.

"But nobody really knows him," Eván said. "Not even a Cuban baseball expert like *mi padre*, the one and only Billy Bryan."

I grinned at her teasing. "When it comes to Cuba, there are always surprises. Nothing goes as planned," I said. "You know that as well as anybody."

"It's happened before, especially on that field, right, Papa?"

Of course, she knew the story about the night almost a generation ago when I was playing in the old winter-ball league here, the catcher for the Habana Lions. Before our game that evening against the Marianao Tigers, a group of protesters stormed onto the field and hooted and hollered when one of their own decided to take the mound. Instead of signaling for the authorities to drag him away, I settled in behind the plate and nodded for the kid protester to throw a few pitches. Just for grins and giggles. This interloper had a fine curveball, and he struck out an American hitter who dared step into the batter's box against him. Only later did we discover that kid pitcher was a young Fidel Castro.

I've told this story so often over the years that it's taken me places, as they like to say. Cuba and the infatuation with the island have never fallen too far out of favor, and what began with me being quoted in newspapers about the latest defector ballplayer to wash ashore in America soon mushroomed into on-camera appearances for several award-winning documentaries. When it comes to Cuban baseball, especially the old winter-ball league, which saw such stars as Brooks Robinson, Jim Bunning, Don Zimmer, and Orestes "Minnie" Miñoso play on the island in its heyday, I've become the expert on the subject. An old man with so many stories about the game back in the day on the Big Pineapple. Put me in front of a camera, with somebody genuinely interested in my answers, and I have been compared favorably with Buck O'Neil or Shelby Foote. My other daughter, Cassy, told me to be myself and try to stay on message. That's how it's done these days, she reminded me, and it has led to this—a small part in a feature film. I would have turned it down, perhaps should have turned it down, but both of my precious daughters, Eván and Cassy, insisted that I give it a try.

"Is the kid that good?" Eván asked. After the day's shooting, she had changed into a red blouse and a black skirt, which thankfully fell below the knee, and low heels.

"He could play in the Majors right now," I said. "He's that fine with the glove."

"You can tell just by looking at him? Just for a few moments?"

I nodded. How can I explain that anybody who has been good but not great in something, as I once was with baseball, can so easily recognize real talent in another?

"Then I will keep my ears open tonight," Eván said. "See what I can find out about him."

"No, it's fine, honey," I replied, and she gave me that exasperated look, like I was worrying too much about her again. But how could I not worry? It had taken so much time and treasure to get her out of this country originally, and now she has returned, all because of me. Cuba has changed plenty over the years. Anybody can see that, with the glittering hotels going up, the new money from overseas investors, everything already here except for a complete flood of U.S. dollars. That last piece has been held up for decades thanks to the political dysfunction in Washington.

"You could come with me?" she asked, looking for her purse.

"No, it's okay. Today's filming wore me out."

"Oh, Papa, c'mon," Eván said. "At least Cassy can get you to have some fun."

"Not really. She knows I'm nothing but an old goat with a curfew."

"An old goat who knows Havana better than any gringo I've ever known."

"Oh, listen to your sweet lies. Always spinning a tale, aren't you?"

I watched her go and then returned to the balcony, overlooking the city of Havana, the first port in the New World, the so-called City of Columns. Once more I was surprised by how quickly the past can be conjured up in the lengthening shadows of another evening in Cuba. The Nacional, like any other international hotel, had tried to become like everywhere else in the world. You can turn on the television to be greeted by the standard movie channels—H B O, Showtime, Turner Classic, and the like. Our first night here I had watched some of *Chinatown*, with Jack Nicholson and Faye Dunaway, redubbed horribly in Spanish. But I eventually turned it off. For the Los Angeles that Nicholson confronts in that movie, with its graft, complications, and dead ends, reminded me too much of my Havana, the one that existed decades ago, before Castro's revolution turned everything upside down once again. Tonight, I stayed away from the television and steadied myself with another rum and ice from the minibar.

Out the window, I gazed down upon the city below. Darkness spread across the land like storm clouds rolling in from the Florida Straits. Crowds of young people had begun to line the Malecón, the five-mile-long breakwater and roadway that sweeps along the face of Havana like a come-hither smile. Here and there small fires were ablaze and people gathered to listen to another street musician or simply to talk. Back when I was newly arrived here, as a mediocre ballplayer trying to prolong what was left of his professional career, this city was all bright lights and glitz. The neon glow from the old Hilton and the Riviera, where the action at the blackjack tables and slots went on until dawn, made the city a spectacle unto itself. So much so that it remains the vision of things more than a half century later. Say the word *Havana* and many still think of the well-heeled crowds, the flashing lights, the party that went on and on and on until Fidel Castro took control. "So Near and Yet So Foreign. Only 90 Miles Away," as the travel poster for the night ferry down from Key West once proclaimed.

When you get as old as I am, eighty-two years old next January, the past can sometimes become as vivid as the present day. After all, this is Cuba, which finds a way to worm itself into the soul and pull you back to the times you'd rather set aside for safekeeping. When Nicky Reid and his Hollywood types convinced me to be in this picture, they made it sound like such a great time. How we would sit around the hotel bar until all hours, talking about baseball and the good old days down here. That had lasted a few nights, and it was fun enough. But too soon the powers that be retreated to Reid's suite to study the dailies and argue about how they could make the best of what had been filmed. This movie has serious problems. Everybody on the set knows it, and to complicate things, the government is giving Reid & Company less than a week to finish up. Our visas are running out with too many scenes still to shoot. That said, I remind myself, it is really no concern of mine. What can keep me up at night, what rages inside me like a fever dream, is my own vision of the past. Havana of those bygone times still rolls out like a black-and-white newsreel when I close my eyes on a clear night like this one, on a balcony high above the streets below.

Eventually I nodded off in the chair by the open window, listening to the distant laughter and conversation coming up from the Malecón. That was how Eván found me when she came in later that evening. She ran her hand lightly across my forehead to make sure I was still in the land of the living. That's her way of checking on her aging father, and I enjoy it so much that I will often play possum just to feel her touch.

"Have you been drinking, young lady?" I said, blinking open my eyes.

"Papa," she smiled.

"You had a good time?"

"Yes, we found a nice place for dinner," Eván replied. "A *paladar* down near the harbor with the best seafood—shrimp, scallops, lobster. All on skewers and laid out over beds of rice."

"All food a regular Cuban doesn't get close to."

"You sound like Mama now."

"We need to visit her grave again before this film wraps," I reminded her. "We'll go to Colón Cemetery the day after tomorrow."

"Yes, yes, I know," Eván said. Instead she wanted to talk about her night, not her mother, the beautiful Malena Fonseca.

"At least half the crew ended up at the bar downstairs."

"Here at the Nacional?"

"Even Chuck Cochrane was there. He kept telling me to go upstairs and fetch you."

"I'm glad you didn't."

Eván nodded and broke into that unabashed smile of hers. A beaming grin of merriment and trouble that I've grown to treasure over the years.

"I learned more about that kid. The ballplayer who impressed you so much."

I sat up and leaned closer to her. Eván's breath smelled of fruit and rum, and I briefly wondered how many drinks she had had that night. But my oldest daughter, the one I didn't know I had for so many years, has always been able to hold her liquor. I've seen her drink her share of men—macho fellows who fashion themselves as the next Ernest Hemingway—under the table many a time.

"He knows of you."

"Me?"

"Back when you played ball down here."

"Impossible," I replied. "It's been years and years since I played down here. Well before he was ever born."

"His grandfather was named Tyga Garcia?"

"Tyga, Tyga," I repeated softly to myself, trying to picture that face again. And then it came to me. Tyga was the clubhouse kid, the smooth-skinned mulatto, on our old Habana Lions team. He would often warm up the pitchers if I was tardy putting on my shin guards after another forgettable episode at the plate or on the bases. As a catcher, with no foot speed to speak of, I routinely made the last out of the inning.

"How did you find this out? He couldn't have been at the bar."

Even if he was old enough, hotels are off-limits to regular Cubans.

"One of the producers told me. Besides hitting the town, they sometimes take in the ball games beforehand."

"The Serie Nacional started a few days ago."

"And they've been going, searching for players to use in the action scenes. Everybody needs a little extra money around here, so they've invited the best ones down."

Eván turned and gazed down upon the city. The blare of a car horn, a snippet of conversation drifted up to us here, high above it all.

"It seems like a real stretch," I told her. "Tyga was just the club-house kid."

Eván looked back at me. "According to this producer, the kid knows all about your old team. How it would come down to you and Almendares for the title almost every year. Supposedly, the family grew up Lions fans."

"Then he must know Chuck Cochrane, too."

"He seems to know enough to stay away from him."

I nodded. "Sharp lad."

"Talk has it that he wants to defect. Play in the U.S. Major Leagues."

"Hush, child, you know there are things that you cannot speak about here."

Eván shook her head. "You make it sound like they bugged the room."

I shrugged. I didn't really know, but I wanted this conversation to stop—now. To be drawn back into the genie bottle it had come from and capped off for good. But my daughter had other ideas and nodded for me to stand beside her as she took in the city.

Reluctantly I did so, and Eván leaned in close to me.

"We could help him," she whispered.

We stood side by side, and the way she carried herself I could have been alongside her late mother, the love of my life. Just like that, the years fell away for me.

I shook my head. "It's too dangerous."

Yet Eván smiled and briefly rested her head on my shoulder. "We could do it, Papa. What better way to get back at El Jefe?"

"Shh, Eván. I mean it."

"Why?"

"It will come to no good. I'm telling you."

"Papa?"

"No, that's enough talk for one night."

She shrugged and made her way back into the suite, a double with adjoining rooms that we were sharing.

Later that evening, after Eván finally headed off to bed, I returned to the balcony and took one last look upon the city of my past. The streets, the way they spread out in a spider's web of tangled cross-purposes and off-angled knots, always reminded me of an old catcher's fingers. My fingers. Somewhere down there was Fidel Castro, or what was left of him. I had heard the rumors about how even in poor health he kept on the move, rarely staying in the same place on consecutive nights, always so careful after the repeated assassination attempts by the CIA, decades ago. While his brother, Raúl, technically was in charge of the country now, as long as Fidel was able to draw a breath, he was the one to be reckoned with on this island.

Revenge, in small doses, can be sweet. My old teammate Chuck Cochrane understands that as well as anybody. When we were the last wave of American ballplayers here, when Havana was a great big party that roared on into the night and we regularly rolled dice and played cards at the casino here at the Nacional or down the street at the Riviera. If Chuck lost money the night before, he made a point of returning to the same establishment the next night, determined to win everything back—determined to make somebody else pay.

Still, if anybody has reason to embrace the Old Testament approach (an eye for an eye, a tooth for a tooth) when it comes to Cuba, it would have to be me. Malena Fonseca, my love, died here, caught in the duplicity and accusations soon after the revolution took root. Did Fidel order her to be killed? Or was it another situation that unraveled before wiser heads could prevail? To this day, I don't really know. Yet in looking out on Havana at night, I knew that if I helped Gabriel Santos get off the island, helped him escape to the Major Leagues, my old friend Fidel Castro would never forgive such trespasses. Eván was right. That, in and of itself, made it something to seriously consider.

2.

NICKY REID MUST have gotten on somebody's good side or, more than likely, bribed the right people, because the next afternoon we were filming at the famed Tropicana Night Club. Nearly the entire cast, from the stars down to bit players like me, sat at the circular tables, each with the complimentary bottle of rum, as we watched the glittering show roll out in front of us.

Reid had placed a half-dozen cameras throughout place, filming it like a rock-and-roll show. Every possible angle was on display as wave after wave of dancing girls advanced toward us, kicking up their heels, coming to the lip of the stage only to peel off and make way for the next line of beauties. The assistant directors had told us to look enthralled at the sight of such lovelies and few of us had to act when viewing this spectacle. High above us, more ladies danced on risers and higher up on balconies, pulsating to the frenzied beat. Many of them wore towering headdresses and close to next to nothing else below that.

Chuck Cochrane caught my eye and nodded. Indeed, it seemed like the old days—when Havana was the most decadent place in the world, with the big-band beat and more gorgeous women than one could comprehend. Somehow, decades later, we had turned the clock back to a time when even aging ballplayers could be princes in the neon-glow realm.

It was dusk by the time we began to file out of the Tropicana. We were wrung out, exhausted by the exhibition of light and flesh we had witnessed. For the moment, our director was all smiles and even though I wasn't privy to how many scenes still needed to be finished, how many more takes and angles Reid wanted to film here in Havana, I knew that soon the race would be on to film as much as we could before we had to head back across the Florida Straits to home. Everyone could sense it, especially when Reid let scenes stand that he would have reshot only days before. My mistake in the crowd scene had been long forgotten. Still, Cuba will always be Cuba. The place reminded me of one of the vintage cars that ply the streets of Havana—the accelerator pushed to the floor and the vehicle hardly moving.

As we fanned out onto the street, looking for the shuttle buses to take us back to the hotel, a fleet of black sedans pulled up. The people filing out of those cars further clogged the area, causing more confusion. The security personnel wore elegant suits that wouldn't look out of place in New York, London, or Milan. Moving as one, they surrounded an elderly man dressed in battle fatigues from the revolution. The group moved straight ahead and everyone craned their necks, trying to see over the grim-faced security detail.

"It's Fidel," someone shouted, and the news spread throughout the neighborhood. Soon the crowds descended upon us from every direction, everyone eager for a glimpse of El Jefe himself.

Castro made his way toward our startled director, and I stood nearby, watching the jubilation drain from the director's face as he searched for his interpreter.

"Your . . . ," poor Nicky stammered and for a moment I feared he was about to call Castro his majesty or some other highbrow term, which would generate ugly headlines back in Miami. Yet Reid pulled himself together and simply said, "Mr. President," as he shook Castro's hand.

In response, Castro took Reid's outstretched hand and held it aloft, as if he were proclaiming the winner of a prize fight. Many of the crew and bystanders dutifully applauded. The man always had a sense for the dramatic.

With that, Castro began to move through the ever-growing crowd. A government interpreter came alongside, allowing Fidel to chat with everyone. I glanced over at Reid and saw that he knew that nothing else would be accomplished today. He had lost control of the situation and fallen farther behind in his production schedule.

As Castro worked his way through the crowd, I knew I could slip away. But what good would it do? If Fidel wanted to find you in Cuba, he would do so. I have never met a more aware, certainly not a luckier, person in my life. Back in the late fifties, near the end of the era for pro baseball on the island, he was also the most confident pitcher I had ever encountered. That's what the original Papa Joe, the legendary scout for the old Washington Senators in the Caribbean, had seen first and foremost in him. Something more alluring than even a hard-breaking curveball. If we had done a better job of convincing Castro to pursue baseball rather than revolution, the world as we know it would have been changed forever.

Soon Castro found Chuck Cochrane, pumping his hand and joking as if the two of them were long-lost brothers, when they actually didn't care for each other when we were playing ball down here. For Chuck had been the brash first baseman for the Habana Lions, one of the best sluggers in the Cuban winterball league. Compared to him, I was a Punch-and-Judy, single-hitting catcher.

Castro was smiling at something Chuck had said, when he looked past my old teammate and saw me. I was still in costume, dressed in a white suit and Panama hat, the garb of the old Papa Joe. The players had nicknamed Papa Joe "the Storm Cloud"—

both for his attire and how whatever he wrote down in his small notebook could cost a guy dearly at contract time.

Castro grinned one last time in Chuck's direction and then brushed past him, now moving toward me. Even at our ages, he remained a force of nature, focusing on the next task, the next would-be adversary.

"You go by William now?" he asked, taking my right hand. Instead of shaking it, he simply held it for an instant, squeezing hard before letting it go.

"It sounds more dignified, don't you think?" I said. "'Billy' is a boy's name. I believe you said that once."

"I did? I don't recall."

He spoke to me in Spanish, knowing I would understand. Despite so many crowding in around us, few really understood the native tongue, not in his rapid-fire fashion, so it was like we were having our own private conversation, with all those eyes upon us.

"At my age, 'Billy' doesn't match the face," I continued. "At some point, we all have to grow up, don't you think?"

Castro seemed amused by the notion.

"I don't see why," he said. "Sometimes it's better to let things be." I nodded at this.

"We must get together before you leave," Castro added. It sounded like an order, coming from him. "Have a more private conversation."

"I'd like nothing better," I replied, even though we both knew it was a lie.

"Good to hear," he said, a hint of surprise coming into his eyes. "For us, it could be like the old days."

"The old days," I repeated.

"We have an exceptional team again here in Havana," he said, stalling, just making small talk now. "Many will make the Olympic team. I believe that we will be one of the favorites this summer."

"Team Cuba is always one of the favorites," I said, watching him break into a triumphant grin. "Olympics, World Baseball Classic—it doesn't matter."

"You still follow the game, Billy? That's excellent," he said, with his bodyguards ready to move on. But he paused and looked me in the eye. "Pardon me, I mean William. Perhaps you're right about such things. Gentleman like us, we need to be more dignified, sometimes even more careful, when we reach a certain age."

With that he broke away and moved through the crowd, shaking hands and smiling like a politician or a rock star rather than the dictator who had survived the assassination attempts directed by so many U.S. administrations.

"You know him?" Nicky Reid said, falling in beside me.

"A little bit," I told the director.

"A little bit?" he said. "Mr. Bryan, the way the two of you were carrying on, it was like two old friends who hadn't seen each other in years. I'd heard the stories about how you met him when you were playing ball down here, before the revolution."

"Stories from long ago," I said. "A long, long time ago."

WHEN I RETURNED to the hotel, I had a traditional Cuban dinner—chicken with black beans and rice—brought up to the room. The others, including Eván, were itching to hit the town again. Time was running out in Cuba and there was still so much to see. I didn't have the heart to tell them that today's Havana pales in comparison to how it used to be. Back when one didn't dare fall asleep because the party barreled headlong into the night, every night, like the celebrations that Gatsby once held in honor of the green light at the end of Daisy's pier.

Once again, I sat at the table near the window and cracked it open, thinking about the night I first met Castro. Our game at the old ballpark had been delayed by student protesters. They often came onto the field back in those days, marching back and forth on the glowing, emerald-green grass. Yet on this night, one of their own dared to stride onto the infield and right up to the pitching mound.

The crowd cheered and whistled as this demonstrator reveled in the attention. He was thinner back then and already knew much about the game. So, almost as a lark, I rolled a ball out to him. As the catcher for the old Habana Lions, reigning champions of the Cuban winter-ball league, I could get away with such things back then.

This kid picked up the ball and we began a game of catch. He toed the rubber while I settled into a crouch behind the plate. We threw a half-dozen times, back and forth, until an angry Rory Guild, the Marianao Tigers' right fielder, decided he had had enough and stepped into the batter's box. Guild wanted to knock that ball out of the park and get the actual game back on track. Always good for a laugh, umpire Raúl "Chino" Atán broke off talking with the rich folks behind the home-plate screen and crouched down behind me, ready to call balls and strikes. Just like that, our little exhibition was on.

Of course, the kid on the mound, the one who dared to throw to a Major League batter that evening at the old ballpark, was a young Fidel Castro. What happened next soon became the glimmer of legends, with as much embellishment as such things require. But as the decades have gone by, I'm one of the few who knows the truth about that evening. And I can tell you, without reservation, that Castro struck out Guild. I would know, because I caught every pitch. Castro did it because he had great stuff and immediately after Guild swung and missed for the last time— "Strike three!" Atán shouted—the security police came onto the field, ready to bust things up as the crowd cheered and booed, unable to fully understand what they had just witnessed. Some kid pitcher, a Cuban, had struck out a bona fide American slugger?

What I'll never forget about that night is the pitch that Castro threw. I've caught more young bucks than I can remember in my years in baseball. Individuals who thought they were the next big thing. But the pitch Castro threw that evening was perhaps the best curveball I've ever seen. On that night, that curveball could have been dropped from heaven above, and Guild missed the offering by a good six inches. Imagine a clock face and the ball falling downward from the one o'clock spot to the number seven position. Beautiful, just beautiful. Sometimes, when I cannot sleep at night, I wonder how something so perfect, so full of grace, could have put so much heartbreak in motion.

Back at the Hotel Nacional the knock came at my hotel door, as I knew it would. I opened it to find a soldier, telling me a car was waiting out front. I pulled on my Teva sandals and accompanied him downstairs.

A black suv with tinted glass sat near the hotel's main entrance. Another uniformed guy, this one with more ornamentation than the one who had retrieved me, held the back door open. As I slid inside, the tourists walking up the long horseshoe sidewalk, the main entrance to the Nacional, slowed to take a better look at what was going on.

As soon as my door closed, the suv sped away and soon we were accelerating toward the sweeping seawall of the Malecón. Along the sidewalk facing the sea, more kids had gathered this evening to sing along with a cheap guitar or just to gaze out on the water and what might lie just out of sight. How I wanted to be with them rather than heading toward this rendezvous with my past.

We slowed only briefly at the signal near the base of Old Havana and soon broke free of the traffic, making good time in the left lane of the boulevard that hugged the rim of the famous deepwater harbor, the place where the Spanish conquistadors brought their loads of treasure stolen from the hinterlands of the New World. On the far side of these dark waters, the searchlight atop the Morro Castle, where so many were

TIM WENDEL

executed in the months after the Cuban Revolution, in 1959, still sprayed its light across the ancient city. A hard turn took us away from the harbor and we sped past the old railway station. It was followed by a quick left and then another right and then another. We could have been a boxer putting in time on a speed bag. Jabs and swings, cuts and misses. Soon I wasn't sure exactly where we were. Only that we were far away from Old Havana, the hotels, Chinatown, the ballpark—all the parts of town that I really knew.

Twenty minutes later, we pulled up in front of a low-slung villa, where almost all of the lights were off and figures moved among the lush vegetation that sheltered the walkway leading to the front door. My car door opened and I followed another soldier away from the street and farther into the shadows. In front of me, the door swung wide and I went inside. The far wall sported three flat-screen televisions, with all the games from the West Coast that evening, the Giants-Dodgers, Twins-Angels, and Red Sox–Diamondbacks.

"I love watching this Mike Trout play," a voice from the darkness said. "He could almost be Cuban, don't you think?"

I took another step into the room, letting my eyes adjust. Dressed in a black silk robe, with dark slippers, Castro sat on a leather couch with the remote control in his hand. "Billy, I mean William, please come and join me."

I reached out with my left hand to make sure I could navigate myself to a place on the far end of the couch.

"A drink, William? Still a Manhattan. Fruit muddled?"

I had to smile. Even though it had been years and years, Castro had done his homework. He wanted me to think that he actually remembered my favorite elixir.

"I haven't had one of those in a long time," I replied.

"Then perhaps it's time for another."

Castro nodded to the bartender, who made up one of those

devils. The guy then refilled Castro's glass, a Dewar's with water, and disappeared back into the shadows.

"Which game do you wish to watch?" Castro asked.

"This is fine," I said, nodding at the Red Sox–Diamondbacks, who were tied at two apiece heading into the fifth inning.

Castro brought up the sound, and for a while we settled in, watching the game and nursing our drinks.

"You could be the lord of baseball with that thing," I said, nodding to the silver-colored remote.

"If people only knew," Castro answered.

With that, Boston's David Ortiz took a mighty swing and the ball sailed over the right-center-field fence at Chase Field in Phoenix. Castro chuckled, sounds of delight that bumbled up from down deep inside him until they became genuine laughter.

"I love that Big Papi," he said, shaking his head. "I truly do."

Moments later, a door from farther back in the compound opened and a younger man dressed in a tailored shirt and pants, purple tie askew, and a cigar in hand strode into the room.

"I don't believe it," the younger man said. "He gave Papi a fastball right down the middle. Center cut."

For a moment, Castro was taken aback, not sure what to do. Instinctively, he began to talk, looking to smooth things over, a skill he was most adept at. "Señor Bryan, may I introduce my son, Tony. He is the true baseball fan in the family."

I stood and extended my hand. Reluctantly the younger man shook it. He must have thought his father was alone, both of them watching the games from different parts of the house. At first blush, they could have been a well-off American family holed up in the suburbs for another evening. The designer clothes Tony Castro wore were freshly pressed. He had to have been watching the game as he prepared for a night on the town, an activity I guessed he was well experienced in.

"You saw that it was Omar Rodriguez pitching?" the son asked.

"Of course," Fidel nodded.

Rodriguez was another Cuban defector. He had somehow left the island a few months earlier and was already in the U.S. Major Leagues.

"He's struggling a bit right now," Castro said.

"And if he keeps serving up pitches like that, he'll be back down in the Minors," Tony Castro answered. He could have been one of those incessant commentators on sports talk radio. "If the score holds up, this will be his third loss this month."

The way the younger Castro acted this could have been as serious an issue as the pending sugarcane crop or an important business contract that had gone unsigned.

"Those Diamondbacks haven't developed him properly," the son continued. "Omar never should have gone there in the first place. It was a huge mistake."

With that he shook his head and nodded in my direction. As he turned to leave, I saw that another man, much older but just as well dressed, was waiting for him in the doorway. This guy was taller than the rest of us, including Fidel. He had well-cropped gray hair and black-framed eyeglasses, the kind my daughters have urged me to consider wearing. I studied this face, trying to place him. He had his eyes on me, too, as if perhaps we had met many years ago. Then he turned and disappeared into the shadows after the younger Castro.

"So how would you pitch to a batter as successful as David Ortiz?" Castro asked, gesturing for me to sit back down. That it was just the two of us again.

"Start him off inside," I replied, "but well off the plate."

"Then he would wait you out," Castro said, warming to the subject. He reached for the remote and turned down the sound. "He would wait for something on the outside half and drive it the opposite way."

"Then we'd have to mix it up. Mostly pitches off the plate. But be ready to push one inside when he's looking for it on the outer half."

Castro smiled. "You catchers make it sound so easy. But if I miss by an inch or so inside, he hits it out of the ballpark, as he did right there. The pitcher soon gets pulled from the game and the catcher is still out there."

"Hazards of the business," I replied. "As we know, life is rarely fair in how it plays out."

"I wish my son could hear you talk about the game. He thinks such things are so easy. That you can fix everything in a hurry. But you and I know that baseball can never be that way. Sometimes things are best left to mystery."

Once more I pictured that beautiful curveball Castro had thrown years and years ago at the old ball stadium here in Havana. How he never really duplicated it again, despite weeks of practice under the keen eye of the real Papa Joe. How the plan, at least for a short time, had been for Castro to sign with the Washington Senators.

"So why didn't you give the game an honest try?" I asked.

"Do you think I could have made it? Could I have pitched in the Major Leagues?"

"You had some talent," I replied. "And nobody has made more of his opportunities than you."

Castro finished his drink and set the glass on the end table.

"Malena Fonseca," he said in a soft voice, for once rid of his usual bravado.

"Malena?"

"Near the end she asked me to forget about our deal. To remember our nation and the struggle."

"That doesn't sound like her."

"Doesn't it, William? I suspect she appealed to your higher sense of duty, too. If not, you would have never left Cuba. Or you would have been more determined in taking her with you to America."

"And for that she had to die?"

"Careful, my friend," Castro said. "Sometimes things aren't as simple as we believe them to be."

For a moment, I pictured her. The raven-black hair, cropped short. The infrequent, yet radiant smile. And those defiant brown eyes that weren't afraid to stare down anyone who crossed her. Those eyes are what our daughter, Evangelina, still carries into this world.

"Malena Fonseca," Castro said, almost wistfully, "she still haunts the dreams of us both, doesn't she, Billy?"

With that Castro punched a few buttons on the remote and the sound of the Red Sox–Diamondbacks game faded, replaced by the reassuring voice of Vin Scully doing the play-by-play from Los Angeles.

"What I would have given to play in a stadium as beautiful as Chavez Ravine," Castro said. "To hear a famous one like Vin Scully call my name."

I didn't answer, and Castro noticed.

"I've upset you, Billy," he said. "I'm sorry about that."

And, for once, his apology actually sounded genuine.

Once more we allowed the game to wash over us, eager to have it heal the past. But my mind kept returning to Malena. How I could have saved her, if only I had been more determined, more sure of myself.

"I'm not as all-knowing as some will have you believe," Castro said.

"That's good to hear."

"In the old days, you wouldn't have been in Cuba for an hour without my knowing it. Now I fear I've become like a lion in winter, as they say," Castro said. "All I have left sometimes is my reputation."

"Maybe that's how it needs to be," I said, feeling the liquor burn through me, perhaps making me too bold for my own good. "If Cuba wants tourism, maybe it needs to be less fearsome, more open."

"Perhaps," Castro said, "but sometimes my brother, and certainly the rest of them, takes things too far."

The dictator turned toward me in the darkness and for a moment I expected him to be angry with me, as he would have been back when we first met. Instead he shook his head in quiet resignation.

"Ah, Billy," he said, "you're the best catcher I ever had."

I breathed a sigh of relief.

"If only you had stayed, if only I had signed Papa Joe's contract," he said. "You could still have talked some sense into me."

"Never an easy proposition," I said.

"I'll admit it—it's true," Castro shrugged. "But you were brave enough to tell me what I needed to hear. There's only been a few like that, who've had the courage. You, sometimes Raúl, maybe Che."

While I didn't appreciate being lumped in with such company, I somehow bit my tongue.

"Your movie director wants more time here," Castro said. "He was so excited to get permission to film at the Tropicana."

"As always, it was quite a show."

"The Tropicana," Castro said, almost to himself. "Sometimes I cannot believe that we kept it open. It makes no sense, as many have pointed out. That a socialist country would have such an attraction. So decadent. But it is a magnet for the tourists and their money."

I couldn't argue with that.

"But as for your director, what's his name again?"

"Reid. Nicky Reid."

"Him getting more time here? That's not going to happen."

"I suspected as much."

"I met with him earlier this evening," Castro continued as the cadence of his voice picked up, becoming more like a speech. "The schedule is the schedule. That's what I told him. Visas cannot be extended for such a large group of outsiders. What would the people here say?"

"Fine by me," I offered. "I'm looking forward to going home."

Castro nodded at this. Once again, he muted the sound of the ball game play-by-play, adding, "Make sure it happens with no complications, my friend."

I didn't answer, unsure of the turn the conversation had taken.

"You and I are cursed with another sense of things," Castro continued. "Seeing things where others see only shadows."

I looked at him, determined to hold his gaze.

"We know baseball talent, my friend. It is our gift and it is also our curse."

I couldn't believe it. Somehow, he knew I was intrigued with Gabriel Santos, the kid shortstop. It had gotten back to him as did anything of consequence on this island.

"Let things be, Billy," Castro said. Then he reached again for the remote and I realized that my time with him was about over. "Take it from an old friend. Another attempted rescue from this land? How would our friend Chuck Cochrane say it to be? Ah, yes, I remember now. He'd say, 'It doesn't have a snowball's chance in hell.'"

I tried to smile and set my empty glass down on the end table.

"We're both old men, Billy. We need to let the past be. If not, it will certainly devour us."

IT WAS WELL after midnight when the government SUV dropped me off in front of the Hotel Nacional. The spillover crowd from the bar, drinking their rum drinks and smoking their fragrant Cohiba cigars, glanced again in my direction until it was decided I was nothing to them. The lull in their conversation ended and things became loud and boisterous again. Once more the night in Havana tried to soar to the heights of the old days.

Upstairs, I quietly opened the door to our suite, careful not to wake Eván, if she had returned from the night's fun. My daughter likes having a good time and I cannot blame her. Not after she spent her childhood growing up here, in the shadow of a tyrant who once loved her mother.

"Papa," she whispered.

She stepped out into the half-light, reminding me briefly of Malena Fonseca's ghostly elegance.

"Yes, honey?"

"We have a visitor," she said, and behind her I saw somebody in the shadows.

That's when I saw it was the kid shortstop—Gabriel Santos. He edged a half step into the light and tried to hold my gaze, only to look away.

I couldn't believe it and turned to my daughter for an explanation. But she didn't say anything, either. And it didn't really matter, did it? What sweet words could smooth over this transgression? We all knew our remaining days in Cuba had just become much more dangerous.

3.

"I COULD REALLY use another week down here," Nicky Reid said. He was still excited about how Castro had sought me out during his surprise visit outside the Tropicana. "You could get through to him. With a bit more time, we could have a really beautiful picture."

Today's filming was in the cobblestoned square before the cathedral in Old Havana. Tourists craned for a look to see what was going on. Above us, seagulls called to one another, riding the ocean breezes.

"I've come to love this place," the director said unabashedly. "It takes a while to wrap your mind around it, doesn't it?"

I nodded, trying to ignore him. But Reid pressed on. "That's why another week down here . . ."

"I don't think he'll, they'll—"

"I've been dealing with this office," he said, forcing a slip of paper into my hand. "I would go by today and ask again, but I'm up to my eyeballs, as you can see. My sense is it would mean so much more if you paid a visit."

I gazed at the slip of paper in my hand. It was for an address across town.

"C'mon, just give it a try, Billy. What harm could it do?"

Plenty, I thought, but Reid still stood in my path and I realized there was no getting around the director's request. He was like a kid on Christmas morning, all hepped up about what could be if he stayed on his best behavior. I had to at least go through the motions or he would find out what else was in play on my end. That's the kind of place Cuba is. Secrets are rarely held for long.

"Okay, I'll try."

Reid smiled. "I knew I could count on you."

I didn't have any scenes for the rest of the day. In fact, with the crowd shots at the old ballpark completed, my involvement in the film was drawing to a close. After lunch on the set, I hailed a cab, one of the old classics, a '58 Chevy held together with prayer and duct tape, and took the fifteen-minute ride to the office address at the Plaza de la Revolución.

Speeding out Simón Bolívar Avenue, away from Old Havana and the harbor, it wasn't difficult to imagine how grand this part of the world had once been. Royal palm trees still rode the center median as we moved in and out of traffic, passing everything from Audi sedans to donkeys pulling carts. Just past the wide plaza and the José Martí Monument, the cabbie pulled over and nodded at the Soviet-style building with the eight-story iron mural of Che Guevara that flanked the front door. He didn't want to go any closer to this home of government bureaucracy, and I didn't blame him.

After giving him a hefty tip, I made my way across the wide expanse, what was supposed to be the beginnings of a new city in the old Spanish capital. But it hadn't worked out that way. Except for demonstrations and public outcries, when people could fill this space for as far as the eye could see, I was one of the few heading across the plaza on this hot Havana afternoon.

Inside the revolving doors, large ceiling fans moved the stale air as best they could and I walked up the stairs to the Office for Permits and Official Permissions. Pushing the door open, heads turned in my direction.

"I'm with Nicky Reid, the movie director," I said in Spanish and not trying to soften my American accent.

My declaration brought the office to a standstill until a young woman, only a few years younger than Cassy, approached me.

"Our director would like another week here," I said. "To fully complete his filming."

"What is this about?" she asked. "Please start again."

"The movie crew that's in Habana Vieja today?"

"Oh, yes, the film people."

"My director? You see, he needs more time."

After I finished, she walked back to her desk, returning with a thick file.

"But he's been given his answer," she said. "That's what it says here. The production visa officially ends this Sunday."

"Perhaps the application could be reviewed again. As I said, he really would like more time."

The young woman leaned closer and said in a half-whisper, "You know, señor, this decision comes from the highest levels." Then she briefly stroked her chin. As if she had an imaginary beard—the universal sign in this country for Fidel Castro.

"That's what I was afraid of," I replied.

She shook her head. "But somehow I think you already knew that."

"Maybe."

"So why come here? Waste your time?"

I shrugged. "Sometimes one has to go through the motions, right? For appearances' sake?"

Now it was her turn to smile, as if she were in on the joke. "You know Cuba much better than most gringos," she replied.

"My director asked me to ask, and I'm trying to help him out."

"Please sit down, señor," she said, nodding at her desk. "What is your name?"

"Bryan. Billy Bryan," I replied, as we sat down across from each other, and as her coworkers kept glancing over.

"I'm Señorita Perez," she told me. "I deal with permits for the *paladares*, the restaurants. But I can check again if you'd like."

"If it's possible."

She almost winced at my reply. I wasn't making this easy for her.

"It's going to be a marvelous film," I lied. "We were filming the other night at the baseball stadium."

Perez seemed reassured by this. "We are crazy for the game," she said almost respectfully.

"So, my director wanted me to put in a formal request for more time down here," I said. "He wanted me to take it directly to Fidel Castro himself. Did you know he visited the set the other day? But how does one reach out to Fidel?"

"How indeed," Perez said, shaking her head.

For a moment, we sat there in silence.

"I could go to another office in this place," I began. "Ask someone else."

"It wouldn't do you any good," Perez said, lowering her voice. "You know as well as I do that it doesn't work that way here."

"Yes, I know."

Perez paused and glanced over her shoulder at her coworkers, who were still watching us.

"Your request will be duly noted," she said, taking out a small notepad and scribbling down a few sentences. "There's really nothing more you can do."

"You're sure?"

"I promise you that I will take it the highest levels that I can. You're staying . . ."

"At the Nacional."

Perez briefly smiled at this. Of course, it had to be the Nacional, the most expensive tourist trap in town.

"All right then," I said, standing up, suddenly eager to be out of here. Nothing was more demoralizing than to edge too close to the Cuban political machine, see how business was done in this country.

"I promise I'll submit this to the proper channels," Perez said. "You have my word, Señor Bryan."

Outside, the heat had grown worse and I began the long walk across the plaza in hopes of hailing another cab. The mural of Che stared down at me, those furious eyes following me as I hurried on my way. I had never encountered Comrade Che. He came along after my time in Havana as a ballplayer was drawing to a close. He and Fidel had first met in Mexico, during Castro's exile there. After joining forces, they returned to Cuba aboard the *Granma*, an overloaded cabin cruiser, with the rest of their ragtag bunch of revolutionaries. Even though the government troops were waiting for them when they landed, ready to blow them to bits, enough of the major players—Fidel, Che, Raúl—were able to escape into the mountains. Three years later, they had taken control of the island. That is why I never sell Castro short when he sets his mind to something.

As I came upon the main boulevard, another old taxi appeared and soon I was being whisked back to the movie set. Thankfully, Reid was too busy to ask about my fool's errand, so I sat in the shade and watched them film. By midafternoon, the heat had gotten too much for me and I caught the first shuttle back to my air-conditioned room at the Nacional, where another rum and ice could be easily secured. The small van swept up to the hotel's main entrance and soon enough I was inside, where the cool air sweep over me, momentarily stopping me in my tracks. As I made my way past the front desk, one of the receptionists called out to me.

"Señor Bryan?"

"Yes," I replied, surprised that she knew me.

"There is a message for you," she said, and held out a small white envelope.

Walking toward the elevators, I opened it and pulled out a small sheet of white paper with government letterhead.

"Tell your director that his request is denied—again," it read. "By the way, my son, Tony, was intrigued by how you would pitch to a slugger like Big Papi."

It was signed Fidel Castro.

4.

AS EXPECTED, A pair of plainclothesmen, in a gleaming black Audi, followed us from the hotel late the next afternoon, our last full day in Havana. Thankfully, they left us alone as our old taxi pulled up to the main gate of the Colón Cemetery and we walked inside.

Chuck Cochrane once described Necrópolis Cristóbal Colón as an amusement park in memory of the dead, and I couldn't disagree with him. Founded in 1871, almost 150 acres in size, with more than two million buried here, the mausoleums, chapels, and family vaults were wedged in among the regular graves. Almost everywhere, white-marble statues of angels rose up from the ground. Some had their wings spread wide, while others appeared more hesitant, even resistant to any appeals or prayers, with their arms crossed, or a single finger lifted to the heavens. Everything was packed in so tightly together that one had to stick to the wide boulevards that intersected at the white-columned chapel in the middle of the property or hug the white-stone sidewalks that threaded through it all. If not, a person could become lost and disoriented in this homage to the past.

Eván led the way to her mother's gravesite. The angel statues, which gathered like flocks of birds atop the larger headstones and every other vault, gazed down upon us as we passed by the vault for La Milagrosa or the "Miraculous One." Located at the corner of Calles 3 and F, it is the grave of Amelia Goyri de Hoz, who died in May 1901, while giving birth to a son who also died. The son was buried in the same coffin at the foot of his mother. For some reason, the coffin was reopened years later, and the son's skeleton was found cradled in his mother's arms. A small steel box for donations, surrounded by flowers, sat atop Amelia's grave, and I dropped in a few American coins and rang the small bell attached to the box for good luck.

A short walk beyond that we came to the small marble vault that read "Malena Fonseca, Patriot, 1929–1962." It now stood a stone's throw away from the Mártires del Asalto, a memorial of shiny metal flags that was erected in 1982 to commemorate the students killed in the attack decades earlier on Batista's presidential palace.

As I stood to one side, Eván placed a small white-brown shell, which had come from the beach near Cassy's place in Florida, atop the headstone.

As Eván bowed her head in prayer, I took a long look around. Even though it was growing late in the day, the hot sun still beat down with a vengeance, with little shade to be found anywhere at Colón. The cemetery would soon close, as it did every day of the week, promptly at five o'clock, and after dark some Cubans would scale the walls, feeling that after hours was a better time for their Santería ceremonies. That the night was always more effective for prayers to the shadows and the past that we all shared.

When you've lived as long as I have, the past can become all-consuming—capable of overshadowing the future and even the present. It's easy to picture one's life as a series of seemingly innocent choices that ripple though events, sending one off in one direction and then another. We like to think that one can backtrack at any point. Alter course and regain our bearings. But what one realizes at my age is that's rarely the case. Small, spur-of-the-moment decisions build one atop the other and soon become the path that we have little choice but to follow. What if I hadn't rolled that baseball out to a young Fidel Castro? What if I had given up my pursuit of a big league career a few months earlier and stayed in Havana after my final season here? Could I have protected Malena Fonseca from all that had followed? What if I hadn't glimpsed Gabriel Santos fire a baseball over to first base only a few days ago?

Eván raised her head and took my arm, and together we began the long walk back to the front gate.

"Sometimes I wish she had a bigger presence in this place," I said, almost to myself. "There are so many other graves here."

Eván gave me a curious look.

"She should be more than a ghost in this town," I added. "A name that everyone remembers and takes time to honor."

"Papa, it's fine," Eván said and patted my arm.

As the sun dropped lower in the sky, we walked the main boulevard, past the chapel with two towers, walking slowly toward our waiting taxi.

"Fidel wouldn't allow her to be anything more than a ghost," Eván said softly.

"But why? After so many years?"

"Papa, you know as well as I do that nobody can be bigger in this country than him. Somehow Mama threatened too much of that. You know as well as anybody she was the real saint of the revolution."

"All I remember is that when everybody else tried to be a hero, she was the only true one."

"That's what I've been told," Eván said.

"And for that she had to be eliminated? I mean, it couldn't have been some kind of accident, a misunderstanding?"

Eván stopped and looked back at the cemetery that stretched in all directions. She blinked several times, fighting back the tears.

"Oh, the revolution did away with her—that's for sure. Can't you see, Papa? She was too good for Fidel, the whole lot of them. For that reason alone, she had to die."

I nodded, knowing she was right.

"And that's why I'm going to help that kid, Gabby Santos."

"But how?" I asked.

Eván smiled and leaned closer to me. "He wants to leave here. Play in the Major Leagues. He told me as much the other night."

"There's nothing we can do about that," I cautioned her. "You know how this land works. How it holds on tight to its treasures, to its true angels."

"We will help, if we can," Eván said. "That's what I told him, Papa. That there are people we can talk to, back in Miami, once we get home."

I stopped in my tracks, turning toward her

"Oh, daughter of mine, what are you doing?"

"That's all I said," Eván told me, taking my hand. Together we began to walk again down the wide boulevard to the main gate. "But it's a start, isn't it?"

"I'm afraid it is."

5.

"C'MON, PAPA," EVÁN called out, "we're going to be late for the bus to the airport."

"Almost ready," I replied.

I shoved the last of my things into my bag and laid out my white suit from the movie on the bed for somebody else to have.

"What are you doing?" Eván asked, doubling back to hustle me along.

We both gazed down upon the suit coat, pants, and Panama hat, like it was a fallen comrade in some long-running battle.

"You're not taking any of it home?"

"Seems better off to leave it here," I told her. "Somebody in Havana will make better use of it than me."

"But you looked so good in it, Papa."

"Aren't you the one who told me about how the hotel staff divvies up whatever the tourists leave behind?"

"Sure, they do," she replied. "The loot parties. They'll surely have one tonight after everyone has left for home. But I'm not sure what they'll make of that getup. It looks so, so old school."

"You mean like me?"

Eván shrugged. "Too bad you didn't bring your old cell phone. You could have left that, too."

"Why bother? It's a wreck, like me."

"Someone would want it. They could hold it together with duct tape, like they do the cars and everything else around here."

We both paused, looking down at the small pile of clothes. Eván reached into her bag and pulled out a yellow blouse and a pair of sandals. As I watched, she placed them next to the stuff I was leaving behind.

"Papa, at least keep the hat. A souvenir of our return to Cuba."

I considered this, knowing I would never hear the end of it if I didn't.

"Oh, all right," I said and placed the Panama hat atop my balding head.

Downstairs three tourist buses idled in a row, waiting to take us to the airport. There was much conversation as we boarded and settled in. Yet as the buses pulled away from the Hotel Nacional and began to follow each other through the streets of Havana, heading south out of town, swinging toward the Plaza de la Revolución and one last time past the watchful eyes of the Che mural, everyone grew quiet, lost in their thoughts and memories of this star-crossed place.

I looked over at Eván, trying to read her mood. But she turned away, gazing out the window at the city where she had grown up. I knew she was happy I had gotten her out, pushed through all the mounds of paperwork, bribed more officials than I could count, to bring her to America. She was a U.S. citizen now and proud of it. Still, this was her first home. She knew better than anyone else how this place could haunt one's dreams. Despite being raised as a favorite "niece" of Castro's, going to the best schools here, it hadn't taken long for her to become an unabashed capitalist once she reached the United States.

I remembered the airport when it was called Rancho Boyeros, not the new José Martí International. From a distance, the new gleaming structure could have fit in anywhere—Frankfurt, Singapore, Madrid. Yet as we drew closer, the vintage cars lined up outside, sharing the road with the carts and donkeys, gave it that distinctive Cuban look.

Soon enough we were in a long line that snaked through the main concourse. At the far end was customs and beyond that our plane, a 737 charter, stood on the tarmac. I was ready to be gone—away from this place that held too much of my past.

As we stood in line at customs, nervously talking among ourselves, I remembered the time, in the old terminal, when Malena was coming with me. I was on the verge of taking her to Miami and then home to western New York. Everything was set, we were going together, but she balked at the last minute. Something deep down inside of her couldn't leave this place. It was almost like she couldn't imagine herself living anywhere else but Havana. So I left her that day as I needed to join my new team in Florida for spring training, and by the time I could return she had been killed in what was termed a tragic accident, a misunderstanding with authorities. But in my heart, I knew better. Fidel Castro couldn't let her go, and events had soared out of control from there. Castro and Malena were among the most strong-willed people I've ever known, and disagreements between them could boil over in a heartbeat.

I was in front of Eván as we neared customs. Far up the long hallway, men in brown military fatigues, holding machine guns, stood to one side, watching the line with grim faces. I held out my passport to the soldier behind the counter, who flipped through the document and stamped a page far inside.

"Have a good flight," he said, a faint smile breaking across his face.

The smile jarred me. Those in uniform never smiled. Not here.

As I took my passport, I turned to see several soldiers, including one with a fierce German shepherd dog, move toward Eván.

"Wait," I shouted.

"Papa," she cried out, but they had already gathered around

her, pushing her away, as the others in the movie party looked on with stunned expressions.

"You have a plane to catch," a soldier told me. Several more were on either side of me now. "Goodbye, Señor Bryan."

"Evàn," I shouted, and I began to run toward her.

Yet they were ready for any outburst. Several more soldiers closed in from either side and I began throwing punches, hitting one guard squarely in the jaw and catching another in the chest. But it was no good, there were too many of them and when I looked for Evàn again, she had disappeared. The soldiers hand-cuffed me, and several others took me by the arms, forcing me toward the door to the tarmac and the waiting plane. Overhead the bright sun shone down as if mocking my arrogance and stu-pidity. My worst nightmare had come true: so close to where I had last seen Malena Fonseca, the Cuban thugs had now taken my daughter, too.

Around me, the remaining movie people were quickly cleared through customs and our plane was soon loaded and taxiing out to the end of the runway. Evàn wasn't on board.

"As soon as we're in U.S. airspace, I'll call my people," Nicky Reid said. He had taken the empty seat beside me. The one that Evàn should have been in. "We'll get this straightened out. They don't know who they're dealing with."

Mercifully, the flight between Havana and Miami was a short one and soon we were touching down in Florida. As we cleared security there, Reid's people were waiting for us.

"Did she get in any kind of trouble?" one of them asked.

"Make contact with enemies to the government?" said another.

"No, no," I repeated, but deep down I knew what this was about. Evàn had somehow gone too far in trying to help San-tos, the kid ballplayer.

"Dad, what is happening?"

It was Cassy, my other daughter, my American-born daughter.

She lives an hour or so north of Fort Lauderdale and had come over to pick us up so we could spend a few days with her before I drove north to Buffalo.

"They took Eván."

"Eván?" she said. "But why?"

I opened my arms and she stepped toward me. For a moment, she was once again a little girl and my only job in her world was to protect her.

"But why?" Cassy repeated.

My eyes had welled with tears, and all I do was shake my head.

Cassy moved to one side as Reid's people and more officials in dark suits gathered around me. Soon we were huddled in some-body's office deep in the bowels of the airport. They drank coffee from Styrofoam cups, and in the background I heard the static of security radio and snatches of CNN. Cassy stayed at my side, holding my hand. Despite better relations between the U.S. and Cuba, only a limited number of flights was permitted between Havana and Miami daily. Another arrived from Cuba in late afternoon, but Eván wasn't on it.

Our ranks had swollen to twenty or more when Nicky Reid's cell phone rang.

"Who is this?" he demanded as we quieted down to listen.

"Yes, I understand," Reid continued. "Hello? Hello?"

Then he looked at his phone as if the device had somehow failed him.

"That was someone who said they were with the government in Havana," he announced. "Billy, he said your daughter is on the last flight today on JetBlue, number 667."

"There aren't any more flights from Cuba coming into Miami tonight," somebody said.

"JetBlue goes into Fort Lauderdale," another airport official answered. "It's already in the air, arriving at 10:30 p.m."

"That's in forty-five minutes," Cassy said.

"C'mon," an official said. "We'll be able to get you there in time, sir."

Down the backstairs we went as the suits talked excitedly into their cells. Soon we were joined by men in uniform and as we exited a set of doors, we were close enough to the tarmac that we could hear the planes revving their engines and the baggage trailers rushing by. Within seconds, a black SUV pulled up.

"Sirens and flashers on," one of the suits ordered as Reid, Cassy, and I were ushered into the backseat. "Only stop if you absolutely have to."

With that we were off, making the turn onto the Route 112 overpass and then heading north, running fast in the left-hand lane on Interstate 95.

"Will we make it in time?" Cassy wondered aloud.

"If not, I'm sure security there will be ready for her," Reid said, trying to sound reassuring.

Out the car windows the lights of Hialeah and now Miami Beach spread out in front of us. I couldn't help thinking that more of Cuba would look like this today if Fidel Castro hadn't come to power, if he hadn't been allowed to operate the country as his own little world.

Up ahead, the traffic peeled away from the left lane, doing its best to stay out of our way. At this hour, there were few cars on the highway and we made good time, soon pulling up to the arrivals level at Fort Lauderdale–Hollywood International Airport. Security was waiting and the three of us were shown to a people mover. We were allowed to bypass security and we sped up the long corridors toward the gate.

"The flight just landed," the driver said. "We'll be there in a jiff."

This end of the terminal was nearly deserted as we pulled up to the gate. The first ones to disembark from Flight 667 looked at us with nervous eyes before hurrying past, eager to get on with their regular lives. The line of people coming off had slowed to a few stragglers when several flight attendants came running up the ramp, looking for help. That's when more security personnel stepped in, and they eased Eván into a wheelchair and pushed her the rest of the way to us.

"Papa," she said, as I stepped toward her, with Cassy right behind me.

I was relieved, so happy, until I saw her. Eván's hair was matted down, the small amount of makeup and dark mascara she usually wore, had been scrubbed away and I realized they had tortured her as they once had her mother: holding her face down in a bucket of cold water until her lungs were about to explode. That's what they had done decades ago to Malena, and some twisted mind had decided that her daughter deserved the same fate.

"Are you okay?" Cassy asked.

Eván nodded and slipped a small piece of paper into my hand. I stole a glance at it, growing angry by what it said.

"Mr. Bryan, we need to talk with your daughter for a few minutes," one of the suits said. "We promise to keep it brief. But it is policy."

I nodded and kissed Eván on the cheek before following her down the corridor. Somebody in a suit fetched her bags. Thankfully, security didn't keep Eván long and soon we were together as a family in a suite on the top floor at the Crowne Plaza Hotel, across from the airport.

"It's the least I can do," Nicky Reid said about the room. "I feel terrible about all of this."

"It's fine," I told him.

"No, I mean it," he continued. "Everything is comped. Whatever you need, order it."

As the Hollywood director headed for the elevator, I wondered if I would ever see him again. An exhausted Eván soon fell asleep on the double bed. After calling home, telling her husband that we wouldn't be home until the next morning, Cassy lay down on a rollaway and soon drifted off too.

That left me in a comfortable-enough chair, staring out the window at the runways and the lights of Miami on the far horizon. Once more I looked at the slip of paper Eván had given me, the one that I hadn't shown to the security officials or any of Nicky Reid's Hollywood people.

"She should have known better," it read.

That was all.

I read it one last time before crumpling it up and tossing it into the hotel wastebasket. My old friend Fidel would pay dearly for this.

6.

I AWOKE JUST after dawn to Cassy gently patting my shoulder.

"Dad?"

"Here I am," I said, opening my eyes.

I reached out for her hand and she briefly took it, squeezing hard.

I turned to find Eván, who was still curled up on the large bed. "How is she?"

"Tossing and turning," Cassy said. "She cried out a few times in the middle of the night, but she's going to be fine."

"Poor kid."

"What did they do to her?"

"Scared her but good," I said, thinking about her head being held down into a wash bucket filled with water.

Cassy waited for me to explain it all to her, as I've been doing since she was a little girl. I try not to keep too many secrets from those I love. This time, however, I remained quiet. Such a conversation would have to wait for another day.

"Dad?"

"Yes, honey," I said, returning to the present.

"You're brooding."

"Damn right I am. What they did to her—" And again I stopped myself. Cassy waited for more, but I refused to continue.

"Once she's up, let's get out of here," Cassy said. "The airport people said they'd run me down to Miami so I could get my car. I talked to Bobby. You two will stay with us for now. We can keep an eye on Eván."

I let my daughter's decision wash over me. I had to smile at how she did things: occasional pronouncements with everyone's best interests at heart, and she was usually right.

"Dad?"

"I'm with you," I said, beginning to stand up, feeling the tightness in my back, the familiar ache in the calves and back of the knees from catching too many games in too many Minor League ballparks.

"You keep an eye on her and we'll get out of here soon."

By midmorning, we were all riding in Cassy's Lexus SUV to her place up the coast. Her twin boys, Kyle and Connor, were ready for us when we pulled in the driveway. They often did things in tandem, piling over each other like a pair of puppies, asking questions in rapid-fire fashion, all smiles and curiosity as only five-year-old kids can be. Soon enough they had me out in the backyard, pitching to them overhand, no easy deliveries because Kyle had decided that was sissy stuff. Thankfully, we were only using a white plastic Wiffle ball and for a time the throwing motion felt nice and easy. I pitched to one of them, while the other one retrieved the misses. Sometimes I put just enough spin on the ball to make it move, but not so much that either of them would get too discouraged.

Around us the neighborhood of cul-de-sacs was gearing up for another day. Minivans of various makes and colors, the living-room-sized vehicles that everyone in this part of the world seems to need, were coming out for the day, and Cassy waved at nearly everyone as they passed by her corner lot. She would survey the subdivision and return her attention to our game, just Grandpa and a few tykes playing ball.

"I'm glad you're both safe," she said, and I nodded, concentrating on my next pitch. The way the two boys were changing places, one hitting and the other catching, I wasn't sure which one I was pitching to right now. And it really didn't matter. I was just an old man, an aging pitching machine, and I continued to throw, even though I knew my shoulder would need ice after I called it a day.

"Cuba always puts me on edge," my daughter continued.

"You liked it well enough when we were there a few years ago," I answered, keeping my eyes on the batter and home plate. "If I remember, you were pretty insistent that we make our first trip together."

"That doesn't mean I was ever relaxed down there," she said. "I mean, I loved the city and the people. It's all so beautiful and exotic—like going back in time. But somehow I never did trust it all. It was like it could turn tail over teacup in a heartbeat."

Tail over teacup? That's a phrase my wife sometimes used, and now it had been carried on by our daughter. I almost pointed that out to Cassy. But instead I threw another pitch, and Connor, I believe, sent the plastic ball whizzing over my head and out into their yard.

"Almost an all-time best," I said, and that prompted Kyle to take the bat, now ready to best his brother.

I began to throw again, realizing that Cassy was right—one never feels totally at ease in Cuba. At least an Anglo doesn't. And, of course, that is a large part of its appeal. The glitz, the glitter, the past, the mystery.

Eván opened the sliding-glass door from the kitchen and stepped out onto the gray-stone deck. She held a glass of iced tea and blinked her eyes, looking up at the cloudless sky.

"You need anything, honey?" Cassy asked, and Eván shook her head.

"I'm okay," she replied, as Cassy gave her a concerned look.

I have been fortunate that my two daughters get along so well, even though they grew up worlds apart and had such different mothers. My wife, Laurie, was like me, from the north country between Buffalo and Rochester. I had met Malena, Eván's mother, the same night a young Fidel Castro took the mound in Cuba.

"Don't stay out in the sun too long," Cassy told Eván. My Cassy loves to fuss, and I knew Eván would never get used to it.

"I'm fine," Eván said, as she sat down and stretched her long legs out.

"Two more pitches each," I called out to the twins.

"Ahhh."

"Grandpa is on a strict pitch count," I told them, and despite their protests I soon joined Eván in the shade of the deck.

As I sat down, Cassy brought out a glass of water with ice and lemon. "I'm going to take these two down to the pool," she said. "You're more than welcome to come."

"I'll stay here," Eván said, and I nodded, indicating that I'd do the same.

Eván and I sat together, listening to them change and gather up towels and goggles until the side door shut and they were off, walking the block or so down to the neighborhood pool.

"I don't know how she does it," Eván said, and I raised an eyebrow.

"Being such a good mother," she continued. "So patient when I'd lose it for sure."

"You can always put up with your own children," I said. "That's true for most anyone."

"Whatever you say, Papa," Eván said. She finished off the last of her iced tea and leaned back in the chair, closing her eyes.

I watched her for a while and sipped my ice water. It was going to be another hot one in South Florida. The ice cubes in my drink were already melting.

"You know why he wants to leave?" she said in a low voice. "Why he's so determined about it?"

I couldn't believe we were back to the kid ballplayer again.

"No idea, honey."

Left unsaid was that I didn't care. Let the kid stay in Havana. At least that's what I kept telling myself.

"The last time we talked, right out of the blue, he said he wished he could be you."

"Why me? Gabriel Santos is a much better ballplayer than I ever was."

Eván smiled and looked right at me. "And that's the point he was trying to make, I think. He said that you at least had the chance to play in the Major Leagues. To really measure yourself."

"Little more than a cup of coffee, in my case."

"But at least you got the chance. You know what he told me next?"

I shook my head.

"His exact words? 'If I stay in Cuba I will never know. I may be surrounded by fine ballplayers but too many of us will never know. Never know how good we are.'"

I considered this as both of us fell silent. Eventually I turned to find Eván still watching me, waiting for a response.

"I've been doing a lot of thinking since last night, after what they did to you," I told her. "Maybe we should try to give Santos a chance to find out how good a ballplayer he may be. To see if he can play in the Majors."

7.

AS A PITCHER, Skipper Charles had been too tentative and unsure of his stuff for his own good. Despite an effective fastball, sometimes topping out in the low nineties with quality movement, he was reluctant to challenge hitters. Instead he tried to trick them by going with a mediocre curveball and a more erratic changeup in pivotal situations. As a result, he didn't last long in the Major Leagues. Soon he had gained the reputation as a guy just good enough to bounce between the Minors and the big league club for the rest of his career: the one demoted when a bigger name was acquired via trade or a regular came off the disabled list.

That's why I was surprised when Eván and I turned off the main road to see a large sign reading, Sir Charles's Fine Crafts and Fishing Charters. Sir Charles? While some would have considered that to be over the top, I was heartened by the blowhard business name. After all these years, Skipper had seemingly summoned up enough nerve to stand on his own two feet. That was the kind of confidence we would need to pull this off.

Skipper was waiting for us in the bar of the small yacht club overlooking the harbor in Key West. The dock space was split between the masts of sailboats and the more low-slung cabin cruisers and cigarette boats. Word had it that Skipper owned several of the latter—fast boats that could reach Havana from the Florida Keys in a few hours.

"My old catcher," Skipper said when he saw us. The years had treated him well. Skipper still had a boyish-looking face and the lively step of a man who wasn't about to acknowledge his age.

"Skip," I said, briefly hugging him. "This is my daughter, Evangelina—"

"Evangelina Fonseca Bryan," she said, as she reached for his hand.

Even though Skipper was solidly built, taller than me, my spirited daughter was able to give him a firm handshake. The old-timers at the bar, already into their cups, shifted on their stools to give her the once-over. Even at a distance, with her angelic face, darker skin, and flowing skirt, Eván draws the eye.

"Good to finally meet you," Skipper said.

In all likelihood, he had heard the stories about how I learned I had a daughter back in Cuba after the old winter-ball league in Havana fell apart and the U.S. embargo went into effect. And how I had moved heaven and earth to get her out.

"Here, sit down," Skipper said, and soon we were flush with menus at what I took to be his regular table near the picture window, overlooking the small harbor.

"It's been a while," Skipper said.

"Thanks for seeing us on such short notice, Skip."

"My pleasure."

"We heard you have quite an operation down here."

Skipper motioned to the waitress, and soon he and I were presented with Amstel Lights and Eván a gin and tonic. Together we raised our glasses to the old days—in Havana.

"The best thing I ever did was to invest my last baseball bonus in the boat business," Skipper said. "Nobody came out and said it—that it would probably be my last big-money contract in the game. They never do that, do they, Bill?"

"No, they don't," I replied. "If anything, they lead you to believe that you can play ball forever."

"Exactly," Skipper said, nodding his head. "But something told me that this was probably it. It was in spring training down here with the Dodgers. I was trying to hook on with a new club, but deep down I knew it wasn't going to work. I wasn't getting into many games. Couldn't start one to save my life. The big bosses really weren't giving me an honest look."

"I know the feeling."

"And it wasn't like the old days. When we could go down to Cuba for a sweet paycheck, right? That option and most others were long gone by then. It just took me a while to figure it out."

I love the faraway look that steals into people's eyes when they talk about the old days in Havana. It's a rare form of melancholy that settles over those who have actually been there and lived the life. Even now, so many years later, they can easily conjure up those memories. For a moment I could tell that Skipper was back there—playing ball at the cavernous ballpark in Havana, all of us running wild on the town at night. Yet he flicked a switch somewhere inside himself and returned to us, back at that table overlooking the harbor in Key West.

"That's done with, though," he said. "That's why I decided to build up a respectable-enough fleet. I landed some high rollers, guys from New York and Washington, who love to troll for the big fish farther offshore. They fancy themselves the next Hemingway, riding high out there on the Gulf Stream, angling for the beasts of the deep. They actually say crap like that, and I'm happy to play along. For a price, of course. Nonnegotiable."

"And that led to other opportunities," Eván said, and Skipper turned to her, with a slightly perplexed look. I love it when men realize my daughter is more than a pretty face. That she's often a half step ahead of the rest of the world.

"Well, you have to adjust to the circumstances," Skipper told her. "This business is like any other. You need to change or you go under. There's no holding still in the current, darling."

"So, you've diversified," Eván replied. I had to smile. When Eván first came to live with us (Cassy hadn't married yet), she had practiced her English with real diligence. Among her favorite tongue twisters were *diversify* and *diversified*. It took her months to get them down.

I reached over, my hand briefly covering Eván's. I almost wanted to acknowledge that she had said the word correctly.

"Skip, we need some help with a special project of ours," I said.

He glanced around to make sure no one was eavesdropping. He knew exactly what I was referring to, and he wanted to keep it under wraps.

"That's what I figured, Billy," he said.

"He's got plenty of potential," I continued quietly. "He deserves to see what he can do in the big leagues."

Skipper smiled faintly and looked over my shoulder at the harbor of boats bobbing in the freshening breeze.

"You may not know this, but ballplayers are the worst cargo," he said and turned back to us. "They are watched like nobody's business right now in Havana. I kind of blame your old friend Castro."

I resisted answering that he was no friend of mine.

"Ballplayers from Cuba fetch good coin," Skipper added. "Everyone seems to have a hand in such transactions on the island now. You'd be surprised."

"But you've had success before," I said. "Especially with ballplayers."

"We've had our moments," he said. "But as they say, it don't come easy."

"Good deeds in Cuba rarely do," I agreed. "To get somebody out—for good." I glanced at Eván. "We know that drill as well as anybody, don't we, hon?"

Eván smiled knowingly. Skipper drained his beer and signaled to the waitress to bring another round.

"YOU TWO ARE crazy," Cassy said. "Just plain crazy."

We were back at her house and she was trying to keep her voice down, with the twins already in bed.

"Remember what they did to you the last time?" she said, looking at Eván. "Interrogated you for hours and then tortured you by shoving your head in a bucket of dishwater."

As she carried on, I wished I hadn't confided in her. Still, it's tough not to tell Cassy everything.

"I'm okay," Eván protested.

"You're fine because you were lucky," Cassy added. "Lucky they lost interest. Somebody in Havana had their big joke at your expense. They decided to torture you the same way they did your mother. I mean, what kind of place has that kind of institutional memory?"

I told her, "Cassy, it's fine."

"No, it's not, Dad. That's just plain crazy and downright evil. And here I've been pulling my hair out because nobody ever calls me."

"I'm sorry, darling," I told her. "I couldn't get any reception south of Homestead."

"That does it," Cassy snapped, and Eván and I grew quiet. We were on the couch in the living room, with Cassy pacing in front of us. We knew better than to interrupt her when she became this upset.

"I'm getting you a new cell phone tomorrow," Cassy continued. "Before you drop off the face of the earth again and I cannot reach you."

"But I like my old flipper phone."

"It's a dinosaur, Dad. You can get one for ninety-nine cents on Amazon now."

I realized that Cassy had become fixated on my old phone because there was nothing she could do about our plans with Skipper Charles. She knew we were going ahead with it regardless of how angry she got with us.

"I tried to get him to ditch that phone down in Cuba," Eván said, "but he wouldn't hear of it."

"That settles it," my American daughter said. "You're not leaving here without a new cell."

The room grew quiet and Cassy stopped pacing. Instead, she stood defiantly in front of us. I took a chance, steering the conversation back to our plans for Gabby Santos.

"We can get this kid out," I said in a low voice.

"Of course, you can, Dad," Cassy snapped. "You can solve all the problems in the whole goddamn world if somebody only gives you the chance. Mom was right about you. You wear your heart on your sleeve and then act so surprised when the general population doesn't salute your lofty aspirations."

"Eván and I talked about it," I said. "He deserves better than to rot in their system."

"So, you two are going to be his knights in shining armor?" Cassy said, shaking her head. "Sometimes I think you both still believe in fairy tales. I mean, things don't work that way anymore, especially in a place like Cuba. You two forget I've been there, too. I've seen how it is. So pretty for the tourists on the outside and a sick man's nightmare on the inside."

"That's why Gabby needs to get out," Eván argued.

"Just listen to yourself," she said, her voice rising again. "Gabby? Where did that come from? He's just another ballplayer looking to score the big bucks by playing in this country."

Eván peered down at the floor, knocking away one of the boys' colored plastic balls with her bare foot.

"No, it's not like that," she replied.

"Honey, talk to me," Cassy told her. "Evvy, you sometimes forget we're blood. I got my spider sense out on this one and there's something else at play here. What is it?"

When Eván looked back up at Cassy, her eyes were misty. Both of us waited as she wiped the tears away with the back of her hand.

"He knew all about Mama," Eván continued. "How she was apprehended at the airport, trying to get on that flight to Miami. Trying to get to you in America, Papa. How that was the last time anyone saw her alive."

"So, he knows an old story, a Cuban fable?" Cassy said. "That doesn't mean anything. Your mother was a national hero, Evvy. From what I understand, she was more of a saint than the rest of that revolutionary bunch—Fidel, Cienfuegos, Che—put together."

"No, Cass, it's more than that," Eván explained. "We traced everything all the way back. How his mother and Mama may have been cousins. I probably met him at some family holiday when he was just a baby, before you guys got me out."

"And that's reason enough for this crazy scheme?" Cassy said, as she sat down on the couch between us. She tapped Eván lightly on the knee with her palm. "Everybody is somehow related to everybody else, aren't they? That's what the Good Book says, doesn't it?"

Eván reached for her hand and clasped it. She brought the hand up to her face and stroked her cheek with the back of Cassy's hand.

"I know it seems silly, Sis," Eván said. "Do you know how much I love that word—*Sis*? How happy I was to discover I had a sister, somebody I could call Sis?"

All of us grew still, watching her hold Cassy's hand.

"You guys got me out," Eván said, "and now we have to try and do the same for him. He's family."

"Family?" Cassy said with disgust.

The word hung in the air until I tried to hurry past it.

"Unfortunately, we can't bribe enough officials to get a ballplayer like Santos out," I said, realizing how high the stakes had become. "I've seen him play. He's much too good for that."

"But we can try other ways, can't we, Papa?" Eván said. "We can go with Skipper's plan."

I nodded. "Yes, we can."

8.

BARELY VISIBLE FROM Route 1, the small cove sat hunkered down in a nest of mangrove trees away from the main highway. In my rearview mirror, the traffic sped past, making a beeline for Key West, the next and final destination down the Overseas Highway. As Eván and I made our way down the white-stone road, things opened up to reveal a fair-sized parking lot, squat gasoline storage tanks, and several boats, all sleek cigarette models, bobbing at tether along a weathered dock. Skipper leaned against a full-sized pickup truck, waiting for us.

"How many wrong turns you make?" he asked.

"Just kept the Gulf on my right and the ocean on my left," I replied. "Like you told me."

"Good job," Skipper replied. "As you'd expect, we don't exactly advertise this side of the operation."

The property sported nothing taller than two stories, and the wood was weathered gray from the saltwater winds. Inside the far building, Skipper motioned for us to join him at a circular table covered with charts and tide tables.

"I did us some more homework," Skipper said, as he flipped open a small notebook. "First, we need to go over the rendez-vous point again. Where and when?"

"He will be at the public beach east of Havana, between Villa los Pinos and the Hotel Bravo Arenal, the one we talked about," Eván said. "But not until the middle of the week."

"Why not?"

"The team has games every night until then," she replied, taking stock of the brightly colored maps that lined the walls. "They've had several rainouts."

"They'll have more rainouts to contend with, too" Skipper said. "This weather forecast is plenty dicey."

He took off his Miami Marlins ball cap and scratched his head. The back of his neck was red from long hours in the sun. "Billy, did I ever tell you I hate the start of hurricane season?" Skipper added. "It makes everything a real crap shoot."

Eván looked at me, clearly afraid that the operation would be delayed, even canceled.

"But maybe we could have it work in our favor," Skipper said, as he peered at the charts and tables spread out before us. "Less security along the shore during lousy weather. Usually. If he can be there, we can make this work."

"He'll be there," Eván answered.

Skipper glanced at her, now studying my daughter as closely as he had the charts. "How are you getting word to him?" he asked.

Eván turned to me, uncertain if she should answer. I nodded, saying, "No secrets now, hon."

"An old friend of my mother's," she said. "His father was some kind of mascot or cheerleader at your old winter-ball games."

"Bolo?" Skipper asked, turning to me. "The one and only Bolo?" I nodded.

"Billy, I don't know how you can cozy up to that kind of history," Skipper said.

"It ain't easy, friend."

"What's this all about?" Eván asked. "Your stories go too far back for me sometimes."

Skipper smiled, not knowing where to begin.

"You see, darling, Bolo was merciless on your old man," he said. "Back in the day, Bolo did all the classic tricks. The ones old school mascots and jokers always pull. Bolo stood on top of our dugout with two baseballs wedged into his mouth. He'd chase the fire-eater with cups of water. He'd bang away on this tiny drum of his, getting the crowd going. But if somebody screwed up, like your father here, he made sure the catcalls rained down."

"I think I see," Eván said, smiling.

"And his son is the new Bolo?" Skipper asked.

"No, his son works at the stadium," I said. "Head of the grounds crew. Nobody has stepped into this Bolo's shoes."

Skipper nodded. "When you think about it, how could they?" he said. "You can't duplicate that winter-ball league—the talent, the antics."

And for a moment his voice trailed off, and I'd like to think both of us were caught up again in that golden age when Havana was the center of the baseball universe during the off-season. Where else could you be paid so well to play a game and be serenaded by overflow crowds, with a rumba band in the far-off bleachers to boot?

"It was a time, wasn't it, Bill?" he said to me.

"No doubt," I replied.

"Bolo, Bolo," he repeated, shaking his head. "I haven't thought about that crazy son of a bitch in years."

Skipper smiled again and then turned to the issue at hand. "You trust this guy?" he asked.

Eván nodded. "Like I said, he's an old family friend. We've known him since primary school."

"Ain't that something?" Skipper said.

He pulled a chart closer to him and then a weekly projection of the latest weather forecast. "Wednesday it is then," he said. "The seas will be rough. But, again, that could be to our advantage. You get word to the kid," Skipper told Eván. "Tell him to be on that beach twelve miles past the harbor tunnel near the castle. The small beach, the last one before the hotel. It isn't the biggest piece of real estate, but it will serve our purposes. Tell him to be there by ten o'clock sharp. It will be dark enough by then."

"You've used this property, this pickup place, before?" I asked.

"Billy, let's not get into it. The less you know about this end of the operation the better."

Skipper turned back to Eván. "Our signal will be two long blinks of the light, one short, got it?"

"I'll get the message to him," Eván said. "And there's one last thing."

Skipper gave her a curious look.

"I'd like to go," she said

"Eván?" I said. "We didn't discuss this."

"You don't need to, darling," Skipper said, almost in a whisper. "If he's there, we'll get him. It will be a fast operation—quick in, quick out."

"But I want to make sure," Eván said. "It would help, don't you think?"

Skipper gazed up at the charts covering the walls and shook his head.

"There's always a curveball in the mix," he muttered.

"Eván, listen to me," I told her. "It's too dangerous. Especially after what you just went through, what they put all of us through."

"But if it could help," she said, "I think I should be on board."

"Skipper?" I said, turning to my old teammate.

"Like I said, we can pull off the operation without her," he said. "That said, she does know what this guy looks like. Safety-wise, she'll be fine. My guys and equipment are top-notch for this kind of run."

I couldn't believe what I was hearing. It was like the two of them had planned this out beforehand and sprung it on me at the last minute.

Skipper shrugged. "I'll leave the two of you to sort this out. We're a go for Wednesday, as long as the weather doesn't go totally in the crapper. But I'll warn ya. It's going to be a bumpy ride."

Outside, the three of us made our way to my car. I gazed about us, breathing in the saltwater air, trying to calm my nerves. The half-dozen boats, bobbing in the calm waters, nearly filled the quiet harbor.

"Quite an operation," I told Skipper.

"They're plenty fast, Bill," he replied, "and what you want for a job like this. A quick turn around the bases."

"I DON'T SEE why you have to go," Cassy said. The three of us were gathered around her kitchen table.

"Because I think I can help," Eván said. "Even Skipper had to agree that I'm the only one who can positively identify Gabby."

Cassy looked to me, but I didn't reply.

Over the years, since she had joined us in the U.S., I had learned that so much of Eván's world came down to principle. Things easily fell into black and white for her. Once she latched onto something, she took a stand, often in a major way. Somehow that's what had happened with our rescue mission to Havana.

"Evvy, it doesn't have to be this way," Cassy said in a worried voice. "I checked the weather reports for the straits. It's going to be rough weather."

"Skipper said there will be rain, some good-sized swells," I said.

"Which could help," Eván added.

"With the growing chance of a major storm coming out of the Gulf of Mexico," Cassy continued as if she had memorized the weather report. "There's a tropical depression now east of the Virgin Islands. That could head our way."

Eván refused to buy into her concern. "Or it may not. You never know."

For a moment, none of us knew what to say until Eván began again.

"Dad, I know you're paying Skipper Charles a good amount for this," she said. "So what happens if the weather turns bad? So lousy that he cannot make the run to Cuba?"

I thought for a moment, running through the agreement in my head.

"He still gets paid."

"One hundred percent?" Cassy asked.

"Not all of it," I replied. "But a healthy chunk."

Cassy shook her head. "This is so stupid. That means he'll give it a shot no matter how lousy the weather just so he can get his money. And my sister here insists on tagging along at all costs?"

"I think I have to," Eván said. "To make sure he holds up his end of the bargain."

"This has trouble written all over it," Cassy told us. "I realize that the horse is long out of the barn with you two. That you've made this deal with Skipper. I just wish you'd stop and think things through one last time."

Yet Eván wasn't interested in any soul-searching. "I'm going," she said in a low voice. "Say a prayer for us, little sis."

After that Eván went up to bed and I walked out onto the screened-in back porch to gather my wits. While the sun had set long ago, I could still make out the row of poplars that lined the far property line. Beyond that, the noises of the swamp drifted out to us. Only a few stars could be seen overhead as a thin layer of cloud was moving in fast from the west, the leading edge of the bad weather that was coming our way.

When you get to a certain age, a codger like me, you try to let things slide when you have to. When I was at the tail end of my playing career, trying to hang on in the Southern League, I played pool with an old-timer, a Mr. Evers. Now, Mr. Evers may have been on the downward side of life, as I am now, but he still came to play each day with a smile and dressed to the nines. His penny loafers were always freshly polished and his shirts lightly starched, even in the heat of that summer, which is when our paths regularly crossed.

One afternoon we were playing eight-ball at Landers, the only place worth a tinker's damn in Chattanooga back then, and he told me, "A man cannot be governed by Father Time. One must be knowing of the clock on the wall, the calendar hanging by the door, but we cannot be beholden to them."

I had no idea what he was talking about, but unlike the locals who hung out at Landers I wasn't reluctant to ask what Mr. Evers was getting at exactly. Perhaps that's why he liked hanging out with me. I asked questions.

"What do I mean by that?" Mr. Evers continued. "Well, take someone like yourself. You're what, thirty-five years old or so?"

I nodded, even though I was pushing forty at the time.

"I'll be eighty-one come October," he said. "Not long after you ballplayers have cleared out, another season of yours up and done. Thirty-five years old to eighty-one? That's a hefty range in years. So it doesn't make sense for me to try and live my life like I was still your age, now does it?"

I couldn't disagree with that.

"But look around you, Billy," Mr. Evers said. "How many people do you see who don't make that necessary leap in understanding or even faith. Quite a few in your profession, I'd wager. What I mean is, a man cannot live his life at eighty-one, with the same goals and aspirations and even purpose of intent, that he would at age thirty-five. It just doesn't make sense, but people do it all the time. One of the best lessons I've learned over the years is to remember where you are in life. Certainly, one person may look younger than another and they're both the same age. Some of us are more fortunate than others when it comes to matters of money and health, even love. But one has to acknowledge where one is in life, how old they truly are. What I'm trying to say is it makes no sense at eighty-one to try and act and deal with the world like you're still thirty-five. The ones who do so are only asking for trouble. Trouble on more fronts than an honest man can handle."

I was thinking about Mr. Evers, our times together, when Cassy came out on the deck with my new cell phone. She and Eván had chipped in to get it for me.

"Say hello to an old friend," she said, holding out the all-black gizmo with the large screen. "Maybe he can talk some sense to you."

I gave her a curious look. I wasn't expecting any calls.

"It's Chuck Cochrane," she whispered.

"Chuck?"

"I called him for you."

"But why?"

"I figured that if you're reuniting your band of Cuban brothers, you should at least talk to somebody with a good head still on his shoulders."

"Oh, honey. Why'd you go and do that?"

"Just talk to him, Dad. What have you got to lose?"

I took the receiver from my daughter, who headed back inside.

"How are you, Chuck?"

"I heard about your other daughter, the Cuban one," he said. "Everybody on the charter back home from Havana got wind of it. She okay?"

"Fine. She came out on a later flight."

"Thank God for that."

Then I paused, trying to wait Chuck out.

"So, you're playing ball with Skipper down in the Keys?" Chuck finally asked.

I couldn't believe that he knew.

"Don't worry, Billy. Your sweet daughter there didn't breathe a word of it. But when she called and said I should talk to you and I'd heard about the buzz on the street. Well, it didn't take much to put two and two together."

"Skipper's got a good operation going."

"No disagreeing there. That said, it's Cuba, Billy. That's what worries me about all of this. You're playing with fire again."

"Maybe so."

"This has to do with the kid down there, the shortstop?"

I didn't answer.

"You're going to try and get him out?" Chuck said.

"I really can't say."

"Well, there's my answer right there, Billy. Now I see why your smart daughter, the American one, called me in the first place."

"It's not that big a deal."

"If you say so, Billy. All I know is I wouldn't be heading for the Florida Straits right now. Some piss-poor weather moving in."

"That's what I hear, Chuck."

"You don't need to try this, not now."

Once again, I grew quiet, not sure what to tell him. Did I trust my old friend from my Cuba days? Maybe, maybe not. Perhaps I never did.

Chuck said, "I'm not sure what you're up to, Billy, but once again you're heading into a storm."

"Seems so."

"Is that a smart move?"

I had to chuckle. "Chuck, since when did you become an expert on smart moves? You were never the cautionary sort."

"An old dog, even ones like us, can learn new tricks, Billy boy."

"That so?"

"It's a scientific fact, my friend," Chuck laughed. "I read it somewhere on the internet, so it has to be true, right?"

"That may be, Chuck, but it looks like I need to play this one out."

"All right, Billy. But if things go south with Skipper, give me a call, okay? The number is right there now on that new cell phone your daughters got you. Between the two of us, we still know more about Cuba and how it works that anybody else around. And that includes Skipper Charles."

9.

THE RAIN, WHICH had started as a weak drizzle when we'd left Cassy's place north of Fort Lauderdale, was a steady downpour by the time we reached Skipper's marina late that afternoon. Dark clouds rode the far western horizon as Skipper greeted us in the parking lot, where puddles already pooled in the potholes.

"We just made a run out to the five-mile buoy," he said, as he held up a large golf umbrella that Eván and I ducked underneath. "It's blowing hard out there. But it's still manageable."

Eván smiled at this. I knew she didn't want any delays. Her dark hair was pulled back from her face in a braided ponytail that hung down her back. The ends were already growing wet in the rain.

Skipper led us into a two-story building and through the bottom floor, where stacks of rope and boxes were piled high. Up a narrow set of stairs to the top floor, we came into a room where all of the blinds were closed off and color LCD screens covered much of the wall space.

"You've got my best men for this run," Skipper said, holding out a poncho and foul-weather pants to Eván. He took another look at her—how tall and well-built she was—and he pulled back the pants. He flipped through another box until he found a larger size.

"You're not going?" Eván asked and took the man-sized clothes without a second thought.

He nodded at the wall of computers and flat screens. "Right now, I can do us more good here. We have GPS on the boat, rigged back to the main computer. We've tapped into the Coast Guard communications, too. It's all backed up by an emergency generator on-site, in case the power goes out."

I tried to be reassured by everything he was saying.

"Your father and I will be plenty busy here, at mission control," Skipper added. "With so much going on, I need another set of eyes."

Skipper turned toward me, "Old catchers don't rattle easily. They've seen it all, right?"

I smiled at the compliment. Sometimes it was good to be known as an old, washed-up ballplayer.

On the table in front of the wall of screens and dancing images, a CB radio crackled alive.

"There's a Coast Guard cruiser a few miles off Key West," Skipper said.

When he saw the flash of concern on my face, he added, "Don't worry. He's angling for port. He doesn't want to stay out too long in this kind of weather. After years in these parts, I know all of those guys' tricks."

After Eván was outfitted and I had grabbed a poncho for myself, we made our way down to the dock, where the longest cigarette boat in Skipper's fleet was almost ready to go. It was forty feet, stem to stern, and both of its engines were fired up, spitting and gurgling in the churning waters.

"This is Monty," Skipper said, pointing at a lean guy standing behind the wheel.

"And that's Pote," Skipper added, nodding at a shorter guy in the back of the cockpit.

They glanced at us and nodded and then returned to the tasks at hand. Monty was firing up and then throttling back the engines, while Pote lifted up the floorboards, checking the bank of gasoline tanks. He tapped the dials, making sure all four were topped off. Only then did he come toward us and hold out a hand for Eván to step aboard.

"Stay next to Monty or in the cabin," Skipper said. "These boys make a great team. Nearly a hundred passages to their credit. Let them do their jobs and they'll only need you coming up to the beach at Santa Maria."

"How long will that be?" I asked.

Skipper looked up at the growing banks of dark clouds.

"Usually three hours," he replied. "But we'll need to keep an eye on the radar."

Monty said that they were ready to cast off, and Skipper untied the lines holding it to the dock. The engines roared louder as Monty gently edged the throttle forward and the boat, christened *Rascal*, made for the red-and-green markers at the entrance of the harbor. The two of us watched from the dock until the craft disappeared from view.

I knew I was a fool to allow her to head back toward Cuba again. But there comes a point when every parent realizes they have no control over their children anymore. They are on their own, standing on their own two feet, with their own aspirations and ways of doing things. Perhaps that's when we parents begin to ask ourselves how much control we ever had in the first place.

"Time for us to get to work, too," Skipper said, and I followed him back to the boathouse.

Inside, the color screens dazzled with various images, and Skipper flicked on several more monitors before settling into a swivel chair behind the long mahogany table. He pointed for me to take the seat to his left. On the largest screen, a red dot blinked in the lower corner, making steady headway now toward the center of it all.

"We can follow their progress from here," he explained, "while keeping an eye on everything else that's brewing, too."

He turned toward another screen, which was almost as large. "You help me with this one," he said. "It's the latest weather in time lapse. That's the wild card now. That storm is building up, but we should be able to slide by it without too much trouble."

For the next hour, we watched the small blinking dot as *Rascal* made its way on the large screen, heading across the Florida Straits straight for Cuba. Too soon we began to concentrate more on what was happening on the screen next to it as a long line of green, flecked with yellow, was sweeping in from the Gulf of Mexico.

"I'll be honest, Billy, I don't like the looks of this weather pattern," Skipper said. "Things are happening faster than forecast. Just how good is this kid?"

"Good enough that I'm not sure when we'll get another crack at him."

Skipper nodded. "I was afraid of that."

"Remember the stories about Yasiel Puig? Those numbers he put up?"

"He's that good?"

"Very well could be," I said.

Skipper considered this for a moment and picked up the shortwave receiver.

"*Rascal, Rascal*, this is Papa Bear," he said.

"Papa Bear, this is *Rascal*."

"You've got some heavy weather bearing down on you," Skipper said.

"It's already here," Monty replied from aboard the *Rascal*, and both of us could hear the scream of the wind from their end.

"One pass at it," Skipper said. "No more."

"Roger that," Monty replied.

As we watched the screens, the flashing red dot gained purpose, heading directly for the Cuban coast.

"He's got pedal to the metal now," Skipper said. "But it may not do us any good," he nodded at the storm radar. "This storm is increasing in wind and size. Warnings going up around the Gulf as we speak."

"So do we call them back?" I asked.

"We can play it out a bit longer," Skipper replied. "As you say, we may not get another chance."

On the largest screen, the red dot made a quick left and slowed.

"They're less than a mile out," Skipper said. "I'd imagine the waves are smacking them at midships now. Pretty hairy ride."

With that Skipper picked up the short-wave receiver again. "Two long beams, one short," he told Monty.

"We're on it, Papa Bear."

"And?"

"Nothing. Breakers on the beach. No package for pickup."

"What's your depth?"

"Twenty feet and falling."

"Give it another minute," Skipper said, his voice rising. "Get in as close as you can."

He turned up the volume and both of us waited out the seconds.

"Nothing, Papa Bear."

"Give the signal again."

"We are. Repeatedly."

Skipper shook his head.

"No response, Papa Bear. Wind's picking up."

"Pull out," Skipper ordered.

"Aye," said a relieved Monty. "Turning for home."

"Watch the swells coming around," Skipper warned. "This baby is blowing up quick."

Both of us focused on the red dot now picking up speed, racing to return to the far corner of the screen.

"Billy, he wasn't there," Skipper said.

"Maybe he couldn't see them with the storm."

Skipper shook his head. "*Rascal*'s equipped with the best illumination rig that money can buy. It can tan a seagull from a half mile away."

"You know how things are in Cuba," I said. "Maybe the authorities were onto him. Wouldn't let him slip away."

"Maybe."

The crackle of the radio interrupted us.

"Papa Bear, Papa Bear, we've still got Big Daddy on the prowl out here. Need to swing wide and go code black."

Skipper replied, "Aye, *Rascal*. Deal accordingly."

He set the receiver down, muttering under his breath. "Worst weather in months and the Coast Guard cruiser is still prowling around a few miles offshore, blocking their way."

"Why would he do that?"

"Who knows? Maybe he got tipped off somehow. But where he's sitting isn't going to make this any easier."

Skipper tinkered with the settings for the largest monitor, widening the picture, and the cruiser appeared as a dark rectangular block. The Coast Guard rig now sat in the lower right-hand corner, directly between Skipper's port and *Rascal*.

"It won't go any farther out," Skipper said. "It's just messing with them. Somehow they know that our vessel is out there. So, your tax dollars at work are going to sit there and make things downright difficult for everyone involved. My boys are going to have to run farther up the Gulf side and then come around to us through the back door. Damn, that's well out of the way, and my lads, and your lady, are going to take an awful pounding because of it."

For the next hour, we watched our red blip give the cruiser a wide berth, moving well past Skipper's cove, until it was safe enough to turn south and troll back down the coast.

"I swear the feds are screwing with us bad," Skipper said, nodding at the big screen. "They haven't moved. Wasting how many gallons of fuel to hover in that position. They know we're out there, and if *Rascal* had tried to cut in front of them, the Guard would have collared them for sure."

AT NEARLY TWO in the morning, *Rascal* limped into the harbor. Skipper and I were at the dock, ready to help them tie up. The deck and cockpit, everyplace I could see, had been scoured clean by the breaking waves.

I reached for Eván and her fingertips were cold to the touch. Unsteady on her feet, she stepped onto the dock and into my arms. Once the engines were off and everything tied down, we followed Skipper back to the boathouse. Inside, Eván peeled off her wet sneakers and the foul-weather gear.

"We didn't wait long enough," she said, massaging her forehead. Her thick hair was matted down. "We were there too early. We didn't give him enough time."

"Please don't start, darling," Skipper said. "In those conditions, things never run like clockwork, anyone would realize that. If he was going be there, ten minutes either way doesn't matter."

"That's all the information he had."

"The clock ran out," Skipper said, as he turned toward the screen. "Game called due to bad weather." The radar screen had come alive with streaks of yellow and orange moving westward. "This storm will be a tropical depression within a few hours. This is the latest projection."

"But we left him there," Eván said.

"We had our shot," Skipper said. "It just didn't play out."

"When can we try again?" Eván asked.

"Not anytime soon, I'm afraid. That Coast Guard cutter lying out there? That just wasn't something random. Not in this weather."

"Skip, c'mon," I said. "I've put honest money into this operation."

"Billy, I love you like a brother," he replied, refusing to look me in the eye. "You sure did a lot for my career back in the day."

"Skip?"

"I'm sorry, Billy. With this weather, the kid's situation—it all seems jinxed to me."

"Don't be like that."

"I'm serious," Skipper said. "I'm out of this game. Nobody's worth this kind of aggravation and expense."

Later, in the car, driving back up the coast to Cassy's place, Eván and I tried to sort things through.

"There are plenty of other smugglers," she said.

"I don't think Skipper Charles would like to hear you calling him a smuggler," I said.

"That's better than being a swindler, which is what he really is."

Rain buffeted the car and I had the wipers turned up high.

"Whatever you call them, we can't just find another one, not with a boat like that," I said. "Near as I can tell, it's a close-knit bunch. That's why I went with Skipper. At least I had a connection with him, even if it was years ago. Word will get around now and nobody will give us the time of day."

"They will if the money is good enough," Eván said.

"And that's something I'm not exactly made of," I reminded her.

10.

"CHUCK COCHRANE CALLED while you were in the Keys," Cassy told me. "He saw the radar. How bad the weather had gotten."

I didn't answer right away. My bag was packed and I was ready to start the two-day drive north to Lockport, New York, and check on the old farmhouse, which has remained my permanent address through the years.

"Dad?"

"I wish you hadn't told him," I said, taking a sip of the Cuban coffee she had made me. It went down thick and sweet. My daughter may look like the all-American kid next door, but she can make coffee as well as any Cuban señorita.

Cassy was at the kitchen sink, cleaning the last of the breakfast dishes, with the boys already out in the backyard, playing baseball.

"I didn't tell him anything important."

"You told him enough so he was able to figure out the rest."

"Maybe he could have helped, Dad. He certainly could have done a better job than Skipper Charles."

I had to smile at that. "It's funny but back in Cuba, Chuck certainly wasn't a Boy Scout. He was never the one to come to anybody's rescue, especially when it came to gambling, drinking, and women."

"And you were right there with him. At least the way he tells it."

I looked at her and tried to smile. How does one explain to your child about when you were so young and stupid? "Sure, I was."

"Until you met Malena Fonseca."

I nodded at this. "Yes, until I met Malena. Chuck didn't like her smoothing over my rough edges. He wanted me to stay the same in Havana. As wild as he was."

"Why don't you see him before you go?" Cassy urged. "He's close by."

"What good would that do?"

"It's not like you have a lot of options right now, Dad. Not when it comes to getting that kid off the island."

That's how I found myself taking a detour before driving north. I gave the guard my name at the checkpoint to Chuck's subdivision and the gate went up. My old teammate was waiting for me and together we went inside his two-bedroom condo, just a few blocks from the beach.

Inside, I accepted a Pabst Blue Ribbon and we sat across his kitchen table from each other.

"The weather got too much?"

I nodded. "I'm beginning to think that the kid may be better off in Cuba."

"Few things ever work out when it comes to Skipper. You know that as well as anybody who played in Havana, Billy," Chuck said. "I mean, how many games did you have to talk him through another rough patch? Put a few men on base and old Skip came apart at the seams. Anybody could see it."

"I suppose."

"Every time he pitched, you had to go out to the mound to chat him up. That's where you earned your pay as a catcher in Cuba, Bill. It certainly wasn't with the bat. I know—I was there. Sometimes you sweet-talked Skipper. Other times you browbeat him. It was an amazing thing to watch. It really was."

Chuck got up and clicked on the TV remote. His curtains were already drawn against the midday sun and soon images began to flicker on the large screen, which dominated the far wall. I immediately recognized the agility on display, the impressive arm gunning the ball across the infield. It was Gabby Santos—in action.

"Where did you get this footage?" I asked.

"Does it matter?" Chuck answered. "There's no doubt that the kid can play up here, be a star in the Majors."

I stared at the screen. "Like I said, maybe it's not meant to be, Chuck. This Santos kid may be as jinxed as the country he comes from."

"Enough. You're sounding too much like Skipper," Chuck answered. "This kid's got the goods, Billy. I mean look at the footwork, the arm. Sooner or later, somebody is going to get him out of Cuba. It might as well be us."

"I don't know."

"Besides, Billy, it has Cuba written all over it."

I took a long pull on my beer and glanced at him. "What are you talking about?"

"I was thinking the other night," Chuck smiled. "It's typical Cuba, isn't it? So much of it is always out to break your heart."

"I don't know what you're driving at."

"Yes, you do."

Chuck paused for a moment, unsure of how to continue. "People sometimes ask me about the old days down in Cuba and I tell them about playing ball, hitting the nightclubs, all the glitz and the glamour. But no matter how much I tell them, they'll never understand the place like we do, will they? They see it as a sports yarn or some kind of political thriller with the revolution hovering in the wings. But that's not it, is it?"

"What was it then?"

"You know as well as I do, Billy. It was a love story, with so many different angles."

"A love story? You might be reaching there, Chuck."

"Hear me out, hoss." he replied. "First you had old Fidel talking about his love of country. But as we soon witnessed, his love was more for power. A setup where he was calling the shots. Look at what the revolution did to the whole lot of them. Drove them to such disagreements and distractions that they couldn't believe in much of anything when it came to their country's future and how to decide things."

I couldn't disagree with that.

"You fell in love with Malena, who had a much different version of love of country than the rest of her crowd. Just imagine if she had had her way. How different that part of the world would have been."

I didn't answer. I didn't want to go there. It hurt too much.

"And then there was us," Chuck continued. "At first, we went to Havana to play a game we've loved since we were boys. We were so eager to take the field on another sunny day in paradise. God knows we played it to the hilt."

"When did you become such a philosopher, Chuck?"

"Cuba will do that to you, won't it?"

I tried to laugh it off.

"So how does this all come back to the kid shortstop, to Santos?"

"The way I figure it, we're about the only ones who really understand all of this," Chuck said. "We know how long a shadow this ghost of a land has. In my book, that makes us the best ones to help this kid out. Like it or not, we're the only ones who can pull this off."

"Maybe you're right."

"You know I'm right, Billy. Stew on it a while, brood about it, like you always do," he said and nodded at the T V where another highlight of Gabby Santos flashed across the screen. "Just remember that I'm here when you're serious about helping this whiz kid escape."

11.

I DON'T FLY much anymore. Not since 9/11. The lines, the security—they have become too much for me and I'd just as soon drive while I still can. Leaving Florida, the most direct way home is up Interstate 95 to South Carolina and then over to Interstate 77 and the long haul north to Cleveland, hugging the shore of Lake Erie to Buffalo. That route usually takes two long, long days. I listen to my CDs, sometimes books on tape, but mostly old crooner stuff, as Cassy calls it. Frank Sinatra, Nat King Cole, and Tony Bennett, with an occasional switch over to NPR, so I can say I know something about the world. When I grow too tired, I find a motel, the cheaper the better, and that's how I can find my way home again.

Like I say, that's the most direct way, the AAA route. But over the years I've made some great friends along the way, real *compadres* who have helped me move past the disappointment and heartache. So on this trip home I soon angled over toward Atlanta, where I could pick up Interstate 24 near the Tennessee line. From there I headed up the long, dangerous hill that truckers have nightmares about, and Johnny Cash once sang about, until I reached Monteagle and Kate Sinclair's place.

Even though it was going on midnight, I had called ahead and she was waiting up for me. Kate is the kind of woman a guy makes a long detour for.

"How was the grand return to Cuba?" she asked, as I came up the red-brick sidewalk to her front door.

Despite the hour, Kate was swinging gently back and forth in the porch swing. Even in the shadows, she was drop-dead gorgeous.

"Fidel and his bunch had to take their pound of flesh."

"Oh, Billy," she said, as I sat down next to her on the swing and we looked out on her quiet street in her peaceful part of the world. "What did they do?"

"They wouldn't let Eván leave, at least not with the movie charter."

"They detained her?" Kate asked and took my hand in both of hers.

"It ended up being only a couple of hours," I replied. My chest grew tight and for a moment I was as anxious as I had been for the time they held her.

"But she's okay?"

"Yeah, she got out on the last flight that evening, one into Fort Lauderdale. But they couldn't resist roughing her up."

"Oh, darling," she said, and kissed me on the cheek.

"They dunked her head in a pail of water. Just to teach her some kind of lesson."

I hesitated about telling her any more. This wasn't her battle. It had never been.

"Payback from the old days?"

I nodded. "For her mother."

"The mysterious Malena Fonseca?"

"Batista's secret police got ahold of her, on the eve of the revolution, and they didn't even ask her any questions. They just kept dunking her head in a pail of water. Only a few people still know about it. Me and—"

"Castro?"

"Yeah, Fidel."

For a while, we sat there, listening to the night fall into a deep slumber.

"I must admit that I was a tad jealous when you didn't take me along this time to Havana," Kate said. "But now I see you were protecting me from this."

"You don't need any protecting."

"It's a place with a black heart, isn't it? Cuba?"

"Let's just say that it has a lot of ghosts. More than most places."

Kate stood up and took my hand. "C'mon, it's late."

She led me upstairs to her bedroom with the four-poster bed. Without saying another word, she had me sit down on the bed's edge and then she pushed me back and began to strip off my clothes. After turning off the light, she stepped out of her long skirt and moved atop me.

"Kate?" I said, briefly trying to rise to a sitting position.

"Hush," she said, pushing me back down with one hand. "Let's see if we can forget about that devil land Cuba for a while."

We tried our best to do so, but I knew as well as anybody that Havana doesn't fade from view that easy. After Kate curled up next to me, I gazed out her bedroom window at the silhouette of the barn where she did her artwork. I tried to make my last memory of the day be the line of hedges that marked her far property line, the evening breeze in the treetops that could have been a quiet prayer. How I wanted that to be the last thing I remembered before I nodded off. But once more Cuba proved to be too much for me. As I settled down, what came into my head was the Malecón seawall and how it runs along the edge of Havana, rising like a fishhook into the Florida Straits, ready to snare anything in sight.

"You're thinking about Cuba again, aren't you?" Kate said, as she rolled over to face me.

"How could you tell?"

"You slow down a touch, like you're moving in some kind of dream."

"Don't worry," I told her. "I can still return to the land of the living." And I pulled her close.

"Tell me about it," Kate said. "Where did you stay? What wasn't a nightmare for you this time?"

I chuckled. "Oh, they put us up in the Nacional, one of the last of the grand old hotels there."

"The Nacional," she repeated.

"Yeah, it's on a small hill near the water. A palace of a place. All white stone and spires back in the day."

"Sounds decadent."

"It's where all the Hollywood stars stayed—Frank Sinatra, Ava Gardner, John Wayne."

"You ever see them?"

"No," I said. "But I told everyone I had."

Kate laughed. "Billy Bryan, you're such a liar."

"How do you think I got to where I am in life?" I said and kissed her again.

I STAYED WITH Kate for three days and could have lingered longer. But that's the nature of our relationship: glorious times together and many more weeks apart.

The filming in Havana had run into mid-March, avoiding the worst of the summer heat on the island. From that standpoint, it was almost the same schedule we kept during the old winter-ball days when Chuck, Skipper, and I played for the Habana Lions. Yet even with the two weeks I'd spent in South Florida at Cassy's, with the unsuccessful rescue attempt, winter wasn't that far gone back home. As I headed north, the land faded from green to a gray, with few if any buds to be seen. By the time I pulled into my driveway off Slayton Settlement Road, it felt as if I had never really left. Once again, Havana faded into the distance, far beyond this new horizon.

Sometimes Eván rides shotgun with me on these trips north. For a girl who grew up in Cuba, she has adjusted well enough to the colder temperatures and enjoys visiting Niagara Falls and downtown Buffalo, with its sweeping parkland and Havana-like boulevards. This time, though, she decided to stay behind in Florida. She sometimes works in a friend's jewelry store in Naples. That's how she tries to forget about Cuba.

Back at home I busied myself with the little things that can prop up a life. The winter hadn't been kind to the outside of my four-bedroom rambler, which was way too large for a person so late in life. The trim around the windows needed to be scraped and repainted, and there was an executive decision about what to do with my old barn. The structure, like me, was beginning to list to one side and wouldn't last many more years.

I was in my upstairs study, just gazing out the window, when my new cell phone rang. The caller ID read Cooperstown, New York.

"Billy, it's Tom Schlesinger at the Hall of Fame."

Over the years, I've helped Tom and the folks in Cooperstown. My involvement with the permanent exhibit "Viva Baseball" had led to those appearances in documentaries and eventually to the small role in Nicky Reid's Hollywood feature.

"How you get this new number, Tom?"

Schlesinger tried to laugh. "Your daughter warned me you'd be prickly about this. But you never pick up your home line."

"Too many telemarketers. I should cut the copper for good."

"Cassy gave it to me. I hope that's okay."

"What's on your mind, Tom?"

"We've been able to secure more artifacts from the Cubs, either on loan or as outright purchases."

"Sure you're not taking some, too?"

"C'mon, Billy. You know we don't operate that way."

"I know, Tom. I'm just rattling your cage."

Schlesinger gathered himself and told me about how they had come into a huge swath of black-and-white photographs, real vintage stuff from the island. His goal was to match it up with contemporary American photojournalists, with strong Latin roots. Guys like Victor Baldizon and José Luis Villegas.

"Our problem is that we have so little background about these new images," he told me. "We'd love to know the back stories, who the photographer was, getting an ID on everyone in the picture."

"When were they taken?"

"The late 1950s on up to the revolution itself. Right when you were there, Billy. We were hoping that you could take a look at them and see if you recognize anything about them."

I gazed out the window at the fields in back of my old farmhouse. My land hadn't grown anything but weeds and grass for years.

"Tom, I'd love to help, but I'm not really up for a drive your way right now," I told him. "I mean that's a solid three hours down the thruway."

"There's no need, Billy. Your daughter said you have a computer."

"So?"

I needed to talk with Cassy about laying out so much of my life for anybody who called.

"We can send the images via attachments or whatever works for you. Our tech guys will set it up. Then you can scroll through them on your own screen and tell us anything that stands out."

"Tom, I don't know."

"It would be a big help to us, Billy. Sometimes you forget that you're one of the few baseball guys who really knows this time, this fantastic era of baseball."

"Yep, that's me," I said. "I'm the last of the Mohicans."

After some arm-twisting, I told Schlesinger I'd do what I could.

The next afternoon, after I gave the Hall of Fame guys access to my aging desktop computer, nearly a hundred photos arrived, and I had little excuse but to begin clicking through them.

Schlesinger had been right. They were impressive shots. There's something to be said about quality black-and-white images. They remind me of the dreams that come to me late at night. The way everything rolls out in shades of gray and black, inviting the mind to fill in the rest—the color, the conversations, even the meaning, when it suits one's self.

The first photo was of Martín Dihigo, one of the best players of all time, and only Babe Ruth was better on and off the mound. Dihigo could play any position, and he pitched no-hitters in Cuba, Mexico, and in the old Negro Leagues in the U.S. Yet Dihigo never played in the Major Leagues because he took the field long before Jackie Robinson broke the color barrier in America. Dihigo had a wry smile on his face, as if he knew that the world wasn't ever going to be square with him.

In comparison, the next Cuban star stared directly into the camera, almost with contempt. Here stood Adolfo Luque, the so-called Pride of Havana, who pitched for two decades in the Majors, mostly with the Cincinnati Reds. The only real difference between Dihigo and Luque was the color of their skin. Luque's was pale enough to gain acceptance into the game's upper echelons and make good money in the big leagues.

I continued to click through the file, allowing myself to be won over. It promised to be a fine exhibit in Cooperstown, and perhaps I would even visit once it opened. That's when I came upon an image that stopped me in my tracks. The subject was Orestes "Minnie" Miñoso, the first black-skinned player to star in a big-market U.S. city—Chicago. Unlike Dihigo and Luque, the onetime White Sox star was dressed in street clothes and his sad eyes gazed into the camera. Hall of Famer Orlando Cepeda, Señor "Cha Cha" himself, once told me that

Miñoso "is to Latin players what Jackie Robinson is to U.S. black ballplayers."

Years ago, I had the good fortune to speak with Miñoso on the set of a public television documentary. He briefly mentioned the racist threats he had had to endure when he came north to play in the Midwest—the taunts, the popcorn boxes, and worse that were thrown in his direction. But then he told me something, almost in passing, which I've never forgotten. "I never let the world hurt me," he said in a soft voice. "None of it stayed with me. I never wanted them to know my feelings on the inside. On the outside, I just gave them my smile. My smile all the time."

Miñoso wasn't smiling in this photo, however, and I began to realize why. In the background, over his right shoulder, stood his trademark black Cadillac, parked along one of the alleyways in Havana. The date was January 1959, when Fidel Castro and his victorious armies, nicknamed Los Barbudos, or the Bearded Ones, were sweeping into Havana, with huge crowds cheering their arrival. I once met a woman, the landlady of a fourteen-story building in Vedado, the city's west end, who had grown up on the eastern end of the island. Someone asked how she came to Havana.

"With Fidel," she answered, and we realized that she had been in the army. That she was one of the conquering heroes on this memorable day in the island's history.

None of it had worked out that way for Miñoso, though. The story goes that several in Castro's army recognized him that day and called out to the baseball star, waving for him to join them, be a part of the victory parade. Miñoso began to move toward them, ready to clamber atop one of the rebels' jeeps or tanks, which had become impromptu parade floats. But he suddenly stopped. Something deep inside tugged at him, saying not everything was right about all of this. That this moment, which so many had prayed for, wasn't going to be a joyous scene for very long. That Fidel and Che and all of the rest of them would soon prove to be as evil as the dictators they had replaced. Despite the cries to join them, Miñoso turned and walked back to his Caddy. Within months, he would depart Cuba for good, losing several real estate investments and leaving family behind in the process, too.

"Author unknown," read the photo caption. Of course, I knew who had taken this melancholy image. It had been Malena Fonseca. I could have told the Hall of Fame, updated their exhibit information. But then I clicked to the next photo in the collection. I had decided long ago that some secrets are best kept close to the heart.

12.

"WE'LL JUST POKE our nose out into the big lake," Greg Downs said. "See if all the pieces are still in working order after the long winter."

"You're the boss," I replied, just happy to be out on the water.

Greg's Pearson 35, a fine-looking sloop, cruised down the Niagara River, making for Lake Ontario. A breeze with a cool edge built from the Canadian shore. Greg was at the wheel and I was along for the ride.

Frankly, I couldn't believe how excited I was to get Greg's call. A spur-of-the-moment invitation to join him down at the Youngstown pier and to take his boat out for a quick spin, a tune-up, really, after it had been put back in the water for another summer.

"I know it's not as dramatic as Cuba," Greg said.

"Cuba can be overrated," I said, as we eased past Fort George on the Canadian side; up ahead loomed Fort Niagara to starboard. Only a few other sailboats were on the river this morning. Most were still set up on their wooden cradles. Their owners doing the final preparations so they, too, could be dropped back into water in the upcoming days. By next weekend, Greg said, almost everybody from the yacht club would be afloat again, with the first race of the season scheduled for the following weekend.

"Don't kid a kidder," Greg said, looking content behind the

wheel. "I'd love to sail down to Cuba sometime. Problem is the politics will likely outlive me, and I won't get the chance."

"The politics can be ugly," I agreed.

"But that movie you were in," Greg continued, "they somehow found a way to operate in Havana."

"Only by finding the right people to bribe. It's like anywhere— grease some palms of the huge and powerful and you've got a chance. But nothing ever works out as planned in Cuba."

"You sound like a man with experience," he said, eager to hear more. But I only nodded and gazed out at the vast sheet of water that stretched toward the northern horizon.

Greg knew about my two daughters. How Cassy was raised up here and how I later discovered I had a daughter in Cuba as well. As my accountant, he had helped me pull together the tens of thousands of dollars to eventually get Evàn off the island.

"It must have been something to go back," Greg said.

"Always is," I said, as we came upon Fort Niagara, and the big lake began to open up to us, from one end of the horizon to the other. "Next time I'll get you down there."

Greg smiled at this. "I've always dreamed of going to Cuba," he said. "What's it really like?"

I considered this as we crossed that shifting line of froth, the place where the Niagara River ended and Lake Ontario began.

"It's like the land that time forgot," I told him. "It's so run-down in places—dirty and noisy compared to what we have. Still, in the early mornings and at dusk, it's easy to picture how it once was. You have these wide boulevards reaching toward the Malecón seawall, which runs the length of the city along the ocean. The streets in the old part of town are just riddled with columns, which makes for one view along the sidewalk and perhaps a completely different one if you're out in the street. The City of Columns—that's what Old Havana was called. It can all be so chaotic and so lovely at the same time."

Greg pulled on one of many lines leading back to the cockpit. As the jib unfurled, he turned off the engine and we turned up closer to the wind.

"It's a memorable place," I added, happy to let the wind take away my words.

"That's why I need to go," Greg said.

As we edged out into the lake, I looked back at the Niagara River, at the distant hotel towers and the rising mist way upriver where the falls went over the precipice.

"We'll get you there one day," I promised.

13.

"ANY INITIAL THOUGHTS?" Professor Alan Yates asked.

His question was greeted with silence.

"We have Señor Bryan's story about the exotic, tantalizing, mysterious island of Cuba."

He smiled in my direction and I wanted to believe that he indeed enjoyed my story, the first effort of mine to ever see the light of day in a classroom setting.

"I just don't get it," said a young lady in her late twenties with long reddish hair.

Professor Yates glanced down at his class roster.

"Yes? Emily?"

"Yeah, that's me," she replied, sitting up a little taller in her seat, eager to weigh in. "I mean, we hear a lot about these streets of Havana, how they're old and crooked and all that, but we don't have much about the people really."

Our first Wednesday-night gathering, in the basement of the English/Communications building at Niagara County Community College, was part of the school's local outreach program. Nobody was in line for any college credit, at least not yet. This was simply a chance to work with a bona fide college professor, a real writer.

"I've heard that it's better to always start with people, strong characters," chimed in a young man in an Oxford button-down shirt and creased khakis. I figured he worked in one of the law offices closer to Buffalo and probably saw himself as the next John Grisham.

"Not necessarily, Barry," Professor Yates said, after glancing again at his class roster. There were a dozen of us in the community class and we had been asked to submit a sample of our writing for a spot in the course. "Sometimes a particular place or locale can work just as well as a quality character, one of flesh and blood. Think about it. A place, vividly drawn, can make us feel a certain way—fearful, happy, on edge, eager for more. It registers with us emotionally."

"I'm not sure how I'm supposed to feel about this," said an older woman in the front row. For a moment, I thought she might be in my camp, but as she continued I knew that she was another killjoy. Somebody who found it easier to pick away at what was wrong with a story than try to imagine what it could be.

"It doesn't help that the writing style is pretty rough," she added. "A lot of typos, and the sentence construction could be better. I mean, if this hadn't been assigned, I wouldn't have finished it, to be honest. John Gardner once said that these things—typos and inconsistencies—break the vivid, continuous dream that we should be having with the story."

"I'm well aware of Mr. Gardner," Professor Yates said, a bit irritated. "Perhaps if we looked a bit deeper here. Really considered what a problematic place Havana may be, especially at this time in its checkered history."

His comment was met with silence and confused looks.

"I'M SORRY THAT didn't go better," Professor Yates told me a few hours later.

We were the only ones left at our table at the Blind Pig, a bar a few blocks off campus in a strip mall. Most of the students had stopped by for a quick drink and then soon headed home to prepare for another working day. I knew Professor Yates had class the next morning, but he stayed for another round, which I appreciated. I don't know if he felt sorry for me after the verbal shellacking that I'd taken earlier or whether he wasn't in any hurry to go home.

"I really thought they'd enjoy something set in Cuba," he said. "But sometimes you never know, William."

"William sounds too highfalutin," I told him.

"That was your byline, the name on the paper."

"I know, but perhaps it was a reach, in more ways than one."

"So what's best then?"

"Billy's fine," I said, deciding right then and there to give up trying to be William in the world. My old player card said Billy Bryan, and I realized that's how it would always be.

"Call me Alan then," Professor Yates replied.

"You sure, Professor?"

"Positive. Old-timers like us need to stick together."

I looked up from my glass of beer. Professor Yates had to be twenty years younger than me.

"Let's just say a class like tonight can be so disappointing," he said. "You think it's going in one direction and the naysayers take it in another."

I nodded and took another sip of my beer. It felt good that he had said that.

"How long were you in Cuba?" he asked me.

"Three winters as a player. That started soon after I signed with the Washington Senators. Then I was just back there for the movie I told you about."

"God, I'd give anything to visit there," Alan said. "It's the forbidden fruit, isn't it?"

"Americans can visit now."

He shook his head.

"High-priced tours and beach resorts aren't for me," he said. "I'd like to be able to go there and roam around on my own."

"You can do that, too. At least for now. It just takes some planning."

I almost began to explain how Airbnb was well established on the island. How the Obama administration had done what it could to open up Cuba to American visitors despite the embargo that went into effect in 1962. I realized that many Americans hold on to a romantic view of the island and the difficult history between our two countries. Time does heal wounds when it comes to how people depict Fidel and his revolution that ran out of steam a long time ago. But obstacles to travel, the reasons not to visit, still exist in people's minds. That's why I decided that it's better to let it all go. Allow people to think what they're going to think, dream what they're going to dream.

We poured the last of the beer from the pitcher into our glasses. We were both seemingly in no hurry to head home.

"Billy, do you know any artists?" Alan asked. The words rolled out a bit slurred and less polished than back in the classroom. "You know, painters or writers and the like?"

"I know a woman who does stone sculptures down in Tennessee," I said.

"Sculptures?"

"Yeah, I met her when I was looking to manage in the Appalachian League years ago. That job didn't work out. I didn't have the patience for it."

"She's a good friend?"

I smiled. "Yes, sir."

"Does she read any of your stories?" Alan asked.

"No, not really."

"Send her something. Hell, send her this one from tonight's class."

"Why's that?"

"Because I'm afraid this community class of mine isn't going to do you much good," Alan said. "It's riddled with too many apple polishers, to use an old expression. Ones who like to talk rather than really think about the story right in front of them."

I was disappointed to hear him say this. Despite having my Cuba story roughed up tonight, I liked being back in school, trying something different.

"You ever hear of Joseph Campbell?"

I shook my head.

"He was a teacher who was really into myths and their impact, their power upon us." Alan continued. "And he knew how the world worked, too. He once warned his students about trying to please their teachers and their classmates too much. In trying to answer the question 'What do they want?' you renounce the gem of an idea that you may have. What he called the jewel. In doing so, you can renounce the particular insight or outlook on things that is yours and yours alone in favor of pleasing the immediate public. You do that one too many times and your particular insight can be lost forever."

I wasn't sure what the good professor was talking about. But his talk gave me some courage.

"How do you feel about my writing?" I asked.

"It's honest, with a hard edge that draws my attention," the professor replied. "But it will just get watered down and compromised by coming to class every week."

"Then what do you recommend?"

"Billy, you have to find your own supporters, maybe form your own writing group," Alan added. "I'll be happy to read anything you send my way. I'll give you notes and suggest directions you could go with it all. That said, you need more good souls in your camp. That's why I asked about other people in the arts that you might know."

"Just send it to them?"

"That's right. I may have another one or two in the department that would be open to your kind of work. Let me see what I can do, but I'd recommend dropping this class."

"I like going back to school," I protested. "It gets me out of the house, around other people."

"Then take a lit class, catch up on the classics. I'm teaching a seminar about Hemingway and Fitzgerald next semester. I'll email you about it. But I'd ease on by this workshop. I'm afraid it won't do your kind of stories much good."

14.

"I ENJOYED IT," Kate told me a few days later. She had called, out of the blue, which was our habit. No set ritual, like every Sunday night, as some people did. We just called when the other one was on our mind, which seemed to be more and more these days.

"I liked how you took us through the city," she continued, "along that street by the water . . ."

"The Malecón."

"And the old hotel."

"The Nacional, where we stayed for the movie."

"All the way along the flank of the city, past the cathedral toward the tunnel underneath the entrance to the harbor and past the castle and to the countryside."

"Thanks for reading it, Kate."

"I'm not a writer, so I can't give you any full-blown critique."

"I wasn't looking for one. It's just good to have someone else read it, enjoy it."

"And I did, Billy."

I couldn't help but smile at that.

"You know, when I close my eyes, I can still see so much of it," I told her. "Being back down there for the movie somehow moved it front and center again."

"Is that a good thing, Billy?"

"Some days it's like a dream and other days—"

"Like a nightmare."

"Yeah, it can be a nightmare, too."

We paused, not knowing what to say next. Kate and I had met years ago now, when I became bored with another night in a bar, this time in Chattanooga, and I wandered down the street and into a reception of her work at a local gallery. I was captivated by her statues before I ever met her. And once somebody introduced us, I couldn't decide what was more enthralling—the way her works of stone seemed to look right through you or the way her light-blue eyes settled upon you and wouldn't let you go.

"I should have taken you to Cuba this last time," I said.

"No, it wouldn't have worked."

"How can you be so sure?"

"It's like I told you, Billy. I had a project to finish here. Besides, your daughter was going. You two needed to be together on a trip back to her homeland."

"It sounds like you're not sure what to make of Eván," I teased.

Kate laughed. It was a playful kind of murmur that a man will go to great lengths to hear time and again.

"How could that be, dear one? I've never even met her."

I knew that was my fault. I should have gotten them together years ago. Same with Cassy.

"What then?"

"You two have a special bond. She's the daughter you found late in life, so that recent trip to Havana was for the two of you. I would have been a bad third wheel in all of that."

"But we'll go to Cuba together someday?"

"Whenever you want, lover."

"It'll be a little while."

"No need to hurry. Cuba will always be one of your angels."

"Angels?"

"That's right, Billy. Places can be angels, too, don't you think?

Places where you've learned something important, met someone special. Those are the places you can always picture when you close your eyes."

"Yeah, that sounds like Havana to me."

I gazed out the kitchen window at the fields that once held tomatoes and beyond that corn. But that was years ago now.

"I like your part of the world, too, Kate. High on that hill near the university. That's an angel."

She laughed again. "It certainly is for me."

After we hung up, I went for a walk along the Erie Canal. Thick clouds were building to the west, blocking out much of the setting sun. I thought about Kate and her barn studio, only a few blocks from the University of the South campus. How it would be good to spend more time there, with her. But then my mind drifted back to Cuba and maybe the next story I could write about the island. If Kate was right, that places could be angels, then they could be demons, too, with enemies to battle and scores to settle.

15.

YEARS AGO, I turned the guest bedroom, which overlooks the driveway and the road beyond, into my office. The plan had been for me to write my life story up here. I had gone as far as a trip to the new Lowe's out on Route 31, on the outskirts of Niagara Falls, to buy a folding table—big enough to spread out the old photos and newspaper clippings from my playing days in Havana and elsewhere in the Minor Leagues. The scrapbook that Cassy assembled from the best of that material sat on a nearby shelf and I reached for it.

When it comes right down to it, though, I don't like talking about my years playing catcher for the Habana Lions all that much. I know I should swing for the fences, as Cassy likes to remind me. Cuba was all the rage a few years back and that will only continue, if and when the country opens up for good. More tourists from America will be ready to make the short plane trip when Fidel finally dies. Sometimes I feel like I've become an exile myself, ready to light a candle to El Jefe's death, counting the days to when the embargo between the U.S. and Cuba ends and things can begin to return to the heyday of how it all used to be. Nicky Reid's movie, which Eván told me is scheduled to be released this summer, may push things more in that direction.

Reid and the others in Hollywood want me to go along on

the press interviews, be there at the scheduled premieres in Los Angeles, Miami, and even Cannes. Eván is eager to go and will be plenty irritated if I beg off. But I might just let it be.

I took up the old scrapbook and settled into the easy chair Cassy gave me for Christmas years ago. I began to flip through the pages and, once again, I heard my daughter's warning that I really needed to scan all of this onto a disk or up to "the cloud." Preserve everything before it faded away. Undoubtedly, my new smart phone could do it if I had any clue how to perform such tasks.

If and when I log everything for posterity, I'll start with the photo I'm gazing at right now. To this day I'm not sure who took it, as the only one in the frame is Malena, with her favorite camera, that familiar Leica, held alongside her face as if she just took another shot herself and is now contemplating what to focus upon next. In this photo of unknown origin, Malena sports a thin smile and her short black hair has been pushed behind one ear. But it is those eyes that still hold me after so many years.

When I watched her take photos, I knew that she saw the world far differently than I ever would. Her eyes would become riveted, even concerned with what was playing out in front of us.

"It's like she's a bigger part of things," Chuck Cochrane once said, and it had to be the smartest thing that ever came out of his mouth.

My phone rang and the caller ID showed it was Eván. I smiled, happy that she had reached out to me.

"Papa?"

"Yes, honey. I'm here."

"Prowling around like a ghost in that old house of yours?" she asked.

"I suppose."

"You got the hang of your new phone?"

"You know it isn't easy to teach an old dog that many new tricks."

"So, what are you doing then? Looking at pictures from Old Havana? Another trip down memory lane?"

A bit embarrassed, I placed the scrapbook and the photo of Malena on the table. "And what if I am?"

"Because we need you back in Florida," she said the excitement rising in her voice.

"Why's that?"

"Chuck Cochrane just called me," Eván replied.

"Chuck?"

"He wants to be in on this, and I think he could help us."

"What are you talking about, Eván?"

"The Cuban team is coming to Mexico to play an exhibition series. And Chuck Cochrane has confirmed that Gabby Santos will be with them."

"Mexico?"

"All games at the new stadium in Monterrey, Papa. Who knows when he'll be this close again?"

16.

ONLY TWO PEOPLE were in The Keg when I walked in late that afternoon.

"If it isn't our own man of the world," said Terry, who was behind the bar. His father, Warren Connelly, who still owned the place, swiveled around on his bar stool to size me up.

"Speak of the devil," Warren said. "Word has it that you've become a movie star."

"Hardly," I said, and nodded when Terry held up an empty glass. "Genny draft."

"Your taste in beer is still hometown," Warren said. "That's good to see, Bill."

"What have you guys been up to?" I replied.

"Watching the national economy take us under again," Warren said, as Terry shrugged. "I don't know what our fearless leaders in Washington are thinking, but things have about gone down the tubes around here. As you can see, our business establishment isn't exactly busting at the seams."

"We still get a crowd on Friday and Saturday nights," Terry countered.

"Only after we extended happy hour clear through to nine o'clock," Warren said, as he gestured for me to take the stool next to him. "I can remember when happy hour was a way to draw some women into the place. A chance to serve those expensive foo-foo drinks with the umbrellas in them. Now it's become our only chance to try and fill the place."

"We still get some regulars after the late shift," Terry said.

"But let's face it," Warren interrupted. "There ain't a whole lot of people working at the Delphi plant anymore. Most people are scrambling to find a job or hold onto the one they have. All of that crap trickles down to us."

The Keg had been in the Connelly family for three generations, located on the last corner in town, right alongside the lift bridge that spanned the Erie Canal. A few years back, the waterway still saw the occasional barge pushed by a tugboat, making the trip from Albany to Buffalo. The bridges that crossed the canal were either lifts or on steel-girders, stacked atop soaring concrete embankments so that water traffic could squeeze underneath. Now such arrangements bordered upon the ridiculous. While the Erie Canal had once opened this part of the country, the major commercial link between the iron mines and wheat fields in the Midwest and the factories and mills along the Eastern Seaboard, nobody really used it for industry and commerce anymore. Pleasure boats were about the only ones on the water, with joggers and walkers pounding along the towpaths where mules had once pulled packet boats.

"We heard about your movie," Terry said. "They had a write-up in the *Sun & Journal*. How long were you down in Cuba?"

"About a month," I said. "By then we'd worn out our welcome and they gave us the boot."

"Ah, Billy, did you get in trouble again?" Warren asked, and held up his empty glass for his son to refill.

"You're drinking the profits," I said.

"Profits?" Warren said, giving me a puzzled look. "We haven't shown much of a profit for months."

"Our only chance of staying afloat may be getting this place listed as a national historic landmark," Terry said, as he placed another cold draft down in front of his father.

"A historic landmark?"

"Now don't be turning up your nose at my latest get-rich scheme," Warren told me.

"Dad, I wouldn't exactly call it a get-rich scheme," Terry said.

"All right then," Warren continued. "Our latest save-our-ass, keep-the-creditors-at-bay, stay-out-of-hock scheme. We know for sure that this place has been around since the late 1800s."

"And we have the cracks in the foundation to prove it," Terry said.

"It's been a roadhouse and small-time hotel," Warren said, his voice building in enthusiasm. "And the canal was the main thoroughfare in town, the great byway west in these parts. I've actually been down to the main library in Lockport. The first time I'd been in there since nearly flunking out of high school. Still, it's amazing what you can find in such an establishment. How anybody who was anybody had to visit Niagara Falls back in the day and they for sure came through here. I mean, we're talking about Charles Dickens, President Martin Van Buren, the kings and queens of Europe. We're going to say that they all slept here."

"All of them may be a stretch, Dad."

"No guts, no glory, son. If we're going to go down this historical register path, we have to sell it hard. Really hard."

"We could get some documentation."

I sipped my beer and let them argue a while before adding, "They do the same thing down in Havana. Every hotel that was a casino—the Nacional, the Riviera, the Libre—they all claim that Humphrey Bogart, Lauren Bacall, and Ernest Hemingway were regulars."

"See," Warren said, "if they can get away with it, we can, too."

"So, you're done with Cuba then, Bill?" Terry asked.

"Well, I'm certainly not going back anytime soon," I told them.

"Things never work out exactly right for me down there, going back to when I played ball with the Lions."

Warren grew quiet, just watching me. I remember a drunken evening in here years ago when I told the elder Connelly about Malena. How I hadn't been able to get her out of the country, to save her from Castro and what the country became.

Warren asked, "If you're not going back down there, then what are you doing, Bill?"

I thought about this and took another sip of my beer. "Maybe I'm going to help somebody get away from Cuba. Change somebody's life for the better."

"Sounds like heavy lifting," Warren said.

"When's this adventure of yours due to begin?" Terry said, as he busied himself behind the bar.

"I'm heading down south tomorrow," I told them.

Neither of them replied, and for a good long while we simply sat there—the only ones in the place. Eventually, I finished my beer and set the empty glass on the bar.

"One more for the road, Mr. Bryan?" Terry asked.

"I'm good," I replied. "Thank you, though."

"Be careful out there, Billy," Old Man Connelly said. "Be sure to come back home to us in one piece."

17.

"CUBA? IT'S LIKE anything major and impactful, I guess," Chuck Cochrane said, as he stretched out in the passenger seat. "You don't realize the full force of it all until it's over and done with."

"Those were good times," I answered, keeping my eyes on the long stretch of nothing that stood between us and the U.S.-Mexico border.

"How can you go wrong with just four ball clubs?" Chuck answered. "With some of the best prospects the Major Leagues ever saw? Sometimes I don't know how we beat those teams, especially Almendares."

"Our old rival."

"And the crowds for those games," Chuck added.

"They'd be lining up hours ahead of the first pitch to get in."

Chuck took a long swig of the beer he had nestled in the cup holder. We had picked up a six-pack at our last rest stop on Interstate 35.

"Sometimes when I watch a game on TV," Chuck began, "I have to laugh about how much is manufactured—from the announcers hyping the game to the fake crowd noise."

"The jumbotron blasting away," I added.

"The Cubans didn't need any of that," Chuck grinned.

Behind us, Eván was spread across the backseat, fast asleep. She had been adamant that we join forces with Chuck Cochrane, and I had to admit that so far it had worked well. Chuck knew a car dealer in the Austin area. We had flown there together from Fort Lauderdale and Chuck did all the talking as we took possession of a blue BMW for the week. We had decided I should be behind the wheel when we hit the Mexican border early that evening. Chuck and my daughter agreed that I had the most honest face.

"I loved that they always had a rumba band," Chuck said. "Does she know that part of her mother's past?" he nodded behind us. "That she loved to dance to the beat of the rumba band at the old ballpark? How we turned her to the glitz and glamour when she hung with us?"

"She doesn't have a clue," I smiled, enjoying how the car handled—low-slung and solid on the road. "She only knows that her mother was a saint for the revolution."

"And you never told her?"

"No, not yet."

"Told me what?" Eván said in a sleepy voice from the backseat.

"Nothing, dear," I said.

"Oh, the stories your father could wax on about," Chuck chimed in. "About walking on the wild side in sinful Havana."

"Oh, those I need to hear," Eván said.

"Another time," I said. "Here we are, we're coming up on the border."

Far down the road a ribbon of red-and-white flashing lights came into view.

Chuck finished off the last of his beer and flung the can into the desert darkness. "Time to button up and fly right," he muttered to himself.

I tried to pretend it was like crossing the border back home. I had gone back and forth into Canada, usually going over the Lewiston-Queenston Bridge, more times than I could remember.

Yet as we drew closer, perhaps it was the dry heat or the long line of cars and trucks, our situation felt more intense, more foreboding.

We idled in line for a good half hour before we finally approached the first checkpoint, the last one on the American side. We paid the toll and then headed into Mexico itself. Here the customs officer, a tough-looking guy in green fatigues, eyed Eván sitting in the backseat and ordered me to pop the trunk.

"Crazy bastard," Chuck mumbled under his breath.

We sat there as he rifled through the trunk, and other uniformed guys soon joined. They spoke in rapid-fire Spanish, too fast for me to really follow.

"Maybe I should get out," I said. "Talk to them."

"Stay here, Papa," Eván warned.

"What are they saying?" Chuck asked.

"Hear that, Papa? *Puta* this, *puta* that. They think I'm your whore. That you're a couple of drunk gringos on a joyride with a prostitute."

"That's what they're really saying?" Chuck said.

Eván shook her head. "Idiots."

"Then I need to talk with them," I said.

"Don't, Papa."

But it was too late. I was out the door, too worked up for my own good.

"*Ella es mi hija,*" I repeated to them. She is my daughter.

They looked at me as if I was crazy, and for my trouble I was spun around and pinned face first against the hood of the BMW. Behind me, I heard the others get out of the car, and Eván seemed to be talking with all of the men in uniform at once. She had her passport out and told them that it was true. She may have been born in Cuba, but I was her father. That she had lived in the United States for a decade or longer.

The commotion grew louder and somebody gave me an extra push to keep me down. But then it all grew quiet, like a storm does after the first crack of thunder. A new guy, the boss man I suspected, asked to see our passports. Chuck held out his and then fished mine out of the glove compartment. When the boss had them all in hand, he ordered us to follow him inside. The rest of the uniformed guys fell back to let him pass.

Inside a cement-block building, we were led into a conference room. There we cooled our heels for a good half hour. Chuck was still muttering about how we had been treated until Eván shook her head, urging him to be quiet. We were being watched through the one-way glass at the far end of the room.

When the boss returned, he still had our passports in hand. He sat down at the head of the conference table.

"What are you doing here?" he asked.

"Doesn't our documentation check out?" Chuck asked.

"Of course, it checks out," he replied. "But I cannot decide if you're the Three Musketeers or the Three Stooges. I mean, two old guys and a Cuban-born diva."

Eván bristled at being called a diva but kept her mouth shut.

"We're just going to Monterrey," I said. "To see some baseball games."

He smiled. "Or to be more precise, the games against the Cubans."

"Are they down there?" Chuck asked.

"Don't play the fool with me, Mr. Cochrane," the boss man said. "We both know that you sometimes scout for the Miami Marlins. That you're on a small retainer with them. And we know that Mr. Bryan here was recently in Cuba, with his daughter. That he's become a movie star at the ripe old age of eighty-one."

None of us knew how to answer.

"I cannot stop you from going into Mexico, from attending the games in Monterrey," he said. "You're correct—your documentation is all in order."

Yet now he leaned forward, resting both his hands, palms

down, on the polished tabletop. "But be careful my friends. The Cubans don't screw around, especially when it comes to their precious ballplayers."

All of us nodded at this.

"And whatever you're trying to pull off—don't come back this way. As you saw, I have plenty of hotheads under my command. Too much pepper blood, as the gringos would like to say. Who knows what they're apt to pull if I'm not around, ready to step in?"

"What's a better option then?" Chuck asked.

The room grew quiet when the boss man didn't respond right away. He just sat there, glaring at us. So, Chuck decided to try again.

"I mean, what do you suggest, sir?"

The boss man shook his head at Chuck's meager attempt to show some respect.

"Now you didn't hear this from me, but I would strongly suggest that you return to the United States through a less-traveled point at the border," he replied. "Say Del Río or Eagle Pass or even Los Ebanos. Stay away from Laredo. This is not a healthy place for the likes of you. Not in times like these, with the drug money flowing back and forth, the words from Washington flaring tensions. Remember that in no way am I your source regarding any of this. Don't bother using my name if you end up in trouble again, which I think the odds strongly favor. I will disavow ever seeing you, let alone meeting with you. Do we understand each other?"

"Yes, but—" Chuck began.

"Do we understand?" the boss man interrupted.

We dutifully nodded our heads in agreement again.

"All right, then. Good luck and goodbye. Remember what I said. Don't come back through Laredo."

With that he fanned our passports out on the table and we waited for him to nod that we could take them back.

The boss man smiled. "I hope the ballplayer is worth all this trouble."

18.

"I'LL GET OUT here," I told Cochrane. The traffic had crawled to a standstill approaching the Crowne Plaza Hotel in Monterrey, Mexico. "We're sure not going to find out anything stuck in this traffic."

"All right, then," Cochrane said, as he drummed his fingertips on the steering wheel. "You walk past, case the joint, and I'll pick you up a few blocks down. I'll be on the same side, same street, which is?"

He craned his neck, trying to find a street sign as a horn blared behind us.

"Primera Calle," I said. "First Street. We're only a few miles from the stadium. It's where Team Cuba wanted to be."

I opened the passenger door, glanced left and right, moving as fast as I could to the sidewalk. Up ahead, Cochrane signaled to turn the powder-blue BMW down an alley. It struck me that the car's color was the same shade as Chuck's precious Hudson convertible when we were first together down in Havana.

"Be careful," Cochrane barked out the window.

When another car honked behind us, I waved him on and pulled the brim of my Tampa Bay Rays ball cap down to hide some of my face. A construction crew had set up farther along the street, with workmen moving back and forth under a yellow canopy. Several storefronts were open with people milling around in front. Dressed in my khakis, polo shirt, and Rays cap, I looked exactly like what I was: a washed-up ballplayer—an old man.

The hotel was two blocks away, on the left side. On the road Team Cuba usually stayed at high-end places, like the Crowne Plaza. Over the years, it had become a reward for making the elite team. That, free gear, and a better-grade of apartment in Havana were about the only things the socialist government could offer its star players these days.

"*Mi amigo*," somebody said, tapping me on the shoulder.

My attention had been on the hotel and the two security guards posted on either side of the front entrance. I turned back to find a young hustler, who was talking a mile a minute. I picked up enough of it to determine he wanted to show me the sights. Be my private tourist guide for the day.

"And we'll find you a woman, too," he smiled sweetly in Spanish.

"Buzz off," I told him, and I pulled a five-dollar bill out of my pocket. "Leave me alone or you don't get a whiff of this."

He reached for the fiver.

"Deal?" I said, pulling it back.

"Deal," he nodded.

I watched him take the bill. Then he hesitated for a moment before turning to go.

"You could use my services," he said in English over his shoulder. "I know this town better than anyone, my friend."

"Yeah, okay," I mumbled to myself.

From there I fell in with the small crowd milling around outside the hotel. As I drew closer, I took in as much as I could without drawing attention to myself. Besides the two guards out front, this alley, the one right next door, was blocked off, and I suspected that the one on the other side of the building was, too. Normally, three lanes of traffic would be moving past, heading in either direction. Yet the construction crew had cut things down to one lane each way. In addition to the orange cones, a healthy section of Jersey wall angled into the lane directly in front of the hotel itself, well into the center of the street.

Despite the setup, no work was actually being done. In fact, it was pretty quiet for a construction zone. No jackhammers tearing up the pavement or idling trucks. Two yellow tents had been erected over manhole covers on both sides of the street.

I walked slowly toward one and lifted the flap. Nobody was inside and the manhole cover still covered the round hole in the pavement.

"Hey," somebody shouted out.

It was one of the guards from across the way, near the hotel's entrance.

I turned away and walked as fast as my old legs could carry me away from the scene. Thankfully, nobody was worked up enough to follow me. My prayers were answered when I saw Cochrane waiting for me in the powder-blue BMW a few blocks up.

"REACHING HIM AT the hotel is impossible," I told Eván and Chuck.

We were in our hotel suite at the Sheraton, on the other side of the stadium. The first game of the exhibition series was scheduled for tomorrow evening. From our window we could see the Crowne Plaza, its top floors towering over the mishmash of apartment buildings and low-slung stores.

"We get a suite at the Plaza," Cochrane suggested.

"Remember, it's completely booked," I replied. I was sprawled out on the couch, my calves still tight from my brief hustle away from the team hotel. "Besides, if they have guards outside, imagine how many more they have in the lobby, checking the elevators. Up on the floors themselves."

"They had control of the street?" Eván asked.

"Somebody did. Like I said, nobody was in those construction tents. It's all show to keep a handle on things."

Chuck and Eván grew silent.

"Maybe we've bitten off more than we can chew," I offered. "We knew this was going to be tough, but this security is over the top."

Cochrane gave me a hard look. "What are you suggesting, Billy?"

I couldn't hold his gaze. "Maybe it's time to reassess things. I mean, from top to bottom. Starting with, what are we really doing here?"

"We're trying to give Gabby Santos a chance at reaching the Major Leagues," Eván said in an angry voice. "A better life."

"Billy, this is probably our only shot for a good long while," Cochrane said, growing annoyed with me. "God damn, I cannot believe it. We hit a snag and you're ready to throw in the towel."

"I counted a half-dozen security guards between the front entrance and the fake construction zone," I snapped. "Who knows if they're Cuban, Mexican, or a combination of both? That's more than a simple snag."

"But when will the Cubans be this close again?" Cochrane added. "I mean, they'll be at the Olympics next, where the security is even more over the top. By the time we get another crack, so close to home, Señor Santos will be so old—"

"That he'll be desperate enough to try to get out on a raft," Eván added. "Or worse yet, cast his lot with the Mexican crime syndicates."

I held up my hands in resignation.

"I'm just telling you what I saw," I replied. "Right now, the Crowne Plaza is a little piece of socialist Cuba, complete with the security detail, plopped down in the middle of Mexico. The Castro government may be hundreds of miles away, but they're controlling this area."

"So what if we change things up?" Cochrane said. "Swing the odds more in our favor."

"Easier said than done."

"Papa, don't be like this," Eván warned.

"And you don't have to take his side," I told my daughter.

"But what if he's right, Papa?"

"He's rarely been right in his life, except to guess right on a 3-2 changeup instead of a fastball."

"And I smacked that sucker out of the ballpark, too," Cochrane said, standing up. For a moment, he pretended to swing an imaginary bat and watch the ball he had clubbed soar far over the outfield fence. "Don't you remember, Billy Bryan, how I won us that game in the old stadium in Havana?"

"How can I forget when you never stopped talking about it? Years later, you're still running your mouth."

Eván took my hand, trying to calm me down.

"Aren't you the one who's always said that you get only one chance?" she said. "If the moment is there, you have to try? Try as hard as you can, right?"

"But all I see are the wrong signs."

What I couldn't help thinking was that these were familiar signs. Of real trouble.

"The Castro government often sends along its own guards and security," Eván said. "I know that as well as anybody."

"All the more reason to be careful here," I said, trying my best to make her understand. "If something were to happen to you? I don't know what I'd do."

"That's why we have to do this," Eván insisted. "We cannot let the bastard somehow win again."

After that nobody said a word for a long time and the sound of the traffic drifted upward, masking the room's air conditioning. The car horns, the noise from the sidewalk below, all of it could have been the random thoughts and fears we were having.

That's when Eván smiled and looked at Cochrane and me. "I have an idea," she said.

19.

TEAM CUBA WAS scheduled to play two games in two days against a squad of U.S. college all-stars. Between those contests, the Cubans were under lock and key, leaving immediately for the airport before dawn, the morning after the second game.

"It's a small window to get anything done," Cochrane said.

"At least we know," I said, "they're leaving at 6:00 a.m. sharp, right?"

Chuck nodded. "Buy enough people beers and it's amazing what they'll tell you," he said.

The two of us were back in the hotel suite, waiting for Eván. First pitch for game one was only hours away.

"Your daughter's the one who drew the short straw."

"If anybody can pull it off, she can."

Chuck shrugged at my show of confidence. "If the credentials people are anything like the bunch over at the ticket office, it ain't going to be easy. Everybody's on edge at the ballpark. They want these games to be over and done with and send the Cubans packing. That's what one guy told me. 'We can't wait for them to be out of here.'"

We sat in silence and I saw my old teammate take a long glance at the minibar.

"Did I ever tell you about the first time I met Eván?" I asked.

Chuck shook his head.

"It was the first full day back in Havana," I said. "When I went back there with Cassy."

"I remember that I was a bit sore you didn't ask me to come."

"Frankly, the only reason I returned after so many years was because of Cassy. Both of my daughters, in their own ways, can be pretty determined when they want to be."

Chuck laughed. "Most women are. They put their minds to something and there's no stopping them."

"We had just come downstairs at the Hotel Inglaterra that morning."

"That's where you stayed? Say it ain't so."

I nodded.

"Oh, Billy, you are such the romantic. I mean, of all the old places left in Havana. The Nacional, the Libre, you and your daughter stayed at the Inglaterra on her first trip to the island?"

"Some traditions die hard."

"Billy, buddy, you're haunted by too many ghosts. You and I both know you were back at the Inglaterra because of Malena Fonseca. The woman you can't ever forget."

I couldn't disagree with him, so I didn't try.

"We were downstairs, in the dining room," I said, intent on finishing the story, one of my favorite family tales. "They have this great spread all laid out—grapefruit, bananas, plantains. They even had eggs and some meat, and, of course, plenty of pastries and bread."

"Cuba with an abundance of food is a grand place," Chuck said, closing his eyes. "I can picture it now."

"We had filled our plates, ready to dig in, when this young Cuban woman barges into the place, looking for us. And she's not taking no for an answer. The waiters, the maître d'—everyone's trying to get in her way, but she's barreling ahead."

"Did you recognize Eván right away?"

I paused to consider this. "I guess I did," I replied. "There was something about the way she carried herself—so proud, so determined—that reminded me of her mother."

"She's not exactly the same build," Chuck said. "I mean Malena was a petite doll of a thing. You can describe Evàn as a lot of things, but petite ain't one of them."

"But there's a fierceness with both of them. You can see it in their eyes. Nothing really scares them."

"Maybe that's why you can't help but fall for them."

"Maybe so."

Once again, we sat in silence, both of us lost in our memories about that glorious time when Havana was Vegas before Vegas. When Malena and I would drive down to the waterfront late at night and watch another boatload of Americans surge off the night ferry from Key West. A steady stream leading to the great city, back when Cuba was alive with laughter and bright neon, and it seemed as if the party would last forever.

We heard the electronic key in the door. Evàn entered—all smiles and business—moving much faster than either of us seemed capable of right now. That's what memories and ghosts can do to you: slow everything down until it's difficult to catch up with what's at hand, what needs to be done in real life.

"Success," she said, holding up a laminated slat with her ID photo hooked to a dark-blue string lanyard. "We are in."

20.

FROM MY PERCH high above home plate, I sat in the shadows below the upper deck. I watched Eván make her way between the home dugout and the third base line, speaking and smiling with everyone in her path. When she decided to dress up, as she had done today, in white blouse, unbuttoned to reveal some cleavage, and a black skirt, not quite a mini but revealing plenty of leg, any guy with a pulse would pause to give her another glance. "You could be Jennifer Lopez," Cassy once said when Eván decided to dress for an occasion. And it was true. With her long black hair combed back, held in place with the help of a pair of Ray-Bans, my Cuban daughter was a knockout, no doubt about it.

Eván also knew when to call in favors, and that's how she had put herself in the middle of the action during batting practice before the first game. She knew somebody at Univision, who knew somebody else in the sports department, who knew someone covering these games with the Cuban national team. The bottom line was she had gotten a media pass, which put her on the field hours before the opening pitch between the Mexican and Cuban squads. It would be our best chance to reach out to Gabby Santos.

I had no such pass and had gotten in through an unlocked side door, a few down from the press entrance. Despite my lack of credential, I was in position to watch her talk up the players. We had swung by a local Office Depot earlier this morning and gotten Eván a digital recorder, with an extension microphone. She had no idea how to use it. I wasn't sure if it even had any batteries, but I watched her wield it like an expert, holding the mike out for the next interview, smiling and nodding along with the answers, and nobody was the wiser.

From my vantage point, back in the shadows, I counted at least six security guards. Two were in uniform, one each along the first and third base lines. I took them to be City of Monterrey cops. Still, as I continued to survey the field with a small set of binoculars, I picked out four more, guys in suits and ties, who moved among the journalists. They had earplugs and didn't really focus on the interviews in progress. Instead they surveyed the field, even studying the seats, which were mostly empty. When they looked my way, I hunkered down in the seat.

Our plan was simple: Eván would reach out to Santos and tell him that we were here and ready to help. If he wanted to escape, we would do everything we could.

Down on the infield, Santos was taking turns fielding groundballs at shortstop. The kid sure was a wonder to behold. The way the ball left his hand, with plenty of zip and on target time after time, I knew he was the real deal. If he wanted to play in the Majors, he certainly would have the opportunity.

Santos hadn't recognized Eván when he jogged past the knot of media near the Team Cuba dugout, and why would he? He wasn't expecting any of us to be here. I had told Eván not to approach him too soon. Let him get in his warmup throws. Only drift over in his direction when he began to take his turn in the batting cage, letting things play out in the measured, methodical way that baseball conducts itself before another game. While there is rarely enough time in the world, everything and everyone in such a hurry, baseball likes to pretend that it has so many free moments to spare. It is one of the quaint notions that I still love about the game.

In groups of three, the Cubans took their turns in the batting cage, spraying line drives to all parts of the outfield. They rarely muscled up to try to hit the ball far over the fence. It had never been their style, and I wondered if it was because of Fidel. He was rumored to be the real general manager, the one who manipulated everything from afar. Perhaps that had now fallen to his son, Tony Castro. Speed on the basepaths, good pitching, and defense, have always been the Cuban trademarks. That's how the best of them had gotten off the island and made the big leagues. Crafty pitchers like El Duque Hernández, and slick-fielding infielders like José Iglesias and Alexei Ramírez. Gabby could be as good as any of them if he decided to leave the island.

Soon enough it was Santos's turn to take a few swings. He was a switch hitter, so he took his first round, swinging from the left side and then turned around to the right side. I didn't see any hitch or flaw, as the batting strokes were mirror images of each other. The kid was adept with lots of potential from both sides of the plate.

When he finished, with time ticking down before the start of the game, I watched Eván stroll over closer to the cage.

"Easy now," I whispered to myself.

She had the notepad out, microphone in hand, ready to make her play.

Eván had slid her sunglasses atop her head and Gabby still didn't recognize her. After all, what would she be doing here, before the biggest series of games the Cubans would play this season, in Mexico of all places? But then he realized who she was and rocked briefly backward on his heels. Just a wobble. That's how comfortable the kid seemed to be in his own skin.

Watching through my binoculars, I couldn't help but coach him under my breath.

"Steady, kid," I said. "Hear her out."

Through the magnified lenses, I could read Eván's lips as she asked Gabby about how it felt to be on the national team. That's the first question we had agreed upon. What was it like to make the squad at such a young age? At the age of only twenty?

The question was so matter-of-fact, fitting with the moment, and we hoped that it would reassure the kid. And it appeared to work. He began to answer like he would to any media person, telling Eván something like that it was a great honor to be on this team, to be selected.

That's when Eván held out the small reporter's notebook, opened to a picture of me back in the old days, wearing my Habana Lions jersey. "But there are so many other possibilities," Eván was to tell Gabby. "You know this player, don't you?"

The kid shortstop nodded, recognizing the team shot of the old Habana Lions. The one with me and Chuck Cochrane seated in the front row.

Here Santos stopped and looked around, almost in amazement. Eván reached out and touched his forearm in an effort to reassure him. Both of them realized that nobody could say the words Major Leagues in this place, with so many ears listening. Everything had to be in code. So guarded.

"He can help you," Eván said.

"How?" Gabby replied as his face became agitated. I feared his answer was too loud, too excited, and I swung the binoculars quickly left and right to see if any of the plainclothesmen had picked up on this.

Thankfully, Eván smoothed things over, nodding her head, and saying something innocuous like, "It must be a great honor to be here."

She closed the notebook and set it down on the emerald-green grass. She held the microphone, as if she were finishing an important interview.

"It needs to be tonight," she told him. "Our friends will be waiting. Come outside, away from the hotel, and they will find you."

Those were the exact words we had agreed upon when we rehearsed all of this.

Santos nodded as if he couldn't believe what he was being told.

"Our man in the Habana Lions jersey will be there from midnight until an hour before dawn."

As I watched, Gabby didn't answer. He didn't know what to say. We knew the Team Cuba plane was scheduled to leave early, the morning after next.

"Good luck in today's game," Evàn said, and the kid nodded dumbly and returned to the batting cage for his last round of practice swings.

Without a backward glance, Evàn gathered up her gear and notebook and made her way to the gate behind home plate and back into the bowels of the stadium. I lingered upon Gabby Santos, watching him take his remaining cuts. Twice he popped up and once barely made contact. He now appeared nervous, like a kid caught up in something far bigger than he had ever imagined.

"Pardon me, sir," a voice said over my shoulder. I had been so focused on what was happening on the field, trying to read every word, that I hadn't seen the guard approach.

He wore a different uniform, more green than blue, so I decided he had to be with the stadium detail.

"You got in early?"

"Yes, I'm a big fan," I replied.

"And an American?"

I shrugged. "You bet I am. I've heard so much about this Cuba team that I drove down from Texas to check them out."

"How did you get in so early?"

"Oh, you know how it works, don't you? You keep trying doors until the right one opens. When you're my age, you have all the time in the world, all the time in the world to keep trying."

"You'll need to come along with me," the guard said.

"Is that really necessary?" I asked. "Tell you what. I'll go back outside and come in with the rest of them. I have a ticket. I promise you that. I'm not trying to cheat anybody."

The guard gazed down at me. "I'm beginning to think you're a scout, for one of the Major League teams. Those are expensive spyglasses. You don't see those every day."

"No, no, it's nothing like that," I said, standing up. The last thing I needed was to be taken into custody and too many questions being asked. "I'm leaving, okay?"

I reached into my back pocket and pulled out my wallet. I looked around us, and the stands were still empty. "This is between you and me, my friend," I said in Spanish. I let him have a glimpse of a one-hundred-dollar bill and then flashed another. "Both yours if you let this drop, right now."

Now it was his turn to take a look around as I slid the bills out of my wallet and folded them over and then folded them again.

"Deal?" I asked, holding out a fist with the bills balled up inside.

The stadium cop nodded and I gave him the bribe. With that I brushed past him and didn't look back as I hurried down the ramp to the street level and the exit below.

21.

"C'MON, WHERE IS this kid?" Chuck said. "The door is closing fast."

"Chuck if you don't shut up," Eván said from the backseat, "I'm going to slap you upside the head."

"You can come up and try, sweet miss," Chuck replied.

"Hey, hey," I said, trying to calm both of them down. That said, my old Lions teammate was right. Time was running out fast, with it now approaching four in the morning in Monterrey.

Together we had watched the game earlier that evening on TV at a nearby sports bar, listening to the distant roars of the crowd. As expected, Team Cuba had trounced the college all-star team, 12–5. For tomorrow's game, things would be even more locked down when it came to security.

Chuck looked back up at the team hotel. Almost all the rooms were dark and we knew it would be impossible to get another message through to Santos.

"He ain't coming," Chunk said. "God damn, he doesn't have the guts."

"I'm going to tear you a new one," Eván said from the backseat, and Chuck and I couldn't help smiling.

"Where did you hear that one?" I asked her.

"Where do I hear anything in your country?" she said. "The

TV, the radio—it's so much talk, talk, talk in this land. Before too long, it seeps into your bones. It's like you have no choice."

Chuck nodded at this. "I can't disagree with that, darling."

In the hours after the game, after the parking lot emptied to only a few cars, we had changed location and were now parked in an alley a block down from the Crowne Plaza.

"Let me take another walk by," Eván said, sitting up. "See what I can see."

See what I can see? Where did she come up with these sayings?

"I hate to say it, sugar," Chuck told her, "but if you meander past that hotel at this hour, they're going to arrest you for the oldest crime known to man," Chuck said.

"Murder?"

"No, darling, whoring. I mean, I may be old but I ain't dead, and some Hondo is going to think you're selling."

"Chuck, I'm warning you," Eván replied in a low purr that I knew was trouble. She was tired and anxious, like the rest of us.

"Please stay put, Eván," Chuck added. "Here, we'll try this." And he eased the car a little farther up the alley, poking the BMW's nose out so we could see all the way down the street in either direction. Nothing was going on. A doorman paced back and forth, and the neon light reflected off the windows of the store-fronts across the way.

"Reminds me of the old days back in Havana," Chuck said. "When it got too late for anybody's good."

"What was that like?" Eván asked him, the anger fading from her voice.

"Havana?"

"Yes, back in those old days."

Chuck turned the car off and glanced at me with a wry smile.

"In those days, Havana at night was the most beautiful place in the world," he said. "Of course, it was corrupt and dangerous, too. But you can't have everything, right? Everyone loves to harp on that now and for God's sake we knew it back then, too. But most of all it was such a sight to behold. Such a beautiful land when everyone came out to play."

"Why was that?" Eván asked. "What made it so special?"

"Different strokes for different folks, Eván. Billy and your mother used to love to go down to the harbor and watch the cars roll off the night ferry from Key West."

I found myself nodding.

"Me? I liked to listen to Lola. She was my girl, or was supposed to be, or should have been—anyway, she sang at the Riviera. For her last song of the night, she nearly always belted out 'Somewhere Over the Rainbow.' By then it was well into the wee hours of the night, like it is now. The crowd had thinned out, sometimes hardly anybody was left if it was the middle of the week. But she sang that song because she knew I liked it, and I always stuck around for the end of the last set."

"What happened to Lola?" I couldn't help asking.

"You know, Billy, I don't rightly know now. Last I heard she was somewhere in Los Angeles, doing bit parts in pictures. It's how too many things play out, right? You think you have all the time in the world. That you'll stay in touch with the precious ones in your life forever, but it doesn't work out that way, does it? You lose track, and with each passing year it becomes too difficult to find them, downright embarrassing to reach out, and by then what's the point anyway?"

Eván said, "You could still call her."

"I don't know, darling. That's your generation talking. With guys like your father and me, it ain't so easy, even though we do it so much in our heads all the time. I mean, I can close my eyes and just like that," Chuck said, as he snapped his fingers, "I'm back to those late nights at the Riviera. Even at that hour, Lola often had some well-wishers and I'd stay out of the way. I mean, what's a hick ballplayer bring to the table in those kinds of situations, right? And afterward I knew she liked to change, freshen up, so I'd wait by the backstage door, sitting there on the steps, probably smoking another Cuban stogie. Somehow from that small alleyway I could see all the way down to the water and the lights atop the Nacional, and that's where we often ended up. There was always time for a nightcap in Havana right, Billy? Even if we were playing a doubleheader the next day."

"Always time for a nightcap," I agreed.

"And you know what I remember the most? It's the smell of the sea. Even well off the Malecón, farther inland, even near the old Colón Cemetery, you always knew you were close to the ocean in Havana. No matter how much it was built up—I mean heap upon heap of Mafia money and neon glow and big-band music and foolish laughter, so many people carrying on. Through it all, the sea was always out there. It always seemed like it was only a few blocks away. I believe that's what made the town feel so full of ghosts. The sea breeze was always coming off the straits, holding everything so close to the heart."

We grew silent inside the BMW, staring out upon that empty street as the night gathered around us. Everything Chuck had said was as true as anything can be.

Closing my eyes, I was back there, walking along the Malecón in Havana at dusk. Once again Malena was on my arm as we gazed upon the dark expanse of water.

"How far?" Malena would ask. It was a question she loved to ask, even though she knew the answer as well as I did.

"Ninety miles from Havana to the Florida Keys."

"Only ninety miles," she would repeat, as if it was the most important number in the whole world. "And to think, we're almost there."

Then she would smile—a sight I'll never forget.

"Papa," Eván said. "Somebody's out front."

Opening my eyes, I saw that she was right. Chuck saw it, too.

Somebody new, not the doorman, was pacing back and forth in front of the Crowne Plaza Hotel.

"Blink the light twice," I told Chuck. "Just like Eván told him."

Chuck did so and in the quick blast of illumination we saw it was Gabriel Santos. He was dressed in a Team Cuba polo shirt, slacks, and sneakers, with an equipment bag slung over one shoulder. He had a wild look on his face as if he was too frightened to finish what he had begun.

Chuck flashed the high beans again and the kid began to jog toward us. But as Gabby stepped off the curb, the headlights of another car flashed alive a half-block away. The car headed into the middle of the street, bearing down on Santos, who stood frozen in the middle of the street.

"Look out," Eván screamed.

The black sedan roared past, sending Santos sprawling to the sidewalk in front of the hotel. With that, Chuck put the BMW in gear and he sped up the street, screeching to a halt in front of the lobby doors. His front tires were up on the sidewalk, shielding the terrified Santos.

"Check on him, Billy," he ordered, and I was out of the car, kneeling over the kid, as Eván came alongside me.

"Papa?" she whispered.

I was relieved to find that Santos was in one piece.

He blinked open his eyes. "Señor Bryan," he said, "we must get away. Now."

Eván and I helped him up to a sitting position. That's when we heard the sedan pull around, ready for another pass.

"Stupid bastards," Chuck said. He reached for Santos's equipment bag and lifted out the biggest aluminum bat he could find. "Time for a little home-run derby."

All of us stared, wide-eyed, as Chuck strutted into the middle of the street, holding the bat in his right hand. Off in the distance, I heard sirens, but they were too far away.

"Chuck, let's go," I shouted.

"Billy, don't you see? They ain't going to let us be," Chuck said, as he stared at the car bearing down upon him. He bent his knees slightly, raising the bat with both hands. "It's time we took matters into our own hands."

The next instant, he was bathed in white light from the car's high beams. Silhouetted in the glare, my friend from our old days in Cuba appeared to be a sitting duck.

Yet as the sedan closed in, Chuck swung the bat, letting it go directly at the oncoming car. That aluminum stick pin-wheeled through the air and struck with a loud crack, barrel end first, right in the middle of the windshield. Moments later, the sedan's horn sounded as it veered away, sailing up on the far curb and rolling onto its side. With the harsh shriek of metal across pavement, the vehicle hit a fire hydrant, sending a gusher of water into the air. With that it came to a stop and nobody got out.

Chuck stood there, a big grin on his face, looking like he had just hit the biggest home run of his life.

"Let's go," I shouted to him. Behind me, Eván had Santos on his feet and was moving him toward the car. "We have to get out of here."

"I can't tell you how good that felt," Chuck said, as he jogged over to the car and got behind the wheel. "That's a home run in any ballpark."

With that he turned over the engine and we were on our way, heading for the border.

22.

WE KEPT TO the backstreets until we were well out of town. As soon as we were past the Monterrey city limits, Chuck hit the gas, staying within a few miles per hour of the speed limit as we headed north. Over the next two hours, we fell in with the flow of traffic, keeping mostly in the right-hand lane, refusing to stick out. For the longest time, nobody said a word, and Gabby Santos eventually drifted off to sleep.

We had decided to follow the customs officer's advice and stay away from the larger border crossings. Instead we headed for the border post at Falcon Dam station. Even though Falcon Dam allowed a limited number of big rigs, we found ourselves in a long line of cars, a half mile or more, all of us idling under the starry sky, with dawn fast approaching.

"We've gotta wait it out," Chuck said.

"We may not have the time," Eván said, looking behind us.

"Ye of little faith," Chuck said. "We got this far."

He reached for a Cuban cigar he had stashed in the glove department. "Anybody else for a victory smoke?"

"That's what I was afraid of," Eván said and pointed at a pair of black sedans that pulled to a stop a dozen or so vehicles behind us. We saw the doors open and several guys, in dark suits and ties, get out.

"God damn," Chuck muttered. "Now what?"

"We have to get him into the United States," Eván said. "Just a foot across the border, isn't that right, Papa?"

"That was U.S. policy when we left," I replied.

"We're running out of time," Chuck said, as he studied events in the rearview mirror. "Those sons of bitches will be on us soon enough."

All of us turned to see the suits moving methodically up the line of cars, shining flashlights into vehicles, asking a few questions, before moving on. Now wide-awake, Santos slumped down in the seat as if he wanted to disappear.

In rapid-fire Spanish, my daughter went over the border policy with him and he nodded his head.

"We need to get him to the other side," I said.

"Any Cuban knows the drill," Eván replied. "If he sets foot onto American soil, they cannot automatically send him back. It's still the law. Sure, they may arrest him. Hold him for a while, but they cannot send him back to Havana. The exile Cuban community would have a fit, somebody with his talent, and the border guys know it."

"That may be true," Chuck said, drumming his fingertips on the steering wheel. "But right now, we're still a Major League throw from Yankee territory."

"Looks like the first checkpoint is in Mexico," Eván said, nodding in front of us. "It's a different setup than Laredo."

Indeed, the smaller border crossing consisted of a ramshackle building and then a steel-girder bridge across a ravine. On the far side, we saw that the two-lane road widened to several more lanes, with a gleaming office building that could have belonged in Dallas or Washington D C.

"That's where we need to be," Eván said.

"We won't be anywhere close," Chuck grumbled. "Not by the time that posse catches up to us."

By this point, we were abreast a lumbering semi. I rolled down my window and shouted out to the good old boy driving it.

"What's the holdup?" I asked.

"What's that?" he replied as I got out of the car and went up to his rig.

"Papa, be careful," Eván said.

"What's going on?" I repeated to the trucker.

"A flood of migrants closer to Laredo," he shouted down.

"Migrants?"

"They're calling it a caravan," the driver told me. "Thousands of them, and it's rippled right down the border."

He briefly turned up his CB unit. "You hear that?"

I shook my head. It was nothing but static from where I was.

"The *federales* weren't prepared at all. Word has it we'll be sitting here for hours. Officials are pissed off and looking to lock people up, too. This is going to be a long night, partner."

I nodded and tapped the side of his cab in thanks. Before returning to Chuck's BMW, I gazed back at the suits. They were working their way through the two lines of idling cars and would soon be upon us. That's when I spied a sidewalk leading past the trucker and the line of vehicles. The route wound up to the border, where it was encircled by walls of metal mesh. Closer to the border, the fencing was lined by barbed wire. Still, the concrete path kept going, right on up to a narrower bridge that led across the ravine to the American side.

"Change of plans," I said, opening my door. Chuck switched off the dome light, keeping us in the shadows. "Gabby and I are going to have to hoof it."

"Papa, I should go," Eván said.

"Stay here," I ordered. "Slow them down when they get here."

"But your bad knees—"

"You don't have to remind me that I'm an old man. But trust

me, I can still get around the bases. And we'll attract less attention than you would, Evvy."

By then I had Santos by the arm, urging him to get out of the car.

"We'll see you on the other side," I said.

"You sure about this, buddy?" Chuck asked.

The cars in front of us pulled up a bit, making for a small gap in the line. Some drivers behind us saw the opening and sounded their horns.

"Positive. It's the only way," I told him and closed the door.

Bent over at the waist, Gabby and I ducked behind the cars until we were in the open, moving as fast as I could manage toward the pedestrian walkway and the narrow bridge to U.S. soil. Of course, Santos could have left me in the dust anytime he wanted, but he remained by my side and took hold of my forearm, steadying me, as we scrambled up the small embankment to the walkway. God, my legs hurt, and again I was reminded that I wasn't a fast man— never was and never would be.

Once more I pictured myself back in Cuba, trying my best to salvage what was left of my baseball career. "Bolo"—that's what the crowd sometimes chanted at the games in the old stadium in Havana when I came to bat. For in my slowness, I reminded them of the team mascot, the real-life Bolo, the clown who used to twirl lighted sticks of fire atop the dugout roof and lead the crowd in cheers. His favorite trick, I remembered, was when he ran the bases during the seventh-inning stretch and handed the red-and-white-striped Lions banner off to our third base coach, Willie Gomez, as he turned for home. After a few more scuffling steps, he would belly flop across the lid to loud groans and plenty of laughter from those in the stands. Back during those days in Havana, team management once asked if I'd be interested in a race for the ages against the beloved Bolo. I refused. I mean, what was the point? I told them. I was a catcher for the Habana

Lions, a guy with a starting job and I didn't want to risk getting hurt in some silly promotion. But we all knew the real reason I turned them down: I would lose that race to Bolo.

Once more I tried to make myself go faster, really churn those worn-out legs. But truth be told, I wasn't making much progress. Santos helped me up the embankment and together we hustled as fast as I could go toward the bridge across the ravine.

"What papers do you have?" I asked him.

"My team credential," Santos replied, stealing a glance at what was going on behind us. The commotion grew in our wake, and I prayed that the dark suits weren't onto us already.

"Passport?"

"Team officials took them all," he said. "They keep them locked in their room until we go to the airport."

There was no line for pedestrians at the Mexican guardhouse. In fact, it was unmanned, so we raced past, ignoring the cries for us to stop.

For a moment, Santos hesitated, until I pushed him forward.

"Get to the other side," I said. "I'll catch up. Go, go, you have to get there."

That's when the first of the shots rang out and I raised my hands in the air. Still, I nodded at Santos, telling him to keep going. And, thankfully, the kid shortstop took off, really running now, becoming a blur in the shadows, racing toward the lights on the far side of the bridge. I had to marvel at such ability, realizing that I had never run that fast in my life.

When another round of shots rang out, the U.S. side became abuzz with searchlights and noise and shouting. With my hands still raised, I tried my best to catch up to it all.

Several shots whizzed over my head and I was halfway across the bridge by now. Out in front of me all hell broke loose—a thunderstorm of light and barking orders. I saw Santos reach the other side and be swallowed up by a crowd of uniformed personnel. I ran for the chaos as bullets crackled against the concrete walls a few feet behind me and I fell forward and began to crawl toward the American side.

"Stop, stop," somebody on a bullhorn shouted, but I kept going toward the blaze of white lights Santos had disappeared into.

Then somebody in uniform was beside me, pulling me to my feet.

"What the hell are you doing?" he asked, and I was relieved to hear the hint of a Texas drawl. The guy who had taken me into custody wore a blue-issue military shirt, with U.S. Customs in white stitching above the front pocket.

"I'm an American," I said.

"So what are you trying to pull here, Gramps?"

"I'm with him," I said, pointing at Santos, who was surrounded by so many cops.

"He's not American," the customs officer said. "He doesn't even have the proper papers."

"It's okay, it's okay. He's Cuban," I said.

"Cuban?"

"That's right. That kid is the best damn Cuban ballplayer to reach America in years."

23.

EVÁN AND CHUCK didn't catch up with us until hours later. By that point Santos and I were sitting silently in a meeting room under florescent lights, cut off from the rest of the world. Eván, bless her heart, barged in, ready to start kicking butt and taking names. At times like this she reminded me of her mother, unable to let any perceived injustice slip by. When she saw us, my daughter smiled, and I found myself grinning, too.

"You did it," she said.

"We made it across."

"And whatever cock-and-bull story you told them worked, too," Chuck added. "Why do you think they let us come back here so soon?"

Eván shook her head, warning him not to speak so loudly. All of us followed her gaze up to a security camera in the far corner of the room. Somehow being Cuban in this day and age meant always knowing when somebody was eavesdropping on your conversation.

"All I told them was that Gabby here was the star of the Cuban ball club," I said. "That we had to get him into the United States before the bad guys caught us."

"And it worked," Chuck said, with a hint of admiration.

"Because it's the truth."

Soon afterward the only door to the conference room opened and a pair of customs officers walked in.

"It does appear to be the truth," said the older one. His nameplate read Collins. "Mr. Bryan, your story checks out."

I resisted telling him that of course it did.

"We even obtained video of your young friend here in action," Collins said, and he nodded to the other officer.

The younger one pressed several buttons on the wall and a screen at the back of the room descended from the ceiling as a video player hanging above the long table whirred to life. As the lights dimmed, images of ballplayers began to play out for all to see.

"Mr. Santos, I believe that this game was from last year?" Collins said.

Gabby Santos nodded, "Against Pinar del Río." And we watched him turn the double play with the base runner bearing down on him. He threw on to first base and jumped effortlessly in the air as the runner slid underneath him.

"And this one is something," Collins added as the highlight montage switched to Santos at bat, this time wearing the white uniform with red trim of Team Cuba.

"Yes, I remember," he told the customs officers. "It was in Holguín. How do you say, a pretend game?"

"An exhibition?" asked Chuck.

"That's right. Against the American team."

Together we watched him turn on an inside pitch, driving it into the gap in left-center field. The camera followed Santos as he hustled around the bases and slid headfirst into third for a triple.

"I'm sorry it came against your country's team," he said in halting English, perhaps wondering if such a classic hit would get him in trouble.

"Don't worry about it," Collins said. "Now, of course, anybody can say that they're somebody famous and talented. That they're somebody we should let stay in the country. But this last bit of film, I believe, cements your case."

He nodded again and the footage on the screen became darker, with us trying to make out what we were watching now.

"This was taken an hour or so ago," Collins said, and we recognized the two long lines of cars leading up to the border.

"See the guys moving up between the cars?" Collins asked, and the camera angle zoomed in, revealing two, now three figures, fuzzy and frantic with activity in the darkness. "They checked out every vehicle that they could."

We saw them coming up to Chuck's car, glancing at my old teammate and my daughter and then moving on.

"They meant business," Chuck said.

"Yes, they did," Collins said, nodding at his partner. "Watch this."

The images became greenish in color, yet much more detailed. "We were able to put a night-vision lens on them. Dialed it up with some infrared technology. Look at their hands. What they're holding."

"Guns?" Eván said.

"High-powered ones, too," Collins told us, glancing first at Santos and then toward me. "And I have no doubt that they would have used them if they'd found what they were looking for."

All of us were silent, considering what he had said.

"They didn't come any closer to the border, to the official crossing, so there wasn't anything we could do," Collins said. "Except take these pretty pictures."

The lights came up and none of us said a word.

"They're still out there," Collins said. "But they won't get any closer, at least not tonight."

"Can you offer him any kind of protection?" Eván asked, nodding at Gabby.

"You'll all be fine for now," Collins replied. "Mr. Santos, we have some paperwork that will accelerate your path to U.S. citizenship. Give it to your agent or your new team. I look forward to watching you in the big leagues someday."

Collins turned to go. But then he stopped and looked back at me. "That was a very brave thing you did out there, Mr. Bryan. I mean it. All of you really stepped up."

24.

A FEW MONTHS later, with a new baseball season well under-
way, I began to receive Cuban postcards in the mail. The first
one was of the Capitolio, the Cuban National Capitol Building, whose dome looks like a miniature of ours in Washington.
"Wish you were here," it read. No signature. Nothing else except
my name and address.

A few days later, I received another. This one was of the Presidential Palace, an ornate building of white marble, which was
now the Museum of the Revolution. In the far right-hand corner,
encased in glass, stood the *Granma*, the yacht Castro, Che, and
the others sailed from Mexico, in 1956, to start the war against
Batista. "Your friends miss you," it read.

And then, the day before I was leaving to drive down to Kate's
in Tennessee, came a postcard of the Hotel Inglaterra, where I've
stayed in Havana. It had no inscription, only a large *X*. Worried
now, I made sure the front door to my old farmhouse was locked
before I left for my latest trip south.

The next day I was making good time on Interstate 81 when
my cell phone rang. I slipped on the headset Cassy had gotten
for me and shown me how to use.

"Hi, Billy? I need to talk to you about our Cuban prospect." It was J. P. Morse, general manager of the Chicago

Cubs, the team that drafted Gabriel Santos in the first round that spring.

"He's hardly my find, J.P. I just helped get him up here."

"But you've got a great rapport with the kid. You know him as well as anybody, Bill. His makeup, what he had to do to get out of Cuba."

"That may be but—"

"And that's where I need your help, Billy. The bottom line is that I'm worried, heck the whole organization is worried sick about him."

"He's hurt?"

"No, it's nothing like that. It's off-the-field stuff."

"Like what?"

"He drinks some. We know that. But what kid doesn't?"

"Then what is it, J.P.?"

"Billy, let's just say that the front office is wondering where his head's at. He's flying down to Miami about every chance he gets. We know he's running with a fast crowd down there, with the Cuban American exile community."

I had to laugh. "J.P., he's an exile, too."

"We know, Billy. But there's the exile crowd in a place like Hialeah and then there's the exile crowd in South Beach and West Palm, if you catch my drift. He's definitely running with the latter. That's the buzz on the street."

"Okay," I said. J.P. was right; this wasn't good news.

"You know Francisco Peña, right?"

"Of course."

"We put him in charge of Santos and it played well for a time. But I was just told that Peña has washed his hands of the kid. Our old hand wants nothing to do with him now."

"I'm sorry to hear that."

"Peña was staying with him in Knoxville. As you know, that's where Santos is assigned now, playing Double-A ball, and we were hoping to bring him up to the Majors in September."

"So why you'd call me?"

"We need your help, Bill. With Peña out of the picture, we were wondering if you would pay Santos a visit in Knoxville. You obviously know the area after coaching in Chattanooga."

"That was years ago. You know that."

"Just a quick visit to take the temperature of the situation, Bill. That's all we're asking."

"J.P., that's off the beaten track for me right now."

I thought about Kate's quiet place a few blocks from the University of the South campus. That's the only place I wanted to be right now.

"Billy, we'll make it well worth your while. All we're looking for is some insight into the kid. What makes him tick. Just a quick visit. Does he have the intangibles to make it at the big league level."

"C'mon, J.P. Of course, he has—what'd you call them? Intangibles."

"We'll send you a plane ticket down from Buffalo. That's the closest airport to you, isn't it?"

"J.P., I'm not much up for flying these days. Security lines and I don't get along too well. Besides I'm driving on I-81 right now."

"See? It works out great then, Billy. C'mon, just give us a day or so of your time. You moved heaven and earth to get that kid out of Cuba. In a way, you have as much vested in seeing that Santos succeeds as we do."

I gazed ahead at the black asphalt stretching through the green fields and the rolling mountains of the Blue Ridge rising in the distance.

"J.P., you're one of the few folks I'd do this for. You know that, right?"

"And I appreciate it, Billy."

"I'll be there tomorrow, about noon. They're playing?"

"A seven o'clock start."

"And J.P., one other thing."

"What's that?"

"How often is he going down to Miami?"

"At least every other week."

"Every other week?"

"And get this, Billy," J.P. added. "The team's next off day isn't until next Monday, but I've been told that the kid already made a reservation to fly down to Miami-Dade again. Our guess is that somebody's gotten his hooks into him and is pulling the line tight."

25.

"IT'S NOT THAT he's overmatched," Stump Hawkins told me. "Anybody can see the flashes, the potential that's there. But it's like he's preoccupied."

"Preoccupied?"

"Yeah, like a huge gorilla climbed on his back and he cannot figure out how to throw it off."

I flipped through tonight's copy of the team statistics the PR people had given me when I arrived at the Tennessee Smokies' gleaming stadium, with its cushy seats and a smattering of luxury suites. Everything seemed to be renovated or brand-spanking new in the game these days, state-of-the-art as they like to say. Everything, that is, except me. I turned to Gabriel Santos's statistics, but Hawkins, like any manager in a bind, could recite the bad news by heart.

"He's hitting .205 and he'll be below the Mendoza line by the weekend the way he's going at the plate," Hawkins said. "Everyone told me he had power, or at least the chance for it, but I haven't seen much in a real game. Last ball off his bat that had any chance of going out had to be a week ago."

"And in the field?"

"He's as smooth as advertised. But, Billy, right now I've got another guy who can pick it almost as well. Honestly, between you and me, I don't see Gabby Santos rising any higher in the organization as a no-hit, all-field shortstop. You know as well as I do that a guy playing that position has to really drive the ball at the Major League level. Hell, you can say that about almost anyone in the lineup these days, can't you?"

I nodded and continued to flip through the pages of statistics.

Hawkins kept his eyes on me as he swiveled slowly back and forth in his office chair. Anybody who's managed at the Minor League level has been in the spot Hawkins found himself in. The big bosses, especially at the Major League level, always have high expectations. Yet they rarely do the dirty work—making it all come together. That routinely falls to the guys on the lower rungs, the managers and coaches down in the farm system.

I set the stapled set of papers on the desk between us. Except for a team media guide and a few sheets of paper, the makings of tonight's lineup, and a ball cap sitting in the far corner, the desk surface was remarkably bare for it being the middle of a season. Hawkins had already packed the more personal knickknacks and mementos away—a recognition that he would serve out the year and then be fired or demoted.

"I was going to sit him tonight," Hawkins said. "But seeing that you made it down in time, I'll start him."

"I appreciate that."

"Not sure how much you'll like it after you see him swing the bat for real. As they say, he's got all the grace of a rusty gate in the rain."

"You tried talking with him?"

"Sure, I have," Hawkins said, getting a touch defensive. "I'm his manager, ain't I?"

I nodded sympathetically, ready to wait him out.

"I'll admit my Spanish isn't the best. Even if it was, I reckon a Cuban kid isn't going to confide in me, at least not at the drop of hat. Now I may have three decades in this game, first as a player and now as a manager, but this game is changing faster than most of us can get a handle on. Everyone knows it, but I'm probably one of the few to admit it. At least to you, Billy, because we go back some."

"It has changed," I agreed. "Changed a lot."

"Days are gone when the skipper could plant a malcontent's butt on the bench for a weekend series, maybe longer. Now we've got to be all touchy-feely. Try to get inside a player's head, which is next to impossible when all they're really thinking about is cars, money, and babes, with the emphasis often on the latter. The bosses want you to be—what the hell's the word?"

I shrugged, not sure where his rant was going.

"Empathic," Hawkins said, curling his lip as if he had just bit into something sour. "I mean, screw it all to hell. Who am I supposed to be—Doctor Phil?"

I couldn't help but chuckle.

"I mean it, Billy. Don't it beat all?"

"That it does, Stump."

"Damn right it does," the manager said, lifting his Smokies cap off the corner of his desk and bending the bill a tad. "All I know is I've got a full roster-load of players and this Cuban kid is the only one anybody seems to be concerned about."

With that he stood up, the ball cap still in one hand.

"God damn, I don't know what else to tell ya. You know the drill. I need to make the rounds and check in on the ones who are really producing for this ball club. That's the position I'm in, Bill. Do me a favor—if you gather any intel on my prized short-stop, please let me know."

I nodded and watched him slip on his cap and head toward the clubhouse. Hawkins walked with a slight limp. Collision at the plate up in Seattle, at the old Kingdome, I somehow remembered. Broke his leg in two places.

Gabby's struggles that evening would be the moments that

stuck in my mind from this particular ball game. In the second inning, he struck out looking, with the go-ahead runs on second and third base. A few innings later the star prospect tried to bunt his way on, as many in the opposing dugout snickered at the awkward attempt. The ball rolled meekly back to the pitcher, who threw Gabby out by several steps. Through it all, going o for 4 at the plate, he fielded his position well enough. No errors or mental miscues. Yet he didn't demonstrate any of the flair he had exhibited back in Havana. No happiness or joy in simply being out there, between the lines, playing a game for a living.

After the final out, I stayed in my seat a few rows behind home plate. I nodded at a few of the remaining scouts, who were putting away their radar guns in their metal briefcases. I knew several of them, and they took one last look at me, genuine concern on their faces, before heading up the aisle toward the exit. They realized what I was facing; how the most talented kid on the diamond couldn't hit his way out of a brown paper bag. Only after everyone was gone and the cleaning crew began to move in from either side did I head down to the clubhouse.

I found Gabby sitting in front of his locker stall. Except for the losing pitcher, who was still icing his arm, and the clubhouse attendees, we were the only ones in the room. I pulled up a stool and sat down across from him. Gabby hadn't showered and was still wearing his uniform pants. His button-down top lay on the floor and his eye black had run together with the sweat, turning his face into some kind of clown mask.

"Manager Hawkins told me you were here," he said.

"I was supposed to get you out of that slump."

"You need better voodoo for that, Señor Bryan."

I nodded and glanced around the room. Thankfully, we were alone.

"The fielding was sharp," I added, trying to be upbeat. "No errors."

Gabby cringed. "I can make those plays in my sleep."

"So, what's the problem?"

Gabby looked away, refusing to answer.

"You hurt? Hiding some injury from them?"

His defiant eyes locked on me. "Why would I do that?"

"Because you don't trust them? You're a stranger in a strange land. I know how it feels. I was like that years ago, when I played in Havana."

"I know," he said softly. "You're one of the few who can really understand."

"Then what's going on?" I said, allowing my voice to harden. "Damn it, kid, you're the best player on either team. Why not show them that?"

He nodded absentmindedly and then stood up. From the top shelf of his locker, buried under several shoeboxes, he pulled out a photo and handed me the weathered black-and-white team photo of my old Habana Lions, the year we edged out Almendares for the title, the last full season I played in Cuba. So many familiar faces gazed back at me—Chuck Cochrane, Skipper Charles—and there I was in the middle of the first row, still in my catching shin pads, with a thin smile on my face. If I could go back in time, back to that time and place, and put that uniform back on? Well, I'd pay whatever it cost.

"Why you showing me this?" I asked and went to hand the dog-eared photo back to him. Everywhere I turned Cuba reached for me, asking me to shoulder more of the past.

He refused to take the old photo from me. Not just yet. Instead Gabby said, "He's in trouble."

I glanced back at the photo.

"Who's in trouble?"

He pointed to a young kid, a Cuban, kneeling at the end of the front row.

"Tyga?" I said. "Tyga Garcia?"

He had been our clubhouse kid back in those days. The one fetching towels and picking up the uniforms for the wash after another game. The guy who did all of those chores with a smile on his face.

"He's an uncle, on my mother's side."

Then I remembered Eván saying something about that when we were back in Havana, filming the movie. Tyga had to be an old man now. Almost as old as me.

Gabby leaned closer and whispered. "The authorities took him away. That's what my family tells me. He's in prison and I'm to blame."

"No, that's not true."

"Sure it is, Señor Billy. They arrested him days after I got away."

"But that could have been for anything," I told him. "We both know how Cuba works."

The kid shook his head. "They told everyone in my old neighborhood that it was because of me."

For a moment, I gazed down again at the team photo and all those faces from the past. If only life would stop and linger on the best of times. To make sure we truly understood what was at stake. For all its beauty and allure, Cuba remains an Old Testament land. An eye for an eye, a tooth for a tooth. There is always a cost for any action, no matter how well intentioned.

"So that's why you're playing so poorly?"

The kid nodded and then couldn't hold my gaze.

"I know I'm supposed to be strong," he said. "Everyone who has gotten out before me—El Duque, Liván, Puig—they have done it. That's part of the deal, they say. You leave and you're not sure what happens to family, when you'll see them again, if they'll be all right. But I worry so much about him. He's too old to rot away in a prison."

"Aren't we all?"

"Don't you see, Señor Bryan? If it wasn't for him, I might not be playing this game. He's the one who taught me, the one who showed me how to hold the bat, where to position myself on the field. They took my heart away when they locked him up."

For a long time, we sat there in silence, with me still holding the old team photo. I didn't know what to tell him. Finally, I stood up and handed him back that memento of the great Habana Lions team.

"It's late," I told Gabby. "You need to get some sleep. You have another game tomorrow."

"How can I play when they have him?"

"I'll see what I can do."

For the first time, I saw the boyish spark return to his eyes. The excitement that was present when I first met him in Havana.

"Would you do that for me, Señor Billy?"

"Sure, I will."

"But what can you do? Especially here, on the other side of the waters, out of the country now?"

"I don't know yet, kid. But there's always something. I really believe that. There's always something that can be done."

With that he nodded and tried to smile again.

26.

I NEEDED SOME answers, and the only place to start was Miami. Not the old Versailles and the Cubaocho Art Museum—the exile spots that had been left to the tourists long ago. Instead I drove into the suburbs, south by southwest of downtown, where many of the Cuban exiles now lived.

The streets were quiet here with everyone gone to work in the heat of another day. I made my way along a series of lefts and rights on narrow streets until I came to a small bungalow with a red tile roof, almost completely hidden from the street by a long-standing grove of Spanish moss trees. I heard the sound of tool work, metal on metal, mixed with the soft sounds of old-time jazz coming from the garage. As I drew closer, I saw Max Triandos bent over a vintage white Cadillac.

"You could still make a small fortune fixing up old jalopies back on the island," I sang out.

"Who's there?" Max asked, coming up from under the hood, gripping a fair-sized wrench, ready to do battle.

"Whoa," I said, stepping back.

"Billy Bryan," said Max, setting the tool down on a worn towel that had been draped over the front fender. "What the hell brings you to Miami? Bit too hot for your gringo blood, ain't it?"

"It is a mite steamy."

"Well, we better head inside and fetch you a cool beverage. Fix you up right before the real heat of the day sets in."

I smiled. "You're reading my mind, friend."

Max's wife had left him years ago. As a result, the inside of his place could have used a good dusting, but it was clean enough for two old warhorses like us. At first blush, the decor was typical of most bachelor pads—large-screen television, assorted sports memorabilia. Yet upon further inspection, the baseball knick-knacks were something more than old shots of Mickey, Willie, and the Duke. On the far wall hung a black-and-white photograph of the 1937 Ciudad Trujillo, whose roster included Satchel Paige, Josh Gibson, and Cool Papa Bell. On the mantle was a leather glove, now bronzed, signed by Orestes "Minnie" Miñoso.

"What can I do for you, Billy?" Max asked, as he brought out two cool glasses of lemonade from the kitchen. "You need something stronger?" And he nodded at the small wet bar in the corner.

"No, not yet," I replied.

"Ah, it is more than a social call," he said, and held out the cold glass, which I gratefully accepted. "Please sit down. The couch is better for serious conversations."

He settled into a club chair across the table from me.

"You in some kind of trouble again?"

I shook my head. "But a Cuban kid I know is."

"The ballplayer?"

"That's right."

"The one you helped get off the island?"

"You got it."

Max took a long sip of his lemonade and set it on the dark-wood table between us. "I thought you were done messing around with Cuba. I thought we both were."

"That was the plan, wasn't it?"

"But it appears I'm the only one who kept up his end of the bargain. After getting El Duque out of Cuba, I walked away from all that. You and I know it's become too much of a hornet's nest. With the Mexican crime syndicates now involved, they may be in league with some in the Cuban government. You can't trust anybody with so many chips sitting in the middle of the table."

"I understand."

"So, this is about Gabriel Santos? The can't-miss prospect stuck in the Cubs' system?"

"The one and only."

"Tell me more," Max said, and I laid it all out for him. How Chuck and I, with Eván's insight, had spirited the kid away from the Cuban national team.

When I finished, he took another long sip of his lemonade. "You will need something stronger if this is how I think it is."

"What are you talking about, Max?"

"Let's just say that the appetite for Cuban players has grown to great heights," he replied. "Ever since El Duque and his half-brother, Liván, everybody wants a Cuban on their big league roster. It's the price of success, the new currency of the realm."

"That sounds rather extreme. I mean, there are players from all over the world now. Plenty of them coming to America."

"But, Billy, you and I know there's only one Cuba."

He stood up and gazed upon the old team photo of the Ciudad Trujillo team.

"It's really no different than the old days with Satchel and Josh, I guess," Max said. "The money follows the best talent. Always has, always will. In recent seasons, you've seen Yoenis Céspedes land in New York, José Abreu in Chicago and, of course, there's Yasiel Puig. What people forget is, at its core, with that first step off the island, the whole thing remains a totally unregulated industry. If you can get them off the island, do it in a particular way, this talent doesn't fall under the jurisdiction of Major League Baseball's amateur draft and the like."

"Santos ended up in the draft because we brought him straight into the country. We didn't have the time or deep pockets to try for a third country first."

"And in doing so, you pissed somebody off. Somebody high up."

"How? By playing by the rules?"

"Billy, don't be so naive. This is Cuba we're talking about. There are rules and there are rules, especially when it comes to that godforsaken place. You know that better than anybody. I mean, you were one of the last gringos to play down there. You somehow got your daughter off the island."

"With your help."

"We barely pulled that mess out of the fire, didn't we?" Max said. "But this situation, the Santos kid, could be worse."

"Worse? How?"

"Don't you see? Somebody big had other plans for Santos. The question is who?"

"Other plans?"

"That's right, Billy. I bet somebody in Cuba was waiting to sell him off to the highest bidder, working with somebody else to get him off the island by cigarette boat. Stash him somewhere else in the Caribbean and then showcase him. Sell him off to the best suitor and keep a healthy percentage."

I considered this, putting two and two together.

"So, our rescue mission upset somebody back in Cuba?" I asked.

"That's what I'm thinking," Max replied. "Anything unusual been occurring on your end?"

"No, I was home, in New York, and was coming back down anyway."

Then I stopped, realizing what had been happening.

"What?"

And I told him about the postcards, the tourist shots of Cuba. How I had no idea who was sending them or why.

"Somebody is trying to get your attention, Billy. Now we need to figure out who."

27.

WHO INDEED? THAT'S what I was turning over in my mind when I pulled into Cassy's driveway late that evening. My practical daughter, the one who holds so much of our family together, came out onto the sundeck when she heard my car approach. She and Bobby had lived in a beach community south of Vero Beach for five years now. Not that he is home much, being a golf pro and always on the road. That leaves her pretty much in charge of raising their twin boys. Her days of being a flight attendant on the short hauls in the Midwest were behind her, and Cassy had settled into being a wife, manning the home front.

"Just keep it down, Dad," she said, as I came onto the porch. She leaned up on tiptoe to give me a peck on the cheek. "The boys were holy terrors tonight. Must have been the full moon or something, but it took me forever to get them in bed."

"I'll lie low out here," I said, eyeing one of the comfy chairs, "until the coast is clear."

"Let me just check on them again."

A short while later, she returned to the porch with a tray holding two small bowls of rainbow sherbet and tall glasses of lemonade.

"You're too good to me," I said.

"You've had a long day, Dad. That drive up from Miami is no picnic."

"It wasn't too bad," I replied, eagerly accepting one of the bowls from her. I was tired all over, aching deep into the bones. But I wasn't going to tell her that. I liked to foster the image that I'm a father who is still invincible, high above it all, even though nothing could be further from the truth.

Cassy pulled up a chair and huddled close to me. "I spoke with Eván earlier tonight," she said in a hushed voice.

"Where is she now?"

"Up in New York."

"The city?"

"It seems her part in that movie turned some heads. Your director knew a friend of a friend, you know how it goes. Anyway, she may get another acting job out of this."

"She was pretty good—far better than her old man."

"Oh, Dad, what are you talking about?"

"You don't see my phone ringing off the hook, do you?"

"That's because nobody knows where you are. Plus, you never answer your phone half the time anyway. I swear we're going to have your new cell tricked out with some kind of GPS app. Seriously, Eván and I have talked about it."

Together we finished the sherbet and our lemonade. I almost asked for something stronger but then thought better of it. For a time, we gazed toward the beach as the breeze slackened and the world quieted down for the night.

Cassy asked, "What took you to Miami?"

"Catching up with an old friend."

"That's what brought you there from Knoxville? Seems kind of out of the way?"

"Sometimes I tell you too much, kid."

"Dad, most of the time you don't tell me much of anything at all."

I chuckled at this. "Yeah, I guess you're right."

"I mean, Bobby flies around the world chasing his golf. But he doesn't have a schedule as hectic as yours—Havana a few months ago, back home to Buffalo, then down to Knoxville with a side trip to Miami."

"It doesn't make a lot of sense, does it?"

"This all has to do with the Cuban player, right? The one Eván and you helped get off the island."

I nodded. "He's struggling big time in the Minor Leagues and nobody can figure out why. On talent alone, he should be making a case to be in the Majors. Yet he isn't close, and I'm trying to do something about it."

That seemed to satisfy my daughter and for a time we looked out toward the ocean. The house set amid her high-priced neighborhood was so silent that we could hear the waves lapping against the white-sand beach a half mile away.

"How long you here?" she asked.

"A day or so."

"The boys will like that. They love having Grandpa around."

She began to gather the dishes up to take back to the kitchen. "Your guest bedroom is all done up for you. Try not to fall asleep out here."

"But it's so peaceful at night," I replied.

She kissed me atop the head, like I used to do to her when she was a kid. "You should get some rest, Dad."

THE NEXT MORNING, I rode shotgun as Cassy wheeled her SUV out of the subdivision to the boys' golf lesson. The two kids could really stroke the ball, chips off the old block.

"Makes you wonder what they could do with more time in the batting cage," I said, as my daughter and I sat in the shade, watching them hit it off the tee for the instructor.

"Bobby's decided that too much baseball will mess up their mechanics," Cassy said. "Or so he says."

"Are you kidding me?"

"I knew I shouldn't have told you. But don't fret, Dad. The way those two kids fly from one thing to another who knows what they'll be doing next year. They love baseball video games by the way."

"Video games," I grumbled.

"C'mon, let's grab an early lunch. They're going to practice their short game for an hour after this. Bobby set it up with one of the instructors."

Back in her Lexus RX, we headed for Vero. That's when Cassy grew quiet and turned down the radio.

"What?"

"Shhh," she replied, taking another glance in the rearview mirror. "I'm pretty sure we're being followed."

I began to turn, but she patted my forearm, stopping me. "Stay put, Dad," she said. "Let's see what they're up to."

As we reached the city limits, she slowed down and in the side mirror I saw a black Land Rover come into view.

"They ran a red light coming down the strip to stay with us," she said. "And now they won't pass. It makes you wonder."

She made a quick left and the Land Rover continued to follow us.

"Hang on," Cassy said, and she punched the accelerator, cutting across a lane of traffic, making for the entrance to a parking garage. She made a quick turn into the building and took the ticket. As the gate rose, she said, "Now we'll turn the tables on them."

With that she hit the gas again, accelerating up the ramp as the Land Rover waited for the ticket at the gate behind us. As soon as we were out of sight, Cassy took a hard left and came down the opposite side, heading for the cashier and the exit. A series of wide columns kept us in the shadows as we watched the Land Rover roar up the ramp, looking for us. Only when they were out of sight did Cassy slowly pull up to the cashier and we were back in the daylight, free and clear.

"Any idea who they were?" she asked, as she looked again in the rearview. Now I turned, but nobody was following us.

"Nope."

"Dad, what kind of trouble are you in now?"

28.

THE NEXT DAY I was back in Max's living room, watching him pace the floor.

"Of course, it all goes back to Santos," he said. "It has to."

"A kid who can't hit his weight in the Minors?" I replied. "I don't see how Gabby Santos is causing so many ripples in the game."

Max stopped and sat across from me. "His piss-poor play isn't the point."

"If he doesn't start hitting soon, he'll be buried in the Minors. The way the Cubs are talking, he won't be a September call-up. God knows when he'll get another sniff at the Major Leagues."

"Billy, you're thinking too much like a baseball guy."

"Because that's what I am."

"Open this up for a minute, will ya? It's bigger than one particular player. It doesn't matter if Gabby Santos gets to the Majors someday or is cut tomorrow. That's not what's important here."

"What is, then?"

Max nodded and glanced around the room. "C'mon, I don't trust the weather in these parts."

Even though I had no idea what he was talking about, I followed him outside. Past the sliding glass door, Max had put together a patio of light-colored stone with material from the local Home Depot. Two lawn chairs were edged back into the shade, and Max gave them a glance before nodding for me to follow him into the side yard, farther away from the house and into the shade of a towering royal poinciana tree, rich with red blossoms.

"Sometimes I get paranoid," he said in a lower voice.

"About what?"

"About somebody listening in, monitoring my conversations," Max continued. "Sometimes the phone makes strange clicking noises. That's why I insisted you come back down. I don't do serious business on the phone. Not anymore. Then I got to thinking about the house."

"You think somebody bugged your home?"

"You can never be too sure. Not these days."

I remained quiet, wondering what had gotten into my old friend.

"I know it sounds crazy," he said. "But things are never as they appear to be, especially when we're talking about Cuba. You have to remember that when it comes to Havana, baseball is always an important affair of state. You stole Gabby Santos away from Team Cuba. I've heard the story about how you ran with him for the border down in Mexico."

"It was nothing."

"Perhaps the story has been embellished in the retelling. That doesn't matter. All I know is it showed real courage, my friend. You aren't reluctant to fight the powers that be when it comes to such things."

I reached down and picked a pebble off the ground and half-heartedly tossed it toward the chest-high wooden fence that separated Max's backyard from the neighbors.

"I'm no hero. The kid deserved a chance to see what he's got, up here in the real show. Fat lot of good it's done him so far."

"But in doing so, you pushed back against the whole Cuban

sports machine, the underground system that runs everything there," Max said. "Like it or not, we need to do some more asking around."

MOMENTS BEFORE THE first pitch, we settled into Max's seats along the first base line at Marlins Park. With the threat of rain, the retractable roof was closed tight; and past the towering glass wall high above the left-field seats, the lights of downtown were visible.

"Is this an amusement park or a ballpark?" I asked, as Max flagged down the beer vendor.

"Too much of both," Max agreed. "Still, it's miles better than the old place out near Fort Lauderdale. At least we don't have to worry about rain delays. When it starts to pour here," he nodded at the roof high above us, "they just shut the lid."

The Chicago Cubs were in town and for several innings we watched in silence, as old-timers like us are prone to do. I studied the infielders and decided that Gabby Santos would have no problem playing at this level, with either ball club.

While the Marlins weren't a contender by any stretch of the imagination, I appreciated how they scrapped and battled. They were well coached and instead of swinging for the fences with two strikes, they choked up and looked to put the ball in play. Those tactics are part of a bygone era, my era. These days kids swing from the heels at anything coming their way. They know fans, agents, even general managers only pay attention to the home run. The more dingers you can hit, the fatter your next contract will be. A game that used to have layer upon layer of nuance, as mysterious as the crooked streets in Old Havana, has become a toxic mix of big numbers and bigger egos.

After the third inning, an older gentleman, dressed in an off-white guayabera shirt, khakis frayed at the hems, dark sandals, and a straw fedora hat sat down behind us. Max glanced back at him and nodded slightly. I stole a glance at the guy but didn't recognize him.

For another inning, that's how things remained. All three of us watched the Marlins take a 3–0 lead. Around us, the crowd was abuzz, but in our pocket of the box seats, we were quiet, waiting for somebody to make the first move.

Finally, after the Cubs went down in order to start the fifth inning, the older guy took a fat cigar out of his shirt pocket and crinkled up the wrapper. For a moment, I thought he'd have the gall to light it up here, where no smoking was the rule. But he only licked it and then let it sit in the side of his mouth. I stole another glance back at him and saw that he was smiling.

"Max," he said, leaning toward us. His weathered hands rested on the backs of our seats, and despite the noise around us, we were able to clearly hear his low growl of a voice. "Max, it's like this. I did some asking around."

"Thank you, Ambrose. I knew I could count on you."

"You were correct," Ambrose continued. "Señor Bryan here has angered some very important people."

"And what could he do about it?" Max asked.

"He could start by discussing matters with them," Ambrose said. "And he needs to do it in person."

With that he reached into his back pocket and held out a white envelope. Reluctantly, Max took it from him.

"It's all there," Ambrose said. "Plane information, walking-around money for incidentals. Señor Bryan will be gone a day, maybe two at most. But he needs to leave tomorrow morning. That's his best chance to square things with them."

Max nodded and the old man took the cigar out of his mouth and eyed it. "Time to light this up," Ambrose said. "Good night, gentleman."

Both of us turned to watch him climb up the stairs to the concourse level. I took the envelope from Max and opened it. Inside was five hundred dollars in cash and a single piece of paper with directions to the General Aviation Center at the Miami Airport. The private flight took off at 9:30 a.m. the next morning.

"Billy, I can't vouch for these guys," Max said.

I sighed and shook my head. "I know, but if I'm going to get to the bottom of this, I need to be on that plane, don't I?"

"Afraid so," Max nodded.

29.

THE CESSNA CITATION banked for the final approach, and Port-au-Prince came into view below us. Except for the pilot, I was the only one on board the private jet, with the entire cabin to myself. A map had been left open on a table, an unspoken offer to follow our progress on a clear day in the Caribbean. As we took off from Miami, I didn't know where we were going and at first thought it would be Mexico, even Cuba. But then we settled into a more easterly course, over the Bahamas, heading for the Caicos Islands before we shifted course again and I was sure we were heading for the Dominican Republic. Instead, we came in short of Santo Domingo and soared low over a massive bay. It wasn't until we almost touched down that I realized we were landing in Haiti.

As soon as we taxied to a stop, somebody on the outside opened the main door to reveal a black Land Rover waiting for me. The chauffer held open the back door and I climbed in. Smoothly the driver accelerated away from the tarmac and soon we were roaring down narrow streets lined with shacks of corrugated roofs, deeper into the midday traffic as the boulevards widened, sweeping past what was left of downtown after the devastating earthquake of a few years back. The smell of diesel fumes hung in the air, and stacks of cement blocks and wooden frames marked the feeble attempts at reconstruction. Soon the two-lane streets became clogged with more cars, motorcycles, flatbeds, and small buses. We made a sharp right-hand turn and began to head uphill, following a series of switchbacks as we rose above the noise of the city.

The homes were much larger here and protected from the outside world by metal gates and even guards. We rose and rose until I thought we were about to plunge down the other side. That's when the driver sounded his horn and in front of us a metal gate, twice as tall as a man, slid open and we barreled past. Up a steep drive, we came to a circular drive with a stone patio and foundation. A butler opened the door for me and I followed him inside, through the foyer with sand-colored tile floors and a glittering chandelier. We went all the way through the house until we came out the other side, and the butler left me atop a landing of white-stone steps leading down to a baseball backstop, pitching mound, and regulation-size infield. There was no outfield because the property didn't offer enough room. The property ended at a cliff, with the city barely visible in the abyss below.

"Señor Bryan," said a man in white pants and a blue business shirt. He was seated at a small table near the backstop, sheltered by an umbrella. "Please, join me."

As I came down the stairs, toward the mini-ballfield, I recognized him as the man I had glimpsed in Fidel Castro's quarters that night in Havana. While he wore reflector sunglasses in the midday sun, there was no mistaking his towering build, the gray hair closely cropped, and the craggy face. He had been the one that Castro's son, Tony, had followed from the room when Fidel wanted nothing more than to watch Major League games beamed in via satellite late into the night.

The family friend nodded for me to sit down in the other chair at the table. This vantage point gave both of us a panoramic view of the empty field. We sat, in silence, as the waiter set down

glasses of sparkling water and small plates with cucumber sandwiches with the crusts trimmed away.

"The cucumber is a fine vegetable," my host told me. "I find
that it helps clear the mind."

He spoke to me in English but the conversation soon slid
into Spanish.

"Why am I here?"

"To better define things," he said, and nibbled on one of the
small sandwiches. I watched and waited for him to make the
next move.

"We were never formally introduced in Havana," I finally said.
"But I recognize a familiar face."

"My name is Javier Escalante."

"And you're friends with Tony Castro?"

"Yes, good friends."

"And what do you know about me?"

"That you're a good friend of Fidel's. If things had gone differently, you could have been his catcher in the big leagues."

"Ah, now you're telling tall tales."

"Not the way El Jefe sees it. You returning to Cuba opened up
the past for him at an inconvenient time for some of us. Thanks
to you, Fidel got to thinking about what might have been, which
can sometimes be inappropriate for a man of his advancing age,
don't you think?"

"I don't know about that," I replied, taking a sip of water. "It
seems I live in the past more and more as the years go by."

"And that's what makes you a dangerous person, too, Billy
Bryan."

On the field below us, several players wearing T-shirts with
various Major League insignias—the Dodgers, Red Sox, and
Yankees—began to take the field. An older guy, also in baseball
pants and spikes, trailed them onto the field and started to hit
grounders and pop flies. Without being told, the three players

took up the traditional infield positions—second base, third base, and shortstop—as another coach moved over to first base and took their crisp, accurate throws.

"So, Billy, what do you think?"

I watched a few more throws and decided there was no reason to lie. "They're very good."

"What you see before you are the latest prospects from Cuba," Escalante said. "There will be more in a few months and more after that. As you well know, the island gives the world a steady stream of baseball talent."

"Yes, it never seems to end."

"But no matter how rich the mother lode, it doesn't mean we can look the other way."

I took another sip of my drink, determined to wait out Escalante.

"We didn't appreciate you and your friend Mr. Cochrane poaching on our turf, as you would say," he continued.

I wasn't about to get into an argument with a man like Escalante, about what was legitimate or not when it came to a land like Cuba.

"This is where you showcase them? For the big league scouts?"

Escalante nodded and took taking another bite of a cucumber sandwich.

"Believe it or not, this is the best baseball field in Haiti," he replied, as he dabbed his mouth with a linen napkin. "Of course, there are more fields than you can count just across the border in the Dominican Republic. But then we get into so many rules and regulations there, too many curious eyes. Here the representatives for the teams can come and go, easily monitor a prospect's progress. Here we can negotiate the next deal and everyone is happy."

That's when I realized what a financial boon baseball had become for Cuba and those surrounding my old friend Fidel. A significant slice of any contract agreed upon here could return seamlessly back to Havana. Yasiel Puig had said that 20 percent of his Major League earnings had gone to the Mexican crime syndicate Los Zetas—the price tag for getting him out of the country. If those in the Cuban government were behind this particular arrangement, here in Haiti, similar cuts and kickbacks were undoubtedly in place, too. They would be part and parcel to any deal.

In helping Gabby Santos defect from the national team, we had indeed thrown a huge monkey wrench into the whole setup. The powers that be had missed out on a generous cut of his contract. It didn't matter if they were part of a crime syndicate or high up the socialist government in Havana. Either way, they wouldn't be happy someone else had entered the picture.

"Too bad your diamond is a tad small for batting practice," I said, trying to keep the conversation on baseball. "Then you'd have a bona fide field."

"Oh, we have a bona fide field," Escalante said. "Of sorts."

With that he called down to the field, and the coach with the fungo bat nodded and walked over to a small console near the backstop. As the players trotted off the infield, a vast mesh fence began to rise out of the ground a few yards past the bases. As we watched, it soared upward, higher and higher into the air before angling inward, almost encircling the outer half of the field. It reminded me of a manmade spider's web, with all of us caught inside it.

The entire process took maybe five minutes and by the time the fences were in place, the first of the players had already stepped up to the plate, ready to take his batting-practice cuts on deliveries from a pitching machine.

"It's not perfect," Escalante said. "A few balls still find their way through. We let the street urchins sell such finds at the local flea markets. It's a system that keeps everyone happy. Trickle-down economics—Cubano style."

For a while, we watched the players take turns hitting. All of them had potential and would certainly showcase well, whenever the Major League scouts were invited here again.

"You and Cochrane upset a lot of people," Escalante said, as he pushed the sandwich plate to one side. "Of course, you didn't know it, but Gabriel Santos was due to be in the next crop brought here. By going through a third country, instead of straight to the United States, as you did, his contract would have been markedly higher. More parties could have been a part of that. Gotten their share."

One of the players stung a pitch and drove it hard into the air, where it hit against the protective mesh and fell to the ground with a thud.

"Does Fidel know about your little training camp here, Escalante?" I asked.

"Please, call me Javier."

"Does he?"

Escalante looked at me and then back to the field.

"As we were saying, Fidel is an old man. He'll be ninety years old in a few months. At that age, reality can be so subjective, don't you think?"

"You've kept this operation a secret from him?"

"Billy, you make it sound so cut and dried. As you know, Fidel was never concerned so much with the details of this and that. He's more of a big-picture guy, as you Americans would say."

"So, selling off big league prospects becomes like the time after the revolution? The firing squads, people being eliminated, and who knows how much Castro knows about it all?"

"I cannot speak to my predecessors. One has to believe that they did what needed to be done."

"You make it sound so easy."

"Señor Bryan, do you always take things so personally?"

I tried to simmer down, gazing out on the mini-diamond.

The crack of the bat on ball, even here, in such a strange setting, did calm me.

"I've been meaning to ask," Escalante said. "Did you enjoy the postcards? I thought they were beautiful views of Havana. Somewhat traditional but lovely nonetheless."

"You sent them yourself?"

"Not me, exactly," Escalante replied. "But some close acquaintances in the United States were able to help me with them. You'll find that both of your daughters received several, too. I hope it brightened their days."

I couldn't believe what he was saying and I realized that I had to turn this conversation around in a hurry. If Escalante was able to send postcards to Cassy and Eván, there was no limit to what he could do to us.

"I'm sorry we gummed up the works for you and your operation," I began. "At least when it came to Santos."

"Billy, that's nice to hear. But apologies don't hold much weight here, not in this world. It won't get an old-timer like Tyga Garcia out of prison."

"What will?"

Escalate smiled and sipped his sparkling water. "Everyone seems to have an opinion about that. All of which have significant problems and drawbacks, so far as I can see. That's why I decided to invite you here for a personal visit. Let you see things for yourself. Perhaps between the two of us, we can come up with a solution that makes everyone happy."

"Something that would make those in Havana happy?"

"Careful, my friend, we must never name names," he said. For an instant, we could have been sharing a whispered conversation at a bar or café back in Old Havana. "Even here, you're never sure who is listening, Billy."

I couldn't believe what I was hearing.

"You know as well as I do that Cuba will always be Cuba,"

Escalante said, as he glanced at the waiter in the shadows of the veranda. "And, therefore, one can never be too careful. As we both know, the past, in what light anything is remembered, will always be of great consequence in my land. Think of the giant mural of Comrade Che. I'm told you were there your last time in Havana."

Once more I could picture that sight—the eyes that gazed down upon everyone at the Revolutionary Plaza in Havana.

"Consider how important Che, his memory, has been over the years for leadership in Cuba," Escalante continued.

For a moment, I thought about all the billboards, statues, and photographs of Che Guevara that adorned the streets of Havana. Escalante was right. Such tributes not only held the past close, never letting citizens forget, they helped keep the regime in power.

The two of us returned our attention to the players taking their turns playing a kid's game below us.

"Do you have any suggestions?" Escalante asked. "Something I could offer my friends here and there? Those in high places? Something that could liberate the player's old family friend?"

I knew this would be my best chance to free Tyga. Whatever I said now had to be something intriguing to Escalante and his bosses, whoever they really were. And I knew it had to be something with a twist.

For some reason, I remembered a story my father had once told me, back when I was a kid. How his parents had taken my father to Syracuse when he was young, when he wasn't much older than my grandsons are now. How they drove the three hours from Buffalo to Syracuse on a Sunday afternoon in the spring to see a statue that somehow wept tears of forgiveness. My father was struck by the crowds of people that were drawn to that church for a sight that many claimed was a hoax and undoubtedly was. Yet many more wanted to believe. They wanted to believe the tears were somehow real—a sign from God.

"If our mutual friends relish the past so much, why not give them more of it?" I asked. "Why not offer up another martyr in the name of the revolution? A person that they can, in time, transform into a saint."

"What do you mean?"

"Malena Fonseca."

"What about her?"

"I would think she is still remembered by many in Cuba?"

"Of course, she is."

"Perhaps it's time to hold up her memory. Remind another generation of her greatness."

"Tell me more, Billy."

"She cannot become another Che," I began, not sure where this conversation was going. "But as we both know, every church has its ranking of saints and dignitaries. And while some are larger than others in that pecking order, they all play a role."

Escalante nodded for the waiter to bring a box of cigars. They were Mineros, rarely found outside of Cuba. They were so coveted that the government didn't allow them to be sold regularly. It had decreed that they were only for internal use.

Escalante held up the lid for me and I took one. We shared a gold-plated lighter, puffing the slender cigars to life. After we had done so, the servant carried the box back into the shadows.

"Of course, I know of Malena Fonseca," Escalante said, as he blew a lazy smoke ring into the air above us. "Some call her the heart and soul of the revolution. I also know that the two of you share a daughter. That you helped the daughter make her way to the United States."

"None of that is a secret."

"Then why do you mention it here? Bring that part of the past back to the here and now?"

I took a puff of my cigar and set it in the ash tray between us. For some reason, it didn't taste as sweet as I once remembered.

"Maybe it's because I don't believe as much in the past as others do," I told Escalante. "If the memory of Malena Fonseca can help an old friend right now, help get that person out of prison and bring him to America, where he can live out the rest of his days in peace, well, then that's worth the cost. I can live with that."

"And what are you proposing exactly?"

"I have a friend, a guy I played ball with once."

Escalante smiled. "You ballplayers—it's like this hidden brotherhood that you enjoy, isn't it?"

I refused to acknowledge how accurate his comment was.

"He knows some people and I know some people," I continued, curious to see where such talk would lead us. "But they haven't all remained in baseball. Some have become artists and they do beautiful work, paintings and works of stone. If you'd like, if you thought the idea had some promise, I could talk with these people. Explain to them about Malena Fonseca. What she stood for, especially when it came to the revolution."

"And what would they then do?"

"Perhaps find a way to honor her memory, her spirit, in some way."

Escalante took a long draw of his cigar. "And, perhaps, these friends of yours would do us a beautiful work of art?" he asked.

"Perhaps," I said, relishing that it was my turn now to put the brakes on things.

"If the painting or statue—"

"I'm thinking more of a statue."

"All right," Escalante agreed, "a statue. If this statue was done with style and elegance, something that indeed honored Cuba's past, I believe we could easily come to some kind of an agreement."

"An agreement that would free Tyga?"

Escalante nodded. "Certainly."

For a moment, both of us let the unlikely proposal hang in

the air between us. That a statue honoring the past could somehow free an innocent man from prison today.

"He would come to the United States?" I said. "He would live out the rest of his years there?"

Escalante shrugged as if that was to be expected. I could tell by the dreamy look in his eyes he had fallen back into the past. Undoubtedly, he had seen photographs of Malena Fonseca, what a beauty she was. How that ghost of what had been could shine again in some prominent place in Havana. How it would underscore the importance of the government and of Fidel once more.

"We would pay for all materials, of course," he said. "Pay handsomely to see Malena Fonseca remembered in a public way."

"I will talk it over with my friends."

Escalante puffed again on his cigar, wrapping his mind around the proposition.

"This is an encouraging start," he said. "I need to make some phone calls, Billy. Could you put together something more detailed? We have pen and paper, computers, whatever might help you with a more official proposal."

"You know, Señor Escalante, I find I often do my best thinking watching batting practice, kind of like what is going on right here. The sound of the bat hitting the ball can do that for me."

Escalante smiled and stood up. He folded his linen napkin and left it on the small plate. "Then I'll leave you to it. Let's meet again this afternoon. Perhaps we can even have you back in Miami by this evening."

"No rush," I said, even though I wanted nothing more than to be home, the sooner the better.

"All right then, Billy," Escalante said. "If you need anything, please let me now."

With that he turned and walked up the stone stairs and into the mansion. Soon afterward, the butler brought me a legal pad of paper and several pens in blue and black ink. The prospects hit for another forty-five minutes before gathering up their gear and disappearing into a lower level of the mansion, without saying a word. I didn't write much on the yellow paper. In fact, the only words I put down were:

White marble

Full-sized statue

A tribute, with words decided by the government.

I knew what I was going to propose to Escalante and anybody else who would have to sign off on this. For a moment, I wondered what Malena would have thought about my plan. Yet the more I thought about it, the more I knew she would have told me to go ahead. For her, saving a life would be the most important thing. That's what made her different, dare I say better, than anybody else associated with the Cuban Revolution. Back home, in western New York, I had an old photograph of her. She was looking back, over her shoulder, with a look of concern, even anger, in her eyes. That's the pose I would suggest to Kate Sinclair.

30.

"PLEASE INITIATE THE conversation with your friends," Escalante said. "Your baseball friends, your artist friends— whomever they may be."

We were back at the table in the shade, overlooking the ballfield that stood deserted in the late afternoon heat. The butler brought out a bottle of rum and two glasses to celebrate our agreement.

"I'll admit it. This wasn't what I expected," Escalante added. "But if you're able to come up with something, a fitting remembrance, I'm sure we could find a way to have your old friend released."

He slid a card with raised lettering across the table to me. Curiously, the business card had no individual name on it. Just a small image of El Morro Castle and a listing of phone numbers and emails.

"When you have photos, jpegs, and the like, send them to me at the email address here. If we find them suitable, then we will continue the process. More of an exchange really. A beautiful statue of Malena Fonseca that we could unveil in Havana for your friend's freedom."

"I'm sure you'll be pleased."

Escalante smiled and took a long pull of his cigar.

"Billy, I like the way you think," Escalante said. "Some men cannot forget the past, they remain haunted by it. But you seem able to use it for your own purposes. That can be such a rare skill indeed."

"DAD, YOU'RE PLAYING right into their hands," Cassy said.

After the daylong trip to Haiti, the private jet delivered me back to Miami by eight o'clock and I drove to Cassy's place. She must have told Eván about my doings for she was back in Florida, with both of them eager to hear what happened.

"There's not much about Javier Escalante out there," Eván added. She had her laptop open, scrolling the internet for information. "No bio or anything extensive. But look at this photo."

She turned the screen toward us, and Cassy and I leaned in closer. It was a picture of the Cuban national team after their recent performance in the Olympics. They had been upset in the championship game but still took home the silver medal. The team was coming off the field and Tony Castro was in their midst, wearing a bright-red polo shirt, the same color as the Cuban jerseys. Castro and the team were waving their red team hats in the air, saluting the crowd. Behind them, on the edge of the crowd, stood Escalante. His arms were folded across his chest and he towered above the fray, a stern look on his face, perhaps about finishing in second place.

"I have no doubt that he's high up in the government, with the family," I said. "You should have seen their operation in Port-au-Prince. Strictly top drawer."

"They have an operation for smuggling players off the island?" Eván asked.

"It makes total sense when you think about it," I replied. "They get a hefty cut for looking the other way, even helping spirit the players from Cuba to another country. Because in a third country, like Haiti, where they're showcasing these guys, they can then go to the top bidder. That's where we undercut their scheme with Santos. We got him out and brought him directly to America.

That meant they didn't get any kind of dividend, plus they feel he could have brought more on the open market."

"That's so crazy," Eván said. "Gabby signed a fine contract with the Cubs."

"Good money for you and me," I replied. "But for Escalante and the major players in the Cuban government, they weren't a part of it, so they're pissed. That's why they've locked Tyga Garcia up. It is pure payback."

"Another reason for you to steer clear of them," Cassy said. "Friends of the Castros, maybe even Cuban officials, bringing players off the island for big money? The whole setup gives me the creeps."

Even though it was going on midnight, nobody was in the mood for calling it a night. Cassy went into the kitchen and returned with glasses of red wine for Eván and me.

"Don't you see, we cannot run away from them," I said. "We got caught up in something bigger than we ever imagined and I'll admit that it's pretty terrifying. Government officials cozy with smugglers, crime syndicates, and whatever else falls into the equation. But if these people can get Tyga out, we have to play ball with them."

"I bet Fidel is involved," Eván said, looking up from her laptop. "You know him as well as anybody, Papa. The lengths he'll go to when it comes to power."

I shrugged. "I don't know for sure."

"There you go again, sticking up for him," Cassy said.

"Does it really matter?" I told them. "All I know is that Castro, and those around him, excel at using the past—the revolution, Che, all of it—to benefit themselves. We can, too. We can use their belief in Cuba's past to get Tyga out."

"But a statue of Eván's mom?" Cassy interrupted.

"It's what I came up with at the moment. The good news is that Javier Escalante latched onto the idea."

"Yet this plays right into their hands," Cassy said. "You're helping them remake past history to better suit themselves, their interpretation of how things were back then."

"I'll admit it's tricky," I said and turned to Eván. After all it was her mother's ghost I had brought into this.

"To me it doesn't matter, if it will get Tyga out of Cuba," Eván said. "That would be a huge relief to Gabby Santos."

"Listen to you two," Cassy said. "You're talking about dangerous games with some really nasty people. Rewarding them with a statue of Malena Fonseca?"

"A statue of Mama," Eván said to nobody in particular.

"It wouldn't be just any statue of marble," I told them and nodded at her laptop. "See what you find for a weeping statue, use those words, in Syracuse, New York. This would have been in 1949 or 1950. I first heard about it just before I left home, for good."

She typed the words and soon enough a series of stories appeared.

"A statue of the Virgin Mary that cried real tears?" Eván asked.

"That was the claim."

"Totally unverified, it says here."

"But there have been other cases."

"Weeping statues in Japan, Australia, Italy, Korea. Pretty much all dispelled by the authorities, usually by the Catholic Church."

"But search for some pictures."

Soon enough Eván found plenty of images. Cassy and I gathered around and looked at the slide show she put together.

"See, it doesn't matter what the higher-ups say, those statues draw huge crowds," I told them. "The people want to believe. They want to believe in such miracles."

"A stone statue that somehow cries?" Cassy said. "Dad, is that what you're really trying to do here?"

I nodded.

"If it's at all possible," Eván asked, "how do you do it?"

"I know somebody," I replied. "She might be able to pull it off."

31.

WHEN IT WAS time to head north to Tennessee, to put my plan in motion, Eván insisted on coming along. She claimed that it would put her that much closer to New York City, where more movie promotion was planned. But both of us knew better. She wanted to check out the artist who would do the sculpture of her mother.

Neither of us said much as we drove the interstate from Florida and around Atlanta and crosswise through Georgia. For one of the few times that we were together, she was content to listen to my jazz and big-band CDs, looking out the window as the countryside swept past.

It wasn't until we started up the long hill, climbing out of Chattanooga, toward the exit for Monteagle, that Eván began to pepper me with questions. Up ahead of us, the spires of the All Saints Chapel soon came into view above the treetops, and I slowed as we came upon the quiet streets of Sewanee and the University of the South.

"She's good with stone? Doing this kind of art?"

"One of the best," I answered. "Dr. Sinclair was in charge of the recent renovations here on campus."

"And you're friends?"

I smiled. "We have been friends for some time."

It felt good to have a few secrets from my daughters.

When we turned into her driveway, the crunch of our tires on the pea gravel brought Kate Sinclair out to greet us. She was dressed in a flowing skirt, with a reddish shawl around her shoulders.

"She could be a witch," Eván said under her breath as I stopped the car. "Some kind of beautiful witch."

My daughter looked around, taking in Kate's small home and how it was sheltered from view by the poplars and a smattering of evergreens on almost all sides. Yet Eván soon spied the larger barn in back—Kate's work area. Several blocks beyond us stood All Saints, Sewanee's majestic Gothic cathedral, which was based on the original in Oxford, England.

"I've pulled together some sketches from what you sent me," Kate said, as we walked up to her front porch.

She kept her eyes on Eván, and I knew what she was thinking: Put aside the differences in proportion and height, and Eván was the spitting image of her mother when it came to the face. The woman we were about to make a Cuban saint—Malena Fonseca.

"Please, come on in," Kate said, opening the door. "I'll put some water on for tea."

Once inside, Eván and Kate circled each other like a pair of cats before settling down on either side of the kitchen table. Kate made us Earl Grey tea, and nobody said much while we sipped it. It wasn't until Kate led us out the back door to the barn that I sensed that Eván's respect for Kate began to grow. Inside the work space, slabs of stone, in hues of brown and white, glowed in the late-day sun, seemingly embracing the shafts of light streaming through the oval skylights that dotted the roof.

"I'm going to need help with this project," Kate confessed in a soft voice. "I've never tried anything quite like this before."

She reached with one hand and ran her fingertips along a piece of marble that towered several feet above us. "Some look at this and just see the stone. I believe there's so much more there, deep inside. But it needs to reveal itself to us."

"Can one really carve a statue that cries?" Eván asked.

"Your father has told you his grand plan? No secrets with this man."

"Can it?" Eván insisted.

"No, I don't think so," Kate replied. "The science remains suspect at best. But with the right stone, the right indentations, who knows?"

"And you're still going to try, right?"

Kate looked at Eván, sensing for the first time how determined my Cuban daughter was in making this endeavor work. How important all of this was to her.

"I will carve something fitting of your mother's legacy," Kate told her. "That I promise you. As for the rest? Well, we'll have to see."

The three of us turned to look at the slab of stone.

"I'd like to take some photographs of you tomorrow," Kate told Eván. "That would be very helpful to me."

"Whatever you want," Eván said, still gazing up at the rock.

32.

"DID YOU BRING her on purpose?"

"Believe it or not, she insisted on coming along. When it comes to all of this, she's afraid I've lost my mind. Dealing again with the higher-ups in Havana."

"Well, thank goodness for little miracles, Billy. To be honest, I wasn't sure how I was going to do this project based on the old photographs that you sent along."

"You could have done it," I told her. "And it would have been beautiful."

We were lying in her bed on the second floor of the house. Kate had set up the guest bedroom off the kitchen for Eván. Kate had once told me about how the house dated back to the Civil War. How it had survived the raids and burning of the campus because it was so small, overlooked back in the trees between her and the grand cathedral.

"Did she know about me?"

"No, it never worked its way into our conversations."

Kate laughed, digging an elbow into my ribs. "Or you made sure never to mention me."

I pulled her closer, eager to change the subject.

"She knows now."

"So many secrets, Billy Bryan," Kate said, edging closer. "And you're about to add another skeleton to your crowded closet."

Early the next morning, I found Kate and Evàn together in the barn. Kate had taken a number of small photographs of Evàn, printed them out, and pinned them to the far wall. A new block of off-white marble had been brought in on a pallet and it stood in the center of the work space, almost regal in its roughshod appearance, filled with so many possibilities.

Kate and Evàn were huddled over a light table, studying more images of my daughter.

"I'm feeling better about things," Kate told me. "Take a look at those."

She pointed to a small photograph on the wall and several more on the light table. They were variations of Evàn looking over her shoulder. She offered the world no smile in these portraits. Instead the look was one of defiance.

"What will it be like?" Evàn asked Kate. "When you're finished?"

"There aren't many guarantees when you're working with marble," Kate replied. "So often it has a mind of its own. But ours will glimmer and glow. It will be smooth to the touch in most places. Let's hope that it's like the Trojan horse from the old Greek myths. That it will be more than they ever bargained for."

KATE DIDN'T COME to bed that evening. Instead she spent the night in the barn, making the first marks in the stone. And in the morning, I again found Evàn with her huddled around the table.

"I've officially named her my researcher," Kate said when I entered—a bit sheepish that I seemed to be the only one who had gotten a good night's sleep. "Your amazing daughter found more incidents of weeping statues in Brazil, Italy, Australia— all over the world."

"Almost all of them proved to be fakes," Eván grumbled, hunched over her laptop.

"It's the same thing the Cuban government will claim," I added.

"It doesn't really matter," Kate said, as she put on a pot of coffee in the back corner of the studio. "In the end, people will believe what they want to believe."

Still, Eván wasn't convinced. "Why would they want to believe this time?" she asked.

The comment stopped Kate in her tracks. She studied Eván as if she truly understood her for the first time. Realizing that my long-lost daughter had grown up in a land where leaps of faith, beliefs in the impossible, were rarely warranted or ever forgiven.

"Come with me," Kate said, "both of you. We're ahead of schedule for today. I need to show you something."

She picked up her keys from the side table near the door and we followed her outside. Kate nodded at her battered Ford pickup and the three of us squeezed into the front seat and backed out of the driveway. Only a few students were on the sidewalks as we drove through campus at this early hour and soon reached the main road, heading toward the interstate. After a few miles, Kate turned down a side road and then another until we were deep in the Tennessee countryside.

"You ever hear of a writer called James Agee?" Kate asked us. Neither of us answered.

"He wrote a novel called *A Death in the Family* and did some great movies—*The Night of the Hunter* and *The African Queen*, with Katharine Hepburn and Humphrey Bogart."

"I've seen that one on TV," Eván said.

"One of his favorite teachers used to have a place here," Kate said, as she stopped the pickup. "Eastern Tennessee was pretty important to Agee. It was where he was from, where he got his start."

Out ahead of us lay nothing but open fields.

"The teacher's house got to be in such bad shape that they had to tear it down," Kate said, as we pulled over. In front of us was an empty lot. "The chimney, this beautiful stone thing, was the last thing to go. The workmen labored through a hot summer day, looking to be done with it, when a guy drove up in a bigger pickup than my old rig. He asked if he could have some of the stone from the chimney, which, of course was music to the workmen's ears. The more stone the stranger took, the less work they had to do."

"Smart guys," I said.

"Exactly," Kate continued. "So smart that one even asked the guy's name before he drove off with another load of stone."

"Who was it?" Eván wondered.

"Cormac McCarthy," Kate replied. "The writer."

"The guy who did *The Road*, *All the Pretty Horses*?"

"One and the same. McCarthy is old school. I'd like to believe he knows the stories that can be found in stone. Legend has it he built a chimney at his place with the rubble he brought back."

"I love that," Eván said.

"In a way, we're doing the same thing," Kate mused. "We're using new stone, fresh marble, but we're bringing an old story, an important story, back to life. Now I cannot guarantee that it will weep like the ones you've found throughout history, Eván. As you know, most were deemed fakes by the church or authorities. But you know something?"

"What, Kate?"

"People still believed in those statues, Eván. They believed for no other reason than it brings a good story back to life. From what your father has told me, Fidel Castro and his people want to incorporate your mother's story. Make it their own to help themselves stay in power. But you can never be sure what happens when such things are put in motion, who will believe what when it comes to the past."

"What if it just becomes another part of Fidel's myth?" Eván said. "Helps keep his corrupt state going?"

"It's the risk we have to take, darling" Kate said. "I'll do my best to make sure it bolsters our view of the past, not Castro's."

33.

FROM THAT FIRST morning in Sewanee, Eván was fully involved in the project. She joined Kate in the studio, often posing in person, as work accelerated. Feeling like a third wheel, I decided to head a few hours north and check up on Gabby Santos. I had followed his daily progress and the can't-miss prospect continued to struggle, barely hitting his weight, and showing little power at the plate. Perhaps a visit would do both of us some good.

"Be back by next week," Kate warned me. Her blue eyes had gone a touch wild from caffeine and adrenaline. "I'm racing along with this one, baby. It won't be long."

The next morning, I waved goodbye, promising to return after the team's homestand in Knoxville.

When I entered the Smokies' clubhouse, Stump Hawkins nodded for me to join him in his office. It was midafternoon, several hours before the first pitch for tonight's game, and most of the players, including Gabby Santos, had yet to arrive.

"We have new information about his trips to Miami," Stump said, as I sat down in the chair across from his desk. "Here we thought the kid was partying it up in South Beach. Well, he was in the clubs and the like, but he was hanging with some real unsavory characters."

I had a good guess at where this conversation was going.

"They're demanding a hefty cut of his salary," Stump continued. "Up to 20 percent off the top—"

"To leave Tyga Garcia alone," I added.

"How did you know?"

I didn't answer.

"Have you been sucked into this, too?"

"Let's just say I've been working it from another angle."

"Oh, Billy boy, be careful. My front office guys tell me these guys are real sharks and there's blood in the water."

"Don't I know it," I told him, and for a moment I was tempted to tell him about my trip to Port-au-Prince. Instead I said, "Stump, he can't cave to these guys."

"You know it, I know it," Stump said. "But what about the kid? Does he believe it?"

"I'll talk with him."

"Whatever you can do, Billy. That kid may be the most frustrating player I've ever had," Stump added. "Once or twice a game, you catch a glimpse of what he could really be. It may be on a routine throw to first, even at the plate, where he's making a few strides. For an instant, everything will be so crisp, so perfect, that you wonder why he cannot do that every time. Perhaps now we know. Those devils in Miami have his soul in a noose, don't they?"

"I may be able to help him."

"Billy, you and I go way back in this game and I've always respected you for being fair and square with anybody. From what I understand, you were just about the perfect teammate. But if these reports are accurate, I'd stay as far away from these guys as I could. I know you feel you have a vested interest in all of this, after getting the kid out at all, but I wouldn't cross these guys. There's no reasoning with them."

I nodded in agreement and both of us turned toward his office door. The players were filing into the clubhouse and one of the last to arrive was Gabby Santos. He was dressed in a button-down shirt, khakis, and sandals. While his attire reflected the summer, loose and comfortable, one look at his face revealed that he was carrying the weight of the world. He barely acknowledged his teammates—most of them were talking excitedly around him. Instead he kept his eyes cast downward and began to dress for tonight's game. He could have been a commuter headed to a dead-end job he detested.

"Let me talk with him," I said.

"Be my guest," Stump replied. "Talk to him until the cows come home, Billy. I'm afraid it's not going to change much."

I closed the door to the manager's office and walked into the players' clubhouse. I'd been in more of these rooms than I could remember in my years bouncing around the game, and they hadn't changed much. The music had shifted over the years from rock and roll to rap and whatever else these kids listened to these days. Yet through it all, the time before another game remained a mix of conversation and gaps of silence, with everyone dealing with the expectations in their own way as the minutes ticked down to the start of another contest.

"How you doing?" I asked.

Gabby had his back to the room, his game pants already on and ready to pull on his jersey. He was a handsome kid with jet-black hair and the build of a ballplayer. His square shoulders tapered down to a thin waist and long legs built for speed.

He turned and briefly smiled when he saw me.

"I'm fine, Señor Billy," he said.

I glanced around us. Even though the pockets of conversation continued throughout the room, I saw several of Gabby's teammates checking me out.

"When you're dressed, meet me outside, in the dugout," I said.

"All right," he replied.

Soon the young prospect joined me at the far end of the Smokies' dugout as another pregame routine swung into high gear.

Knoxville, the home team, took batting practice as the fans began to fill the stands.

"I hear you've been trying to make deals with them," I said, as the sound of bat hitting another batting-practice ball punctuated the conversation.

"How did you find that out?"

"Does it matter?"

Gabby looked around and even though we were alone, he switched to Spanish.

"I've tried," he said, "but it's no good. They always want more."

"Most thieves do."

Gabby turned from watching the action on the diamond to me. "But I have to somehow help him. Tyga was the best coach I ever had on the island. He taught me so much."

"There may be another way."

The kid's dark eyes widened. "What are you up to, Billy?"

I decided it didn't do any good to keep him in the dark, so I told him about the statue that was being crafted, how it would be ready in a few weeks, maybe sooner. Most importantly, I told him how Escalante and his people supported the idea. That it would free Tyga.

To my surprise, Gabby was against the plan.

"Señor Bryan, don't offer up a gift like this," he said. "It could work too well for them. Don't you see? It's all about yesterday in Cuba and they know how to play that game so well."

"I realize that—"

"But you don't understand. Something like this only gives them more words and ceremony to keep their lies alive in my country."

For a moment, we sat there, watching the activity in the batting cage.

"It will get Tyga out," I told him. "I'm sure of it."

He only shook his head and continued to gaze out on the field.

"It isn't your typical statue," I said, realizing that I would have to tell him everything we hoped with this adventure.

"What do you mean, Señor Bryan?"

"If things play out, when the conditions are right, it won't just stand there, beautiful in whatever spot they decide to place it."

The kid turned toward me, hanging on my every word.

"I can't tell you the science because I don't understand it all myself. And besides it's not all science. We need some magic, some real luck, to happen here, too. But if the gods are with us, sometimes, when the air becomes really humid, like on the verge of a storm, the statue's eyes will appear to cry."

"Cry? But how?"

"If we're lucky and the rumors begin," I told him, not knowing how to explain any more of this. Instead I simply stopped.

"This sounds crazy," the kid said. "Is this how desperate we've become?"

"We have to give it chance," I answered. "Put it out there and see what happens. See if our prayers to Malena Fonseca will be answered."

34.

WELL AFTER MIDNIGHT, I pulled into Kate's driveway back at Sewanee. The lights were on in her barn studio and as I slowly opened the wooden door, I found Kate asleep on the couch. I picked up a quilt from the floor and carefully placed it over her. In the middle of the room, half in shadow, stood the statue of Malena Fonseca. Her head was turned away from me and as I slowly walked around the work of marble, the look on her face, freshly set in the stone, peeled back the decades and brought me face-to-face with my Cuban past. The lines, the expression, reminded me of when Malena and I began our affair in Havana—me so intent on trying to sign Fidel Castro to a big league contract and her watching with concern and bemusement from the sidelines. Much of the time, she kept the world at arm's length, perhaps seeing it as all some kind of cosmic joke, and that's how I expected her statue to turn out. Yet Kate had somehow gone deeper, drawn something more from the past. Perhaps it was having Evangelina as a real-life model, perhaps it was how the stone had chosen to reveal itself, but the sculpted Malena appeared to be more resigned, more serious and, more importantly, more knowing of what lay ahead.

In the statue, Malena's eyes were cast downward, with her head half-turned to the side. She could have been contemplating everything about Castro's revolution, everything that had transpired on the island since her death decades ago. For here was a cautionary tale from someone who had seen what grandiose, misguided actions can do a people, to a country. These eyes of stone warned one to go slow, to be aware of all the possibilities.

"Do you like it?" Kate said from the shadows.

She was up, with the quilt wrapped around her shoulders against the night chill.

"It's beautiful," I replied.

"She was handsome and mysterious, wasn't she?"

"That she was."

Kate stood alongside me and together we admired the piece of stone, which glowed like a distant moon reeled closer to earth.

"I've never had a project like this one," Kate said. "It was downright spooky at times."

"What do you mean?"

"It's like it carved itself," Kate added in an exhausted whisper. "I mean it wouldn't let me be. I usually take longer with a work like this. That's why I was afraid to take it on. I knew you needed it quickly, to help the ballplayer and the old man. What if I was still working on it a year from now?"

"It looks finished."

"It almost is. It'll be done by this time tomorrow because it wouldn't let me be. Once I started it, took away the first bit of stone, it was like it was talking to me."

"What did it say?"

"To hurry—that people needed to see her again."

I put an arm around Kate and pulled her close.

"What was she like?" Kate asked. "In real life?"

I thought about this, not sure how to answer.

"Never afraid to push back against the world," I finally answered. "Especially if she felt somebody or something she loved had been wronged. As has been said, Malena Fonseca was the only true saint of the Cuban Revolution."

Kate looked from the statue to me. "Billy, I can't promise anything else. That's a science, a belief in the stone that nobody really understands."

"It doesn't matter," I answered and stole another glance at the statue. "As they say, it's a face that could launch a thousand ships."

I took Kate by the hand, ready to walk her across the small courtyard to the house so she could get some rest. "Enough ghosts for one night. You need to sleep in your own bed tonight."

35.

THAT NEXT EVENING, I watched the Cubs-Braves on TNT, while Kate and Eván worked on the statue in the barn. Periodically, I'd wander into the backyard and watch them, with the work area lit up like a distant fire. But I knew better than to disturb them now. Both of them were fixated upon the project—Kate as the artist and Eván as the arbiter of the past.

Too antsy to head back inside, I decided to go for a walk, heading along Arkansas Avenue and angling across the Shakespeare Green to University Avenue, the main drag through town. It was well past eleven o'clock and only a few students were out at this hour. Up ahead stood All Saints Chapel, my favorite building on the small campus. Ever since Kate had taken me there for services one Sunday morning, the first time I'd stepped inside any church in years, the place had spoken to me, as they like to say. Sometimes you come into a room or a locale, and you feel like you've been there before. That on some basic level you know it. That happened to me with All Saints. Perhaps I'd light a candle for the statue when I went inside this time. An offering to the gods to nudge things along in our favor. But I never got the chance to visit the chapel on this night. A block away from All Saints, my cell phone rang. It was Cassy.

"Dad, did you hear the news?" she asked. Her voice sounded out of sorts—breathless and frantic.

"What news?"

"Turn on the TV."

"What's going on, hon?"

"Chuck just called, looking for you. CNN is reporting that Fidel Castro has died."

I hustled back to Kate's and found the images. The Cuban exiles were already out on the streets in Miami. After so many decades, their prayers for something better had been answered. Deep down, I was happy for them. I truly was. Yet I also found myself thinking back to my winter-ball days on the island, when Castro first came out of the stands and showed a genuine interest in becoming a big league pitcher. One could argue that if I had done a better job of convincing him that he had the potential to play in the Major Leagues, if Papa Joe, that old scout that I now played in the movies, had done a better sales job, too, then none of this would have ever happened. Fidel Castro would have played a few years in the Minor Leagues, some place like Peoria or Asheville, and soon been forgotten. Instead he'd sailed his Gilligan's Island–style cabin cruiser, somehow making it from Mexico to the Cuban coast with eighty-two would-be revolutionaries. They came ashore in a swamp, where Batista's government troops had been tipped off to their arrival. Pinned down in a sugarcane field, Castro and only twenty other rebels (including Che Guevara and Fidel's brother, Raúl) made it into the surrounding mountains. From such an inauspicious start, Castro's ragtag crew somehow grew in power, taking control of the country three years later and turning the Cold War world upside down. Castro remained Cuba's *jefe* through eleven U.S. administrations. That's what the cable news headlines told the world now.

Could Fidel have played in the Major Leagues? Highly unlikely, and even Castro sometimes enjoyed being in on that joke. But

I knew he was a good athlete. Growing up, he had excelled in track, basketball, and baseball. Reportedly, he formed his own neighborhood ball team when he was a kid, insisting that he be the guy on the mound. At the age of eighteen, leaving his home on the eastern end of the island for prep school in Havana, he was an outstanding schoolboy athlete.

In the Cuban capital, Castro first attended Belen Jesuit Preparatory School. Determined to be the school's top pitcher, he routinely practiced until dusk, throwing a ball against a wall when nobody else was around to catch him. That's been well documented.

After his time at Belen, Castro moved on to the University of Havana Law School, where he became caught up in the growing revolutionary movement and drew crowds with his fiery speeches against the corrupt Batista regime. Revolution had trumped sports, especially his first love, baseball. So much of what we know about Castro today happened after I left the country, stopped playing ball there. After Papa Joe, Chuck Cochrane, and certainly I failed to convince Castro to stick with the game.

I called the girls in from the barn and together we watched the reports from South Florida and Havana, and the parade of experts began telling us what this would mean for the world and future relations between the two countries. Kate mixed gin and tonics, and we continued to watch as the night settled deeper upon Sewanee. In gazing out on her quiet neighborhood at midnight, we seemed to be the only house still up at this hour. Yet news from Havana would be headlines for everyone by the morning.

"What about our statue?" Eván asked.

She hadn't said anything in the longest time, and I couldn't guess what was going through her head. One who had grown up so close to the dictator and his fabled revolution. Grown to hate it so much that she had no choice but to escape.

"Will they still want it?" Kate wondered, a look of disappointment stealing across her face.

"They'll still want it," I said, as they both turned to look at me. "They may not realize it at this moment, but they need that statue more than ever now."

36.

"THE PACKAGE IS ready," I told Escalante.

I called him from a rest stop outside of Chattanooga, down the mountain from Monteagle and the Sewanee campus.

There was a pause on the other end, and then Escalante said, "Sometimes it seems like you're reading my mind, Señor Billy. This is the first good news I've had in days."

"We got lucky," I told him. "The artists involved rose to the occasion."

Both of us knew I wanted Tyga out of their prison as soon as possible. "It's a fine piece of art," I added.

"When can you deliver it? I can be in Miami in a few days."

"That will work."

"Where was the work done? That would be nice to know. Where are you now?"

"Does it matter?" I snapped—determined to keep Escalante as far away from this part of my world as possible.

"No, not if the work is done to everyone's satisfaction. As we discussed, I will need to inspect it before sending it along to Havana."

I gazed out at the interstate traffic.

"I can have it to you in two days. Three days max."

"Very good, Billy. Here, take down this address. It's in the warehouses near the Miami harbor."

Back at Kate's studio, we spent the rest of the morning carefully packing up the statue of Malena Fonseca. Before it was sealed in the wooden crate, Kate took what looked like a small electric razor to the smooth area below both eyes. As Eván and I watched, she briefly touched the instrument to the stone.

"I can't do any more than that or it will show," she said, wiping the surface clean with a small cloth.

"Will it work?" Eván asked.

"I honestly don't know," Kate said, ready to secure the lid for the first part of its journey to Havana. "The best we can do now is pray."

With the help of several workmen from the university, we loaded the crate into the back of a rental truck and I opened the door, eager to be off.

"Papa, I should come with you," Eván said.

"We already talked about this," I said. "You don't need to be dealing with these guys. They're real devils."

"All right. But please be careful."

As my daughter and Kate waved goodbye, I pulled away and began the long drive down to Miami. While I made good time and was tempted to push all the way through, I thought better of it all and turned into Cassy's place for the night.

"So, you deliver it tomorrow?" she asked, as we cleared the table after dinner. The boys were already in the backyard, ready for me to pitch to them one last time before bed. It seemed the golf lessons had been put on the back burner for now.

"Drop it off and do what needs to be done for our friend's release. The sooner we have him in the U.S., get him together with Gabby Santos, the better off everyone will be."

Cassy shook her head as she began to rinse the plates and place them in the dishwasher.

"You know it's never that easy, Dad," she said. "It's Cuba."

Later that night, after Cassy had gone up to bed, I called Chuck

Cochrane on my cell. Cassy had programmed the phone, so it now held all the numbers of family and friends that I needed.

"I'm dropping off a present to some friends tomorrow in Miami," I told him.

"Cassy told me," Chuck replied. "Some kind of artwork."

"That doesn't matter," I told him. "What I'm worried about is that I may need to personally deliver it to the powers that be in Havana."

"Billy, be careful. That could get dicey."

"You're telling me. I need you to do me a favor."

"Anything you need, pal."

"You remember the Pan Am Stadium just east of town?"

"Sure, but what does that—"

"There are some great beaches just past it. One in particular is to die for, so beautiful, especially on a warm night."

"Yeah, Billy, but what are you driving at?"

"I was thinking that Skipper Charles needs to be reminded about that beach, Chuck. Could you tell him for me? Drive down and actually pay him a visit at his marina. Look through the old charts, so he remembers exactly where it is."

"I'll drive down there tomorrow, Billy."

"That's good to hear, Chuck. Just so he knows."

"Consider it done. What else you need?"

"Your prayers and a little luck."

37.

A FEW HOURS north of Miami, I pulled into a Waffle House alongside Interstate 95. There was one more call I needed to make before the delivery was made.

Darr Prescott picked up on the second ring, and I could tell that my call had surprised him. Since meeting on the movie set in Havana, he had been the one to contact me on a regular basis. He had tracked me down in western New York and later on my new cell that my daughters had loaded up with all the bells and whistles. Nothing annoying, mind you. At first, I thought he just liked to talk, especially about Cuba. But over the months, I realized that he had the makeup of a successful freelancer. He was shooting photographs for the *New York Times* now and still doing video on the side. Like it or not, I'd become one of his sources when it came to all things Cuba, and I was about to give him a good scoop.

"Let me get this straight, it's some kind of statue?" he asked, after I told him about the work.

"Of Malena Fonseca."

"Never heard of her."

"Do some homework," I told him. "Her relationship with Castro, with the revolution is something."

"What's that mean?"

"All I can say is check it out. I think you'll find it plenty interesting."

There was a short pause on the phone while Prescott considered this.

"It's all Cuba right now," he said. "I was in Miami doing a piece that will air on HBO next week and I'll be in Havana in a few days for Castro's funeral."

"And I believe they will unveil the statue of Malena Fonseca soon afterward."

"You think so?"

"I'd bet the ranch on it."

There was another short pause, and I heard the rustling of papers.

"Okay, I'll extend my trip," he said. "When it comes to Cuba, you've never steered me wrong, Billy."

"I don't think you'll regret it, Darr."

JAVIER ESCALANTE AND three of his men were waiting for me when I pulled into the parking lot along the canal in Miami, not that far from the towering hotels and the downtown convention center.

The door to Escalante's Cadillac XTS opened and he was alongside the rental before I had a chance to roll down the window.

"The anticipation builds, Billy," Escalante said. "I heard from Havana this morning. If the work is as good as advertised, they are ready to make a deal."

"It's a fine statue—befitting of the woman and her life."

"Undoubtedly so, but let's have a look."

He nodded to his henchmen and they opened the truck's rear doors and carefully edged the wooden crate out.

"Open the top part," I told them, "and you can see the head."

They did so and soon Escalante peeled back the bubble wrap and straw protecting the upper third of the torso. When he brushed aside enough to gaze upon the face, he became momentarily transfixed by the stern countenance and distant gaze of the eyes.

"I've seen photographs of her. But this," he said, running a fingertip down one cheek, "is almost lifelike."

He turned toward me. "And who was the artist? Who among your vast legion of baseball friends?"

"One who wishes to remain anonymous."

Escalante smiled at this. "You've counseled them well, Billy. All right then. I was just trying to make sure that the proper reimbursement was forthcoming from Havana."

"Freeing an innocent man will be thanks enough."

"And it will happen. If the weather holds, this beautiful work will be spirited to Havana as early as this evening."

"And Tyga Garcia will be released?"

"Almost," Escalante said.

My heart sank. Cassy was right. It was always one more thing when it came to dealing with anything regarding Cuba.

"Our friends in Havana have one last favor to ask of you, Billy Bryan. They said that if the statue passed inspection, and it certainly does in my estimation, then you need to join them for the unveiling. This will make for a fine tribute in the days after Fidel's funeral."

"Really, there's no need."

"They insist that you and your lovely daughter, Evangelina Fonseca, be there. It's only fitting that Malena's only daughter be present for the unveiling, don't you think?"

I'd been afraid of this all along.

"I'm sorry but—"

"As you know as well as anybody, when it comes to Havana, there are requests and there are requests. This one, I'm afraid, is nonnegotiable. You both need to be there to take custody of Tyga Garcia. He will be released immediately after the ceremony has concluded."

38.

EVÁN JOINED ME in Miami and we were scheduled to fly by charter to Havana in the morning. She was exhausted from the flight down from Nashville and soon fell asleep in the king bed, while I made do with the foldout couch in our room at the Embassy Suites near the Miami Airport. Unable to get comfortable, I checked my email on the cell phone the girls had gotten for me. I'm not the kind of guy who receives a lot of correspondence in this fashion, so I was surprised to find a message from Professor Yates at the University of Buffalo.

Señor Billy,

I trust that your writing is going well. As I predicted, the community class has become a den of slippery talk and verbal backstabbing. Not much real work being completed. But that's not why I reached out to you. I'm putting together a course next semester about writing in forbidden lands. Forbidden is a loose term and an excuse to focus on works where the artist or the country or perhaps both are under major constraints and external, even internal, pressures. In doing so, I reread Alejo Carpentier's The Chase, *which is set in Cuba. Check out the attachment for a short excerpt I plan to use. It reminded me of your piece. Is Havana still like this?*

Alan

I opened the attachment to find a photograph of Old Havana. It was the part of town a few blocks down from the Hotel Inglaterra, where the narrow streets are lined with white-marble columns that lead down to the harbor that was once the port for conquistadors in their hell-bent search to find any and all gold in the New World. The passage read:

> Walking from shadow to shadow, he reached the end of the trees and passed into the world of columns. Columns with blue and white stripes, with railings connecting them: a double gallery of portals along the royal roadway whose Fountain of Neptune was adorned in tritons that looked like wild dogs pasted over with campaign posters. . . . Hurrying, the hunted man went from column shadow to column shadow, knowing he was close to the market, where at this hour mountains of pumpkins, green plantains, and yellow ears of corn were piling up near cages through whose bars the turkeys would stretch their heads.

I sat on the couch in our hotel room and gazed out at the bright lights of the airport, trying to decide how best to reply to Professor Yates's email. I'll admit it. The passage frightened me. Perhaps it was an omen about what we were about to do. Finally, I pulled together a reply:

> *Alan:*
>
> *In the old days, Havana was like this from the grand hotels down to the Morro Castle at the harbor's entrance. For night—every night, it seemed—brought on a swirl of conversation and shadows. In the old part of town, the marble columns separated what was going on on the sidewalk from what was going on in the streets. The columns sometimes made it difficult to understand what was taking place only a short distance away—say out in the street or down on the next block. Many of those pillars may be gone, but the dividing lines will always run through Cuba.*
>
> *Your friend,*
> *Billy*

After sending the email, I searched my list of phone contacts and put in a quick call to Chuck. I needed to know that he had contacted Skipper Charles—given him my message. The good professor's email had been a reminder that one needed to do everything within one's power when returning to that star-crossed place called Havana. One had to make plans upon plans to successfully navigate the City of Columns.

AS SOON AS I cleared customs, I hurried to catch up to Eván. I feared what this land could do to her. Yet when I passed through the door into the cavernous luggage claim room that smelled of dust and a hint of coffee, she briefly smiled, trying to reassure me.

We only had carry-on bags, and at the exit I saw a group of drivers holding up signs. One of them would be for us. Side by side, we began to make our way in that direction when a young woman in uniform stepped in front of us.

"Passports," she ordered.

"But we just went through customs," Eván protested. "We have nothing to declare."

"Passports," the young woman repeated, and we dutifully handed them to her.

With strawberry-blonde hair, a few strands brushed behind the ears, she was a beautiful young woman. Several random freckles highlighted her face, just below her intense, dark-brown eyes, and even though she was in a light-gray uniform, she had hemmed the skirt up high, revealing as much of her long legs as she dared to do on the job.

"What's this all about?" Eván began again.

"Shhh," the woman ordered and handed Eván's passport back to her.

We watched as she deftly slid a small piece of paper inside my passport before returning it to me.

"One cannot be too careful," she said, almost too loudly, as if she knew we were all being watched and that she was simply doing her job.

Yet as she smiled, her elegant hand briefly brushing my fingertips, the passport making its transfer, she whispered. "Visit her. She's Tyga's great aunt."

Then she turned on her heel away from us, her barracuda eyes once again sweeping the baggage claim area.

Outside, a car from Escalante awaited us and we rode in silence into Havana. It wasn't until we checked into our room at the Hotel Nacional that I dared open my passport. The slip of paper read, "Natalia Gonzalez, Renta de Apartamentos, Calle 21, Piso 11, Vedado, La Habana."

"You know her?" I asked Eván, handing her the paper.

She shook her head.

"We'll visit tonight," I decided.

AFTER NINE O'CLOCK that evening, we slipped away from the hotel—first Eván and then me. Outside the Hotel Nacional, a string of yellow cabs stood gleaming and new at dusk, another sign of the influx of tourism money coming into the island. A few of the drivers nodded in our direction, but we ignored them, preferring to walk the four blocks or so away from the Malecón and the ocean lying beyond the lights and noise. Several times I glanced behind us, relieved to see that no one was following us.

The address was for a towering apartment building built in the Soviet style—concrete, with narrow slit windows. Inside the small lobby, I pushed the intercom button and was greeted by crackles and static. Then a voice answered, "I'm coming down."

Eván and I watched the numbers above the right-side elevator slowly descend until it opened to us. A willowy woman with silver hair waved for us to get on board. When we hesitated, she waved again, insistent until we climbed inside the rickety elevator.

Shoulder to shoulder we rode upward, eyeing each other warily.

The door slowly opened at the eleventh floor, with a half step up required to exit. Tyga's great aunt propped the elevator door open with one foot wrapped in a leather sandal. She wasn't a big woman, but every part of her was muscle. The kind of strength one gains by doing plenty of manual labor over the years.

"Step off," she ordered, pushing Eván and then me up onto her floor.

When we were all away, she hopped away herself and the elevator creaked to a close and disappeared from view.

The floor had been broken up into a series of apartments and she seemingly made a good living by renting rooms to tourists. We appeared to be the only ones there, but the way the hallways led off in various directions, with so many closed doors, I couldn't be certain.

At our host's urging, we sat around the polished wooden table that took up much of the main room. In the far corner, a small television sat atop an end table, and beyond, a patio door led to a small balcony that overlooked the Habana Libre Hotel and the hills leading up to the University of Havana.

"The young woman at the airport?" Eván asked.

Natalia shook her head, as if to say, speak no more of such things.

"A friend of a friend. A darling child," she replied. "One can never have too many friends in Havana, isn't that right, Señor Bryan?"

I couldn't disagree with that.

Natalia brought us coffee from her small kitchen, thick and strong, and for a time none of us said anything.

"I saw you play," she finally told me. "Once or twice. Tyga got us tickets."

Her voice was little more than a whisper.

"You did?"

"To be honest, I don't like the game so much, but I'd go, for him. Where did you play again?"

"My position?"

"Yes."

"I was the catcher."

"It seemed difficult. From what I remember."

I had to smile at this. "It was at times," I told her. "Very difficult."

Eván gazed about the clean, ordered room. On the wall across from us was a framed print of Picasso's *Guernica*, one of his most famous works and a vivid response to the Nazi bombing during the Spanish Civil War. Elsewhere on the walls hung smaller photographs of sugarcane plantations and the mountains far to the east, where the revolution had first taken root.

"But you grew up—" Eván began to ask.

"Near Holguín," Natalia interrupted her. "On the eastern end of the island."

"I know that region," Eván said.

"I know."

"And you'd visit Havana?"

Natalia nodded. "Every once in a while. To see family. Be captivated by the big city."

"So how did you come to Havana for good?"

The elderly woman gave us both a puzzled look. "I came with Fidel."

It took a moment for us to realize what she was truly saying.

"With the army?" Eván asked.

"Yes, with Fidel."

I had seen photographs of that day in Havana and, of course, had spoken with Orestes "Minnie" Miñoso about it, too. The streets lined with people as Castro's bearded gang of revolutionaries entered the Cuban capital. It will always be remembered here as the day that the waiting came to an end. The world was turned upside down, and for a short time Cuba became a better place for everyone.

"Fidel was my salvation," our host continued. "Others may say that, but for me it's the truth. You see, my father was a rich land baron in the eastern lands. But he never married my mother. She was mulatto and too embarrassing for him and his family. But that didn't keep him from fooling around enough to have me."

Natalia took a sip of her coffee and we waited to hear more of her story.

"When I was fourteen or so, I began handing out literature, propaganda you'd say, against the government, against Batista. Well, my bastard father heard about that and decided I should be deported to Spain or God knows where. Well, I wasn't going to have that. As soon as I heard what he was up to, I gathered up what I could and walked into the mountains. There I joined Fidel and the army."

Eván leaned forward, intrigued now. "And how long were you with Fidel?"

"Until the end. Almost three years. I marched into Havana with the rest when Batista fled in the middle of the night."

Eván shook her head, as if she couldn't quite believe—coming face-to-face with a genuine revolutionary so many decades after the struggle had become history. Perhaps our host mistook my daughter's response for skepticism for she briefly excused herself and returned with a paper bag, which she placed in the center of the table. Natalia reached inside and began pulling out medals and citations.

"This is for my efforts in the Battle of Santa Clara," she said. "This one for a short siege of a military barracks."

"And this place?" Eván asked. "You seem to have the whole floor?"

"You are as sharp as they whisper, my child," Natalia replied.

"Yes, better than any medal, don't you think? They gave me the entire floor of this building for my work in the revolution."

I glanced up at the Picasso painting of the horrors of war— the anguished faces on men and animals, the arms reaching to the sky for some kind of salvation.

Natalia followed my eyes.

"I shot my rifle many times," she said in a lower voice. "But I never killed anyone."

I didn't believe her.

"So, what of Cuba now?" I asked. "With Fidel's passing?"

She took another sip of her coffee and turned her gaze briefly to the Picasso print.

"It could change faster than any of us truly realize," she said. "That's why I'm happy that our prayers for Tyga have been answered. He will soon be out of prison and it's time for him to go."

"He will, with us," I said.

"I fear this country will soon turn for the worse."

"How soon?" I asked her.

Her eyes settled on me.

"Be swift, be bold, Señor Bryan," Natalia said. "You know as well as anybody how quickly things can change in this land."

39.

ROWS OF SOLDIERS were followed by lines of tanks and then waving groups of excited schoolchildren. The show of military might and muscle extended the length of the Revolutionary Plaza, easily a mile long, with everyone passing by the reviewing stand, where Raúl Castro stood. I had to hand it to Fidel's little brother. He methodically saluted every new group that marched by below. His eyes would settle upon a particular group, even a specific person or two, and for a moment they would straighten their backs, stand a little taller, all eager to acknowledge him in return. The huge mural of Comrade Che towered behind us, making everyone involved with the Cuban Revolution appear as imposing and as regal as ever.

Eván and I hung back as far as we could. I knew she didn't want to appear in any footage of this event—the unveiling of her mother's statue in a corner of the square. Dressed in a flowing green dress, with a sky-blue scarf, which had been a gift from Kate Sinclair, my Cuban daughter nervously surveyed the proceedings.

"It will be over soon," I whispered to her. Yet, of course, I had no way of really knowing.

For my part, I kept an eye on the far horizon, west of town. A new line of thunderheads was billowing up into the sky above the Florida Straits, that treacherous gap that forever separates the

United States from Cuba. I had no idea what the statue would do if the heavens opened up and it really began to pour. The carefully carved piece of marble seemingly had a mind of its own. What we did know was that any rainwater would collect, at least a bit, in the microscopic indentations that Kate had made. But how much would gather below the eyes and would anybody notice? None of us knew.

After the parade, Raúl rose to say a few words. Unlike his brother, he only spoke for a few minutes, acknowledging that Malena Fonseca was a pivotal member of the revolution back in the early days. How she had advised him and so many others when they were students at the University of Havana and over-throwing the government was nothing more than a crazy dream. Perhaps Raúl Castro kept his remarks short because he recalled how vehemently Malena disagreed with his brother after the revolution took hold. How she maintained that the everyday people couldn't be forgotten. How after they carried the day, the victory needed to belong to everyone, every Cuban. How the Russians could never be trusted. Her ability to foresee the future sometimes bordered upon the fantastic. For Malena knew that the old adage "absolute power will corrupt absolutely" was as true as anything in this world. That unbridled power can be as corrosive as anger or envy or greed, and that it would soon undermine the movement she so believed in. Even though Malena died before the revolution collapsed, and her homeland fell into such disrepair, she seemed to sense what was coming. That Che, with Fidel's blessing, would line up thousands of her countrymen on charges of treason and kill them by firing squad in the early 1960s, while so many others fled the island for good. Somehow, she knew and tried to warn the rest of them. But nobody chose to listen.

When Raúl concluded his remarks, two soldiers came alongside and flanked him as he stepped down from the podium to face the statue itself. It was concealed under a white sheet and when he nodded the covering fell away to thunderous applause. By then, Eván and I were ready to leave.

When we turned away from the show, we found Escalante in our path.

"An unforgettable day," he said.

I nodded. "And now it's time for you to hold up your end of things."

"And I have done so. Señor Tyga Garcia is waiting for you back at the Nacional," Escalante said. "In fact, he is in your room as we speak."

"Thank you," I said

"A car will be waiting for you at six tomorrow morning. It will take you to the airport, where my private plane will return you to Miami."

"I thought we were going home tonight?" Eván said. "On the last flight to Fort Lauderdale?"

Escalante smiled at this. "Why not enjoy the evening? As you know, there is no place like Havana once the sun has set. Why not enjoy your time here? For who knows? It might be your last time to walk these streets, to breathe in the warm Caribbean air."

"So, we cannot leave tonight?" Eván said, a look of concern stealing across her face.

"No, in the morning," Escalante said. "Now let me see if we can get an official car for you."

"We'd rather walk," I told him.

"All the way back to the Hotel Nacional?"

"As you said, why not take advantage of the sights while we can?"

Escalante shrugged at this and turned away. "As you wish, Billy Bryan," he said.

Eván waited until he was gone before whispering, "Papa, I don't like the sound of this."

"Neither do I."

I looked back at the crowd of photographers taking shots of Raúl posing alongside our statue and stole another glance at the dark clouds on the western horizon.

"Stay here," I told her. "I'll be right back."

I waded back into the crowd, the whir of the cameras growing louder until I found the guy I was looking for.

"I need a favor, Darr."

Darr Prescott was down on one knee, framing a vertical shot of the Malena statue, with the setting sun in the background.

He glanced at me and replied tersely, "Bit busy right now, Billy. Can't it wait?"

"Nope," I said and slipped a business card into the front pocket of his sweat-stained, button-down shirt. "You have a direct phone line back to the U.S.?"

"Of course," he said, rattling off a few more shots. "But it's expensive."

"Do me a favor. Call the number there and ask for Skipper Charles."

"Skipper Charles," he repeated.

"Tell him it's *Rascal* Time. That Chuck was right. That's all you have to do."

"*Rascal* Time and Chuck's right?" Prescott said, standing up. "What the hell does that mean?"

"It doesn't matter," I told him. "Just do it. Please."

Prescott nodded. "Sure thing, Billy. You opened up Cuba for me, so it's the least I can do. Now how about you let me get back to my work? I'll make the call as soon as I'm finished here."

"Thanks," I said, and stepped back into the crowd.

A few blocks away, Eván and I found a typical Cuban taxi. Some kind of Chevy held together by sweat, prayer, and duct tape. The cabbie himself perked up when I told him to take us to the Nacional. He was already counting on a big tip. Not a minute too soon, we were speeding through Havana's narrow streets, heading away from the plaza of people that still gathered under the watchful gaze of Che.

"Is it a beautiful statue?" the cabbie asked.

"Absolutely," I replied.

"I couldn't get close enough to see it today," he explained. "But I will do so in the next day or so."

"You should," I told him. "And ask your friends to do so, too. It is something."

Eván reached over clasped my hand. She was right. I was saying too much. But I was suddenly nervous about Escalante's parting comments and all I wanted to do was talk, babble on to a perfect stranger.

"What makes it so special, my friend?" the cabbie asked. "After all we have many statues in this city. More statues than rice and beans for the people to eat."

"There's something about the face of this new statue," I said. "It's so sad, so knowing."

"Sounds so Cuban," the cabbie said.

"That it is."

He accelerated up Calle San Lazaro, past the famous white-marble steps and stately columns that mark the main entrance to the University of Havana, where the revolution took root decades ago.

"Maybe I'll take my mother there tomorrow," he said.

"If she has friends who remember the revolution, bring them along, too," I told him. "I'm sure they will enjoy it."

As we approached the Nacional, which sits regally atop a small hill above the Malecón seawall, I asked the driver his name. He was Orlando Chavez, but everyone called him Jaime. He had been driving a cab in Havana for more years than he could remember.

"Could you come back for us later tonight?" I asked.

"Oh, yes," he told us. "I'll take you anywhere you'd like."

"Shouldn't we stay in, Papa?" Eván said. "Escalante said we could be on an early flight in the morning."

"I was thinking that maybe Escalante is right. We should see the town," I told her. "Who knows when we'll be back in Havana again?"

"Always a good idea," Jaime said, clearly excited about the possibility of more money changing hands.

"Can you come by in a few hours?" I asked. "After dark?"

"No problem. Any time you want."

"But don't pull up to the main doors—not here," I cautioned as we passed the row of modern yellow cabs and turned into the long drive, heading toward the Nacional's main entrance. A uniformed doorman appeared to help Eván out of the old cab. "We'll find you a block or so away, down near the old Riviera Hotel."

I slipped Jaime an American fifty-dollar bill and his eyes grew wide.

"Plenty more to be had," I told him. "But one must stay quiet about such things."

"I understand," he said.

"We'll look for you in a few hours. In front of the Riviera."

"I'll be there."

As we got out of the cab, I glanced up at the sky. It was dusk, with the setting sun hidden behind a bank of angry clouds, and I began to fear that time was fast running out on us.

UPSTAIRS, WE FOUND that Escalante had been true to his word. Tyga sat in a chair in front of the television, watching CNN News. He arose when we entered, all bones in ragged clothes.

"My savior and his beautiful daughter," he said, and flung a thin arm around both of us, pulling us close.

"Are you all right?" I asked.

"I am now," he replied.

I nodded, wishing it was true.

Eván began to fuss over him, ringing up room service and ordering various dishes—chicken over rice, breaded fish and mango, beers—a feast enough for all of us.

Once the food arrived, we gathered around the small table in the room and ate like kings. When CNN ran a short report about today's unveiling, we watched it dutifully, thankful that we couldn't be seen from this camera angle, and then Eván switched off the television. As we finished eating, the hubbub from the street, another night in Havana, drifted up from a half-dozen stories below.

"We could stay in for the night," Eván said. "I don't know what you were talking about with the cabbie, about going out on the town."

"Maybe so," I said. But then I shook my head and motioned for Eván to join me over closer to the window.

As she drew near, I cracked open the long window, letting the noise from below engulf us.

"Papa, you really think—?" she asked, but I raised a finger to my lips, urging her to be quiet.

From our perch well above the street, we could see Havana coming alive for another night.

"We can't risk it," I whispered to her.

"Risk what, Papa?"

"Staying here. Playing by their rules. One slip and it all goes sideways."

"You mean the statue?"

"We can't trust any of it anymore," I told her. "That Raúl and everyone else are going to let bygones be bygones—allow us to just fly away from here. I don't trust any of them. That's why I've made other arrangements."

"You never told me," Eván said, growing angry.

"Hush, darling," I replied. "I wasn't sure until today. But what Escalante told us? To stick around and enjoy the night air? That's when I got really worried."

I told her my plan. How we would make it appear that we were about to hunker down for the night. Even ask housekeeping to turn down the beds, perhaps order up more room service for Tyga. I had a windbreaker with me that would fit him. He would wear it when we slipped away, on the pretense of an evening walk of the sights, if anyone asked. One last look around town.

That's how the three of us came to be walking along the Malecón a few hours later. Walking toward the old hotels, like the Riviera, that used to glow in the night sky when I was a ballplayer here. We were pretending it was the old days, when Jaime pulled up.

"You know the beaches out past the Pan Am Stadium, not far from the Hemingway place?" I asked him. I was riding shotgun in the front seat, with Eván and Tyga in the back.

"But none of that is open now."

"It doesn't matter. There's a small beach there, the last in the string. Get us there and this is yours," I told him and held up several one-hundred-dollar bills.

Jaime nodded and began to ease into the thick traffic along the Malecón. Once we went through the tunnel by Morro Castle, he picked up speed and soon we were one of the few cars on the road, heading east away from the city of my past.

"I just drop you?"

"That's right," I told him. "No questions asked."

I looked back, confident that we hadn't been followed, and soon enough we were passing the stadium where American pitcher Jim Abbott had become a legend in these parts, and then, farther up the highway, the turn for Hemingway's home. Here was where the writer had spent the happiest years of his life, heading out regularly to the Gulf Stream, where he could fish for the monster marlins, the beasts of the deep. If we could reach those waters in the next few hours, everything would be right with our world, too.

Jaime pulled over to the side of the road. Below us lay the beach in the darkness.

"Flash your headlights twice," I ordered and he reluctantly did so.

All of us looked out at the dark waters. Nothing.

"Do it again," I said. "Pull the car around to face the sea."

Jaime repeated the action and this time, out in the darkness, well offshore, came the return signal. Two long flashes and I nodded for Eván to get out and bring Tyga with her.

"You've done well," I said, and I placed the wad of American currency on the seat between us. "Now be a good fellow and keep quiet. At least for a little while, okay?"

I shut the door and hurried to catch up with Eván and Tyga, who were moving across the beach toward the water.

"Skipper?" Eván asked, as I came alongside.

I nodded. "We had to play another ace, hon. We couldn't trust our luck with Escalante any longer."

The three of us waded out into the warm waters. Behind us we heard the cab turn around and make a beeline back for Havana. The clock was ticking now. Who knew how long we had until Jaime told somebody, who would tell somebody else, and the word would spread like lightning, as it always does in a country like Cuba?

We kept going until the water was up to our waists and that's when Skipper's boat reached us. His men pulled us aboard and we turned toward the open sea, the Straits of Florida, and America, ninety miles away.

"You're late," Skipper said. "Chuck said you'd be here right after sunset."

"It couldn't be helped."

"We have to make up time. If dawn catches us in open water, it ain't going to be pretty."

40.

TOO SOON THE sky began to lighten and we saw dots on the horizon far behind us.

"They're Cuban patrol boats," Skipper said, and directed Phil Pote, who was at the wheel, to angle the cigarette boat farther away from the Cuban shore.

"We must be in international waters by now," I said. Both of us were shouting to be heard above the roar of the engine, and we braced ourselves as we soared into the air off the back side of another ocean swell.

"It doesn't matter, Billy. If they're the first to find us they'll take us in. Boundaries on a map don't matter much out here."

For a time, we were able to keep enough open water between us and the pursing Cuban patrol boats. Yet as the sun continued to rise higher into the sky, our pursuers were better able to locate us on the horizon. As they did so, the distance began to shorten between us and them.

"They're fast ones," Pote said, stealing a glance over his shoulder. "Top of their fleet."

Skipper looked around us. The thunderheads from the night before had become a full-fledged storm farther over to the west, and he motioned for Pote to aim for the darker skies.

"But that's farther away from Key West," Eván cried out as she hung on, the wind blowing back her raven-black hair.

"It doesn't matter the way they're coming after us," Skipper shouted. "Time to call for the cavalry."

We watched as he scrambled down into the small cabin and flicked on the marine radio.

"That's going to alert all sides to our position," Pote warned.

"It doesn't matter now," Skipper replied.

"They'll impound the boat. God knows what else."

"And it might just save our skins."

We watched as he hunkered down with the receiver in his hand.

"Mayday, Mayday," Skipper said. "This is the *Rascal* out of Key West. We're taking on water and our steering is gone."

He nodded for Pote to keeping heading for the storm clouds.

"We're on a course for Panama City. Mayday, Mayday."

Behind us, the Cuban patrols had halved the distance between us, easily within a quarter mile now. A burst of machine-gun fire suddenly erupted, spraying our wake with bullets.

Skipper shouted out, "We need to reach that cloud cover."

"Too late," Pote said, and we peered up to see a fighter plane swoop down from high above us. "One of theirs," Pote called out, and turned the wheel hard to the left as the plane roared right over the top of us.

Somebody with a bullhorn on one of the chase boats warned us in Spanish to stop and surrender. Stop or be blown out of the water.

"That plane will be packing next time," Pote told Skipper.

"Keep going," my old teammate said, and then the rain began to fall. Within minutes, the stretch of open water became increasingly choppy, the waves wild with froth.

Despite the heavy seas, Pote kept the throttle wide open and we soared high into the air over the first in a series of white-capped swells. Tyga pitched backward and Eván clung tight to him. Both of them tumbled down to the floor of the boat, while overhead we heard the return of the Cuban fighter plane.

"It ain't giving up," Pote said.

Through the din we heard more announcements, this time in English.

"It's the Coast Guard," Skipper said, as he gazed around, trying to find the source of these new orders in the mist.

"Our lucky day," Pote shouted, and everyone looked to each other, breaking into smiles.

It could have been a perfect ending. The U.S. forces arriving at the last minute and saving us from being taken back to Havana and facing the government's wrath. But once again, this was Cuba we were talking about—a place and even a state of mind where things rarely play out as neatly as they do in any fairy tale or kid's storybook.

As soon as the words were out of Pote's mouth, something exploded in the water off our port side. To this day, I don't know if it was from the plane or something fired by the Cuban chase boats, but the blast sent sheets of water flying high into the air, drenching everyone aboard. Moments later, waves began to batter us from all directions, with more water sloshing in over the sides. The denotation caused the fastest boat in Skipper Charles's fleet to fly one last time high into the air, hold there for a precious second or two, before tipping like a crazed roller coaster to one side and tossing all of us into the angry seas below.

41.

I AWOKE IN a bunk below deck aboard the Coast Guard cutter. Later, I learned it was called the USS *Annapolis*. As I came to, my first concern was for Eván and the others.

"Is she all right?" I asked a kid in uniform, who was the head medical doctor.

"Your daughter is fine," he replied. "In fact, she never lost consciousness. But the others didn't fare as well."

I tried to sit up, but the room began to spin and I flopped back down.

"Easy there," the doctor said. "Your daughter has been waiting outside."

"What about the others?"

"The older Cuban. He suffered a broken collarbone."

"Are you going to send him back to Havana?"

The young doctor rubbed the back of his neck. "Normally, that would be the case. But the weather is kicking up in Havana, too, and nobody wants anything to do with that right now. The bottom line? We're heading home with everyone on board."

"Thank you," I said. "And the others?"

"The younger crewman is fine, but the other one. About your age?"

"Skipper?"

"Yes, Mr. Charles. I'm sorry to report that he drowned, Mr. Bryan. He was likely knocked unconscious in the explosion. We did recover the body. It's returning with us to shore."

Skipper was dead? I couldn't believe it. I pictured him as a young pitcher who couldn't get out of his own way back in our playing days in Cuba. A kid so young he barely had to shave every day and yet he tried so hard to keep up with the likes of me and Chuck Cochrane and the others when it came to going out on the town, back when Havana was the most glorious city in the world.

Eván entered my room soon after the young doctor left.

"He told you?" she asked.

I nodded as my eyes welled up.

"I'm so sorry, Papa," Eván added as she sat on the edge of the bed. "You were right. He did come through for us."

"Skipper was a good man," I said, as I closed my eyes, trying to block it all out.

"Everything happened so fast," she continued. "Just like that, they were all upon us."

"How are the others? Tyga?"

"Everybody's pretty shook up. But we're going back. All of us are going home to America."

CHUCK COCHRANE STOOD alongside me as Skipper's ashes were spread on the waters offshore of Key West. The six remaining boats in his fleet, plus many from the local marina, were lashed together as the minister told us how much Skipper loved the sea. How once during a daylong fishing expedition, the minister was on board with some others from the church, and the weather kicked up. A small squall that came straight across the straits.

"He told us to focus on the horizon," the minister said. "Don't look down because you'll get seasick for sure. But if you can focus on the spot where the water meets the sky, you'll be all right. And, in the end, we were."

Back on shore, while everyone moved toward their cars, Chuck and I lingered in the parking lot, taking a last look back at the sea. During our playing days in Havana, Skipper and I sometimes fished the Almendares Channel, just south of the Río Club, not far from the ocean and the beaches back there in Cuba. While we rarely caught anything, we both knew that wasn't the point. Simply watching the water flow by, hearing the crash of the surf only a stone's throw away—that was enough for us.

"You're welcome to bunk up at my place tonight," Chuck said.

"I appreciate it," I replied, "but I'm going to Cassy's and then up to Tennessee."

"Our boy has taken off."

"I heard he's playing better."

Chuck added, "Three home runs in two games and one of his fielding plays made ESPN's plays of the day."

"Really?"

"You didn't know, Billy?"

"All I know is that Eván got Tyga up there for a visit as soon as she could. Everyone seemed to think it would be good for the kid."

"No doubt about that. And then there's the doings back down in Havana."

I had no idea what he was talking about. Chuck laughed at my blank expression.

"Billy boy, how many times do I have to tell you that there's more to life than baseball? Take a long look around sometimes. That statue of yours is making headlines. Some churchgoers claim that it's shedding tears. The government says that's a lot of old women talking, but, as you and I both know, Havana loves nothing better than a good story."

"I'll check out CNN when I get to Cassy's."

"I think you'll be surprised by what you've let loose in the world."

42.

A CROWD OF older women, many of them holding rosary beads, heads down in prayer, came into view as the TV cameras zoomed out to show the Revolutionary Plaza in Havana.

"They have gathered here to witness what they say is a miracle and what others regard as an omen," the reporter said.

The scenes cut to a conversation in Spanish with one of the women.

"She says Saint Malena sheds tears of forgiveness for us. For those who have struggled here in Cuba for too long. She has never forgotten those who have lost their way."

The next shot showed the reporter on a balcony, overlooking the square. "Since the statue of Malena Fonseca, a onetime revolutionary, was unveiled last week, a growing number of believers claim that actual tears flow from this beautiful work of white marble—a sculpture done by an unknown artist. Certainly not everyone agrees with this depiction or explanation. Cuban authorities say there are no grounds for such claims. A government official we spoke to declared talk of tears as the hysterical imaginings of a few weak minds. But that hasn't stopped a growing number of Cubans from seeing for themselves. They are drawn to the statue to satisfy their own curiosity. And their numbers grow day by day. This is Kris Clark in Havana for CNN News."

Cassy picked up the remote and turned down the sound. "That's been on every hour since this morning," she said.

"Must be a slow news day," I offered.

"Oh, Dad, the mischief you've caused in Havana."

"So, sue me if I try to bring a ray of sunshine to those less fortunate."

Cassy smiled. "How did you do it?"

"Some things are best left unsaid," I told her. "With luck, the legend of Malena Fonseca will continue to grow. But as for me? My lips are sealed."

My cell phone rang and it was Eván. She was in Knoxville, watching Gabby Santos's resurgence as a Major League prospect.

"He's playing so well," Eván said above the buzz of the crowd. "Another home run tonight."

She sounded like a proud parent.

"And how is Tyga holding up?" I asked.

"It will be another month before his arm is out of the sling," Eván replied. "That said, he doesn't seem to care. I don't know who was more excited before last night's game, him or Gabby."

"I could be up there by tomorrow."

"Don't rush, Papa. Rumor has it that Gabby will be called up to the Cubs in the next few days. He's turned some heads, and it appears they're ready to make him a September call-up."

"Where are they playing?"

"Finishing up on the West Coast and then a three-game series in Atlanta. Can you believe it, Papa? Atlanta? It's so close."

"We could all meet there."

"I'll let you know when I know, Papa. Gotta run now."

Cassy watched as I carefully set down the new cell. Despite all my complaining, I was getting used to it.

"You'll meet her in Atlanta?"

"I need to take a detour first."

"Up to Sewanee?"

I glanced at her, trying to figure out how much she knew about Kate Sinclair and my visits to eastern Tennessee. But my daughter just smiled, waiting to see if I would open up about this part of my life to her.

Instead I simply said, "It seems so."

43.

BY THE NEXT afternoon, I was on the road back to Tennessee. It seemed silly to bypass Atlanta and drive several more hours north when Gabby Santos was about to be called up to the big league team. Still, I missed Kate and wanted to thank her in person for her hard work with the Malena statue. It was a striking piece of art that was well on its way to becoming a legend in Havana.

It did my heart good to think that some believed Malena Fonseca to be a genuine saint. For when I look back on those days, my time playing ball in Havana, I realize that so many of us wanted to be heroes and many of us failed at it. Fidel so embraced being a champion for his country that he ultimately served only himself and a small cadre of family and friends, including Che and Fidel's brother, Raúl. Yet Malena saw it all without blinders and did her best to change matters, especially after the revolution took the country in a more dangerous direction. For that she deserved to be remembered and the statue, the bribe that got Tyga out of prison, would serve such a purpose.

It was dusk as I climbed Interstate 24 out of Chattanooga, my car laboring to make it the last few miles to Sewanee and that beautiful plateau in the Appalachian highlands. As I've said, I'm so thankful that I can still drive at my age. When they come to take my driver's license away from me, they might as well shoot me. I've always liked the freedom to go anywhere, anytime I want. To climb behind the wheel and crank over the engine.

I exited from the interstate and followed the wide roads toward the campus. Turning down the volume on the jazz CD, I cracked the window, ready to let the nighttime hush drift over me. Instead of the quietness, though, I heard sirens in the distance. As I turned down the tree-lined street to Kate's place, I saw a glow in the darkening sky. Accelerating, I saw that her place, the house and the barn, were in flames.

When I pulled up, two fire engines were already on the scene, spraying the house with water. The studio barn was ablaze and I hustled for it before a policeman pulled me aside.

"Where you going, sir?" he demanded.

Behind us another fire engine pulled up and other policemen were cordoning off the street.

"Is she in there?"

"No, Miss Sinclair isn't here."

"You sure?"

Both of us paused to watch the flames race across the studio roof.

"Positive," the policeman said. "The boys were able to get in there, give it the once-over before the fire got too hot."

"Where is she then?"

"She a friend of yours?"

"Yes," I told him. "I just drove up from Florida."

"Florida? That so? Been some other cars with Florida plates passing through here the last few days. Sewanee is a small town. You notice things, you know?"

Florida plates? That could only mean that Javier Escalante had discovered who had done the statue of Malena Fonseca.

"I come to see her every now and then," I told the cop.

"You're the old ballplayer?"

"That's right."

"Miss Kate could be out of town," the cop said. "But she usually tells the girls down at the post office to hold her mail when she leaves. That didn't happen this time around. Plus, she was at the campus gallery yesterday. Several folks saw her there at some kind of reception."

"You're sure that she wasn't in there?" I said and nodded at the barn growing brighter in the flames.

"Positive," the policeman said. "Damn shame to see that go up in smoke. That's where she did all of her work."

"I know."

Walking back to my car, I looked around. The firemen might save the house, but Kate's studio would be a total loss. The locals gathered behind the police barricades, taking it all in. They were unfamiliar faces to me. I hadn't made the time to know anybody except Kate in this town.

I was standing there, not know what to do next when my cell phone rang. Relieved, I saw that it was Kate's number.

"Thank God, you're all right," I said.

Yet I was greeted with a long pause of static.

"Hello?" I said, wondering if my mind was playing tricks on me.

"Señor Billy," somebody said.

"Who is this?"

"Don't you recognize an old friend?" Escalante answered.

"What do you want?"

"You pulled one over on us," Escalante replied. "That's not a good way to do business, especially among friends."

"I didn't pull anything over on anybody."

"We need to have a serious discussion about all of this."

"Where are you?" I demanded.

"Nearby," Escalante said. "We have your lady friend."

"Don't you hurt her. I'm warning you."

"She tells us that she recently took you on a sightseeing trip to see an old homestead. Some story about writers interested in rock and stones, and wanting to hang on to them. To preserve the memory? Sounds foolish to me."

"I know the place."

"Find it and keep going out that road. You'll pass a reservoir and the local beach. Keep going another quarter mile and you'll see a road with no houses on it. Turn left there and we'll be waiting for you."

"All right."

"And Billy?"

"What?"

"Make sure you come alone. Don't tell any of the police there. As they say, this is a lonely deserted road far from home. We see another set of headlights and we're gone, understand?"

I looked around one last time, but nobody was concerned about me. All eyes were on the fire. Driving out of town, I soon found the road that led to the old Agee home, where the workmen had been only too happy to help McCarthy take away some of the chimney rock. From there I passed a small football field and, sure enough, the town reservoir and beach appeared farther down on the left side. Only a few lights had been left on. The swimming hole was closed for the night. A little farther along, it was like somebody had flicked a switch. There were only a few farmhouses, way off in the distance, and the town lights soon fell away behind me.

I set my headlights on high and saw the left-hand turn up ahead. I turned off the main road and followed the rutted road toward a thicket of trees. After a quarter mile, I came to a clearing, where Escalante's Cadillac awaited me.

My high beams flashed across Escalante, who was with two of his men. In their midst, trying to be brave, stood Kate.

As I got out, I saw that a thick rope with a noose had been looped over the tall branches of the oak trees between us. One of Escalante's men was digging away with a long-handled shovel, finishing the last of two graves.

"There's no need for this," I said. "We can talk."

"You embarrassed me," Escalante said, almost spitting out the words. "I petitioned to the highest levels on your behalf. I was your friend in court. I was the one who advised Raúl to let the old man go. So, we lost a good ballplayer to America and didn't get anything in return? The world isn't perfect. Those were my exact words. Let your old friend Billy Bryan win one for once."

As I listened, I realized that the powers in Havana could have thought that Escalante was to blame. That he was even a part of the plan.

"And this is how you thank me? By giving Cuba a haunted statue? A piece of stone that somehow weeps tears?"

"Take me to Raúl and the others. I'll tell them how you were innocent of anything."

"They don't even know what I'm doing," Escalante said with disgust. "Do you think they even care to listen to me since the Santa Malena statue was unveiled? I'm nothing to them now. Absolutely nothing. And for that both of you will pay."

One of Escalante's men came alongside me and nudged me closer to the tree and the hangman's noose.

"How does the saying go, Billy?" Escalante asked. "Age before beauty? But don't you worry, Billy. We will kill your beautiful friend as well. The two of you will be together for eternity."

Escalante pulled down the rope and slid it over my head. With both hands, he drew it taut around my neck.

"Wait," I begged.

"No, I'm in a hurry to be gone from this godforsaken country," Escalante said. "I refuse to listen to any more of your sweet lines about Old Havana."

"But Javier."

"Farewell, Billy Bryan," he said. "Your days of being a man of Havana have come to an end."

His men took hold of the other end of the rope and pulled

hard. As Kate screamed, the blow drove the air out of me and I grasped with both hands, trying to relieve the hellish pressure building around my neck. However, the force of the rope clamped down on me, harder and harder, and soon it was no good. Already I was losing the ability to draw in any air and rapidly losing consciousness.

Way beyond us, back toward town, I heard more sirens blaring. Yet they were a long way away. I would be a dead man by the time those sweet echoes reached us.

I had just about faded away for good when bright lights and the roar of an engine flooded the clearing. A new set of car headlights burst upon us, and for a moment I thought Escalante had ordered more illumination to better view my demise.

Still, as I gazed down upon the scene, wide-eyed and gasping for breath, I could make out other men, fighting with Escalante's crew in a grand battle. To my disbelief, the new ones swung baseball bats, taking the Cubans by surprise. I thought I was hallucinating, my last vision of life here on earth blurred and twisted beyond recognition as I danced away on the gallows pole. Was this somehow my version of heaven? Or even hell? No matter, for it soon dissolved into a riotous mess of bodies and shadows that I couldn't comprehend. Still, something told me to watch. That as long as I could keep my eyes open, stay in this world and witness the frantic battle happening below me, I might just live.

Moments later, the rope gave way. To this day, I don't know if somebody cut it or in the fight the ones holding it let the line slip away. Gasping for breath, I rolled around in the dirt until Kate came alongside me, loosening the noose and pulling it free of me.

As I scrambled to all fours, I saw that the battle was coming to an end and familiar faces had somehow carried the day. Eván was there, flanked by Gabby and what I took to be two other ballplayers. Indeed, they had been wielding baseball bats, leaving Escalante and his men battered and begging for mercy.

"Papa, are you all right?"

I nodded, still struggling for breath. "But how?" I whispered. My voice was an angry rasp.

"Your new phone."

"My phone?"

"It was Cassy's idea. She finally programmed it with a GPS app. That way we would always know where you were. She worries about you. We both do."

Kate laughed. "Your ingenious daughters, Billy. They have saved both of us."

"We were on our way to Atlanta from Knoxville," Eván continued. "You already know Gabby Santos. Say hello to Johnny Burke and Shaun Pietrunti. They're all September call-ups and the ball club agreed with me that it would be great if they shared a ride down. Good for team morale, I told them."

"Team morale?"

"Mostly I wanted Gabby to meet Kate. But her street was closed off by the fire. Then I saw, on my phone, that you were here, Papa, and we decided to find you in a hurry."

"Thank God you did."

Off in the distance, more sirens were drawing closer.

"To be on the safe side," Eván said. "I called the authorities."

"There's no need for that," said Escalante as he held his hands in the air.

"Probably not," Eván replied. "But we need some kind of guarantee that you'll never show up in these parts again. That you'll let Gabby and Kate and the rest of us be."

"You have my word."

"Pardon me, Señor Escalante, but promises that begin in Havana don't go very far in my book."

"I know what we can do," Kate said, walking toward Escalante and his men.

"Honey, don't get too close," I warned.

"It's okay, Billy. We need evidence, incriminating proof for them to leave us alone."

Eván knew what Kate was up to and already had her phone out. "Papa, I like the way your lady friend does business. Always thinking, isn't she?"

Kate eased between Escalate and one of his men, ready to pose for the camera.

"As they do in Cuba," Eván said, "Say, 'Whiskey.'"

Only Kate smiled as the flash went off and Eván took several more.

"Should we include your player friends?" Kate asked.

"No," Eván replied. "They were never here. They were heading to Atlanta to join the big league club."

That drew chuckles from Gabby and the rest of them.

"You're free to leave now, Señor Escalante," Eván said. "But you know what I'm up to, don't you?"

Escalante only nodded.

"Photographs of you with the artist who sculpted the famous weeping statue of Malena Fonseca have already been sent to several of my dearest friends in the Cuban American exile community, as well as my ever-resourceful sister. I'll give them specific instructions that if anything should ever happen to my father, Kate Sinclair, Gabby Santos, Tyga Garcia, or any of us, they are to send these images to interested parties in Havana and even the international news services. I'm sure they will reach the powers that be soon enough. Then you will be a dead man in Havana."

"I understand."

"Good," Eván looked over her shoulder in the direction of the sirens. "And maybe you can be gone before the local cops arrive."

With that Escalante and his men scrambled into the Cadillac. Yet before they could speed away, Gabby, who was still holding a bat, took a swing at the rear bumper, breaking a red rear taillight.

"A bit of payback?" I asked, as we watched the vehicle with the broken taillight head for the main road.

"In Cuba, we're told how strict the police are in America," he said. "How a car can be pulled over because of a small thing like a light being out. Especially if there are brown skins behind the wheel."

I looked at Eván and both of us started to laugh. "The kid is a fast study," I said. "He's already onto the ways of his new home."

Sure enough, out on the main road, we saw the police come to a halt and surround Escalante's Caddy.

"C'mon, I know a back way out of here," Kate said. "We can get the players on the road to Atlanta without the locals being any wiser."

"That would be good of you, señora," Gabby said. "I wasn't sure how I was going to explain any of this."

44.

GABBY SANTOS STEPPED confidently to the plate, leading off the bottom of the first inning in the Cubs' season opener, the start of a new season. Any sign of his struggles back in the Minor Leagues, in Knoxville, were long gone. He demonstrated no outward signs of nervousness, even though I knew he had to be churning inside. Thanks to an impressive spring training, the kid we had spirited away from the Cuban national team had earned a starting spot with the big league club.

"He told me he would try and hit me a home run," Kyle said.

"No, he told me he was going to hit me a homer," replied his twin brother.

"Maybe he told both of you," Cassy said to her sons. "Maybe he did so because he's so happy to have you here, rooting him on."

All of us—Cassy and the kids, Eván, Kate, and me—were there, sitting ten rows behind home plate in seats courtesy of the Chicago Cubs.

We watched Gabby take the first pitch from the Reds' starter, which sailed high and outside for ball one. Gabby checked his swing at the next offering, a nasty split-finger fastball down in the dirt.

Just like that, the new kid in the Cubs' lineup had worked the count to his favor—two balls and no strikes. I watched him ripple his fingers along the thin handle of his thirty-three-ounce bat. He took a deep breath to calm himself, focusing on the pitcher, who now nodded in agreement at the next sign the catcher put down.

For some reason, I decided to close my eyes, letting the sounds tell me what would happen next. I heard the crowd grow quiet for an instant, as if we were all holding our breath, and together we waited. Simply waited for what happened next.

If I've learned anything in life, it's that one must concentrate on the little things, concern yourself with the ones you love and try to let the rest of it roll on by. The world can be a beguiling, overpowering place, and there are times when it all can be too much. Over the years, the ones I've come to admire somehow find a way to move ahead, to do what they can, at such difficult moments. As I've told my children, forget about the people who claim they've never failed or lost at anything, especially something dear. Instead, turn to those who have fallen from grace, perhaps admittedly so, and see how they found a way to get up and move ahead.

Out there, somewhere, I heard the distinctive crack of the bat striking the ball. A sound that a friend of mine once described as being like a dry branch you come upon while walking in the woods. How that twig beneath your feet will break just so, and that's the same sound a baseball bat can make when it strikes a Major League offering with solid intent. It tags the ball with such purpose that the ball has no choice but to soar a long, long way. That's precisely the crackle-clap I heard Gabby's bat make as it connected with the pitch.

The kid had really hit it this time, and I opened my eyes, rising with the crowd as the ball began its trajectory toward the bleachers far beyond the outfield fence.

It was really gone this time.

Acknowledgments

LIKE BILLY BRYAN, I once thought my adventures in Cuba were over. That I had put the intrigue of Havana and the story that began with *Castro's Curveball* far, far behind me. But in early 2017, Jacqueline and I joined Milton Jamail and his wife, Margo Gutierrez, on a short visit to the island. Fidel Castro had died eight weeks before, and Donald Trump was preparing to occupy the White House. Even though it had been almost two decades since my previous trip to Havana, a Cuban plainclothesman approached me on the tarmac in Havana, even before we cleared customs. "What brings you back to Cuba, Señor Wendel?" he asked. A question that reminded me that I was back on this star-crossed island, where so many eyes can be upon you.

Much of the Havana area appeared to be much the same—the sweeping views along the Malecón, the tourists peering through the open windows at Hemingway's old home in a working-class neighborhood, ten miles from downtown. (Visitors to Papa's estate can roam the grounds, but only Cuban officials are allowed inside.) When I further studied things, though, I realized so much had indeed changed. There were more visitors, especially from Europe, more money in play and more transactions, legal and otherwise. The days of ballplayers defecting by raft, for example, had largely ended. Instead, the top prospects were being smuggled across the seas in high-speed crafts to declare themselves to the highest bidder.

My infatuation with Cuba and the baseball culture there began decades ago at *USA Today*, where I was a founding member of *Baseball Weekly*. I was fortunate to work with many talented folks there, including Paul White, Gary Kicinski, Bill Koenig, Tim McQuay, Greg Frazier, Rob Rains, and Rick Lawes. Jeff Passan, who was once an intern at *Baseball Weekly*, has done excellent reporting about Cuban baseball. Scott Price's *Pitching Around Fidel: A Journey into the Heart of Cuban Sports*, Tad Szulc's *Fidel: A Critical Portrait*, Aran Shetterly's *The Americano: Fighting with Castro for Cuba's Freedom*, Milton Jamail's *Full Count: Inside Cuban Baseball*, and Tom Miller's *Trading with the Enemy: A Yankee's Travels through Castro's Cuba* helped me once again place my story within the island's sports and political history.

Sewanee, Tennessee, home of the University of the South, would seem to have little in common with Havana. Still, something about looking upon the world from the western edge of the Cumberland Plateau there reminded me of views to the far horizon from the Malecón seawall in Havana. Just as importantly, in my trips to the Sewanee Writers Conference, I met Greg Downs, Kevin Wilson, Brendan Mathews, Michael Hyde, Holly Goddard Jones, and beloved administrator Cheri Bedell Peters.

Almost one thousand miles north of Sewanee stands the National Baseball Hall of Fame in Cooperstown, New York. I was honored to serve on the museum's advisory board for the "Viva Baseball" exhibit, with Rob Ruck, Adrian Burgos, and Alan Klein. Those in Cooperstown have always been in my corner, and they include Bill Francis, Jim Gates, John Odell, Tom Shieber, Erik Strohl, Bruce Markusen, and Jeff Idelson.

When I began to write fiction, I first found a home at the Community of Writers at Squaw Valley. I've attended the summer conference in the Sierra Nevada four times, where Carolyn

Doty, Richard Ford, Tom Rickman, and Oakley Hall showed me the way. That began a journey where I've been fortunate to learn from such outstanding teachers as Alice McDermott, John Casey, Margot Livesey, Elizabeth Rees, Tom Jenks, and Alan Cheuse. When I was about to embark on a nine-month fellow-ship to the University of Michigan, part of the Knight-Wallace program led by Charles Eisendrath, Alan urged me to seek out his friend, Nicholas Delbanco. Nick helped me revise *Castro's Curveball*, my first novel, which became my master's thesis proj-ect at Johns Hopkins University.

Soon after Gary Brozek assured that the book had found a home at Random House, I was asked to teach classes at Johns Hopkins. I wouldn't have found my way without the support of David Everett, Mark Farrington, Karen Houppert, Melissa Joyce, Ed Perlman, and such outstanding students as Monica Hesse, Will Potter, Craig Gralley, Deanna McCool, Karen Hattrup, Mark Stoneman, and Alma Katsu. I soon discovered that teach-ing keeps you honest about your work.

So often in this game, one needs a sounding board, a shoulder to cry on, to really move ahead. At such times, I've bent the ear of Mary Kay Zuravleff, Howard Mansfield, E. Ethelbert Miller, Paul Dickson, Kyle Semmel, Gerry LaFemina, Gregg Wilhelm, Mel Dixon, Michael Kinomoto, Lelia Nebeker, Elly Williams, Cathy Alter, Gerry Rosenthal, Burt Solomon, Dan Moldea, Roger Ludwig, Diane Henderson, Jane Friedman, David Rowell, Rich-ard Peabody, Dean Smith, and Thu Nguyen. (Yep, sometimes I need a lot of help.)

In that same spirit, here's a tip of the cap to Terry Cannon and Joe Price at the Institute of Baseball Studies at Whittier College.

The running group at the Reston YMCA (Marie Colturi, Molly Ascrizzi, Kathy Tracey, Joe O'Gorman, Rose Trapp, Todd Wait & Co.) has heard about my trips to the Caribbean over the years. So has the Sunday crew in Charlottesville (Mark Lorenzoni and the Ragged Mountain runners). I appreciate their conversation, patience, and friendship.

Finally, thanks to Rob Taylor, Haley Mendlik, Karen Brown, and the folks at the University of Nebraska Press. When I returned from Havana this last time and began to write about Billy Bryan and his world again, Rob made sure this new tale found a home.

Lightning Source UK Ltd.
Milton Keynes UK
UKHW010224280121
377819UK00002B/123